Casual Labor: A Book of Short Stories

Jerome McDougal

CASUAL LABOR: A BOOK OF SHORT STORIES

ISBN 978-0-9835161-9-4

J. D. McDougal Publishing
4401 Aurora Avenue North
Seattle, WA 98103

Prepared for publication by Julia Ziobro, JAZyourWords.com.

Table of Contents

The Girl in a Magnolia Tree

The smell of spring was bright and sweet, in the hills of Akinie town.

The flowers so bright, and new born grass, laid a soft carpet upon the ground.

With palette and paint and easel too, I walked the crest of a hill.

And there before me in a magnolia tree, I seen this girl so still.
Standing high, upon a branch, a scarf upon her head.
I stood below and looked up at her, then in a quiet voice I said,
Hello up there; why is it you are standing in a tree?
She put her finger to her lips, be still she said to me.
But why is it you are in this tree? Do you think you are a bird?
Be quiet! Be Quiet! She said to me, Say not another word.
I stood below and looked above, at this wonder in a tree.
The most lovely girl I had ever seen, just standing in this tree.
I sat my easel on a knoll and I began to paint.
This girl up in a magnolia tree, that seemed so strange to me.
Red-breasted robins flew here and there, gathering sticks and twigs.
Building nests upon a branch, stopping now and then to sing.
Soft songs of spring were in the air, as I watched her standing there.
As still as time in a magnolia tree, she stood without a care.
My canvas turned from white to amber and red and green and blue.
As blue bachelor buttons and morning glories shown yellow on the dew.
Nestled in sparkling tufts of green as new as the leaves on the tree.
One by one they opened up, saying hello to me.
Each searching for its time in life, as short as it may be.
Or were they smiling at this lovely girl, standing up there in the tree?
The scarf she'd tied upon her head was so many colors bright.
Had she climbed up there this morning, or been standing there all the night?
She seemed a part of nature, this girl up in the tree.
Lips smiling, eyes twinkling, smiling down at me.

What made her stand up in the tree? Her eyes both shining so.

I thought, she must know a secret. Something I did not know.

They twinkled like the drops of dew on the flowers below the tree

Why oh why would such a lovely girl, be standing in a tree?

As my brushes turned their strokes into a created picture there.

The girl came down from the magnolia tree, to take her place as well.

Into the center of this art, so magnificent now to see.

A perfect painting of life and love, and a girl up in a tree.

At first a leaf then tufts of turf, my brushes began their dance.

Upon the canvas spreading paint, a flower, a leaf, a branch.

My canvas began to turn into a magnificent sight of spring

Surrounded by leaves and singing birds and a smiling girl in a tree.

The morning passed and the sun drew high. As paint began to dry

The colors changed and became so clear, showing what I had painted there.

Her face so young and skin so clean, she appeared so young and pure.

Upon a branch in a magnolia tree, I had fallen in love for sure.

Every leaf and every branch looked completely real to see.

Such a pretty face, and lovely smile up there in a magnolia tree.

"Why are you there? Please won't you say?" I called into the tree.

"Sir, had I not been standing in this tree, would you have painted me?"

Roger

They squatted down beside the bushes, waiting until it was late afternoon, and for the slow-moving train to pass by.

To him, it seemed like it took forever until they seen a boxcar with an open door. He remembered his hands were slippery from sweating, because he was so scared of falling under the train and getting run over. He was afraid they would slip out of the tight grip his mother had on him as she pulled him along behind her, running to catch the passing car. She picked him up and more or less tossed him in through the door onto the hard wooden floor of the car. He rolled over and watched as his father helped her in, then he jumped into the car and slid the door partly closed.

Still to this very day he could remember the odor left from the cattle that had been in the car before them, the feel of the rough boards on his arms, the clacking of the wheels on the track as he laid there trying to sleep. It was supposed to be warm in California, he remembered his father telling his mother about it. 'Santa Monica, the best place in the USA,' he had said. But they had never got there, they were arrested in Nebraska and taken to jail.

It seemed so long ago now: it seemed as though he had spent his whole life sleeping on hard floors or under street overpasses, behind buildings and on sidewalks as he was tonight. He laid there thinking about that day so long ago when the men took his mother and father off the train. They put them in jail for riding on the train. When he went to the school for kids who had no parents, he had never seen his parents again. Sometimes at night he would dream about them, and dream about the woman who had told him, smiling as though she was glad he was alone now and his parents were in the jail, "They don't want you, kid." She had said it as she led him into a bathroom. "They're better off without you, they can't take care of themselves let alone you too, and you're better off without them. Now take off your clothes and get into the shower!"

That was forty-one years ago, when he was seven. Ten years he had been there in school in Scottsville, Nebraska, of all places. He never told anyone he went to school in Scottsville, Nebraska. He left at seventeen and joined the Army.

Four years in the Army in Vietnam, drinking and smoking a lot of pot, then he was twenty-one years old and on the street in Southern California. He had gone to Santa Monica because it was the only name he remembered. For some unknown reason, he stayed on the street. Now he was forty-eight and he had been sleeping on hard floors all of his adult life, the only thing that ever changed was the towns he was homeless in. Then again, by now, it was a way of life and he couldn't change it if he wanted to.

He wished he was back in Southern California under the freeway, instead of here in Seattle in the rain. He missed his place under the on-ramp at the 405 freeway. And Palm Boulevard. He had a nice grassy spot under a tree, behind the cement wall, out of the sun, out of the weather, away from the cops and people. It was quiet at night and it was always warm. He had felt safe there for over four years. He had his bicycle and his route where he picked up cans and bottles. He found discarded things in the dumpsters behind the apartments and sold them at the second-hand store. On a good day he could make over thirty dollars and still spend half a day at the beach. One day he had found five computers thrown away and sold them for five-hundred dollars. He wished he had them here now. Here, had to work eight hours just to get forty-three dollars. He wanted to go home, back under the freeway, get another bike, and go back to where he had been somewhat happy.

"What the hell? I'm just waiting to die anyway," he said it out loud to himself and pulled the sleeping bag up over his head and tried to sleep until morning so he could go to work and save a couple more bucks. If he could save a few more dollars he could buy some new clothes, and then a bus ticket - it was almost impossible to ride the trains anymore. Now they locked every empty car and put slip guards on all the ladders so you can't climb on a moving train. It was either walk, ride a bike, or ride the bus. He needed seventy-five dollars to pay for the ticket, and some new clothes from Goodwill so he didn't smell, or they wouldn't let him on the bus. It was February, and he wanted to be home by March fifteenth if he could. "Just quit drinking for three days and you're home." He said it over and over as he went to sleep in the rain, on the sidewalk, on a street in southeast Seattle.

"Hey! California! Get up, it's four, you going to work?" It was a man named Bernie, a thin, frail man who was several times stronger than he looked to be. They had been friends for almost a year and he used Bernie as the reason he hadn't stopped drinking or spending all his money every day drinking. Because Bernie didn't want to stop or leave, he just wanted to work, do a few drugs and drink. He had his place in the basement of an old house, five blocks from the casual-labor office. He had lived there for almost three years along with several others who at one time came and went. He could have lived there but he didn't like the smell of the place. It smelled like piss and rotten feet so he just stayed outside where the air was clean.

"Hay! You going to work?"

"Yeah I'm going to work, now get the fuck away from me, will ya?"

He raised up and looked at the thin black-skinned man standing over him, looking down. He could smell the stench of his feet from three feet away.

"I'm up! Get the fuck away from me, you smell like piss, Bernie!"

"Hay, fuck you! You fuckin' mother-fucker! Asshole!" Bernie walked away up the street.

"Well, why don't you wash your funky feet?" he called after him.

"Why don't you wash them for me?" Bernie called back.

"Maybe I will, you skinny little drug-sucking fuckhead!" he called.

"Don't call me skinny," Bernie called back, smiling, showing his rotten front teeth. "I'll sign you in if you want me to".

"Yeah, do it! I need to get a cup of coffee." He was up on his knees, folding his sleeping bag inside his pad, and tying it with a belt he had found a long time ago. At least it had stopped raining. "It's still cold as shit here!" He said it to some people in a car driving past, the lady looked surprised at him through the closed window, then gave him a sort of, 'Are you a crazy man?' look.

"Would I be here if I wasn't fucking crazy?" He yelled after the car.

"I got to stop drinking for just three days and I'm home." He sort of prayed it to himself with his hands folded together. "Just three days - Monday, Tuesday, and Wednesday, then Thursday, I'll buy some clothes, go to the YMCA and take a shower, and I'll be home Friday."

He started walking the three blocks to the 7-Eleven for coffee, and counted his change, $1.68; Friday he'd had $98.00. "I

11

should have left right then," he said, but Bernie had started him drinking Friday night and it was gone Saturday morning, along with whatever Bernie had.

He was ten cents short of having enough for a cup of coffee.

"Un-fucking believable!!" he said as he looked at what he had left in his hand. Forty-eight hours ago he had $98.00 in his pocket, and now he had $1.68. He went into the store and told the man behind the counter.

"I'm ten cents short; can I owe you until tonight?"

The man never spoke to him, just motioned for him to get his coffee and held out his hand for the change, he took the change and put it in the till, then looked at him with a sort of disgusted look, "You can do better, Roger!" he said as he left the store.

"Three days and I'm going home! This time, I'm going home!" He said it several more times as he walked to the casual-labor office across the street and up four blocks.

He walked in just in time to hear the short, loudmouth dispatcher telling Bernie he had to go take a shower before he could go back to work.

"I ain't got no fucking shower where I live," Bernie answered.

"Then go sit under a rain gutter and wash, you stink like you shit yourself! Now get out of here and go wash! And don't come back until you do".

Bernie walked past him. "Fuckin' mother-fucker, ass-hole," he mumbled.

"I heard you, Bernie!" The dispatcher yelled back at him. "And get some different clothes, and a haircut, and brush your teeth, you stink like shit!"

"I ain't got no money! You know I ain't got no money to buy all that with!" Bernie answered, then turned and looked back inside.

"Then go get yourself put in jail for a few days and they'll wash you and give you some new clothes when you get out. Now get out of here!"

Then he looked at Roger and said "You're not much better Roger".

"Yeah, I know. I'm going home Friday if I can save three days' wages and buy a bus ticket."

"Yeah, I'm sure you are," he answered. "I been hearing that for almost a year, Roger".

"This time I'm going home, for sure, I'm going back to Santa Monica Friday".

He took a chair and waited for his name to be called. He sat and waited until it was six-thirty and about twenty men had left.

"Roger Davidson," the dispatcher called his name.

"Right here!"

"You want to go load a roof? It pays ten an hour."

"How many hours?"

"You want the job or not?"

"I need the money," he answered, any hours were better than no hours.

"You need lunch money?"

"Yes," he signed his name, then took the ticket and the money and left to get on the bus.

Monday mornings always went half-way bad before they even got started. This one was no exception, he couldn't find the address, it took him almost two hours to figure out it was on the westside and not on the eastside, the ticket hadn't said east or west just the name and number of the street. He was almost an hour late getting there. Then the job wasn't loading a roof it was digging in the mud for a sidewalk, but the job would take all week if he wanted to work here. Then the property owner told him, "I pay you twenty bucks a day extra if you work hard and come every day until were finished."

"How long you think it will take?" he asked.

"A week or two if you work steady."

"Thanks," he answered, taking the shovel and began to dig the slot eight inches deep and four feet wide, tossing dirt up against the wall of the building, covering some pipes that were left exposed. He worked until three-thirty, and left for the casual-labor office to get his check. He had a plan now, and he felt better about himself. He always felt better when he had a plan. He was going to get his check, go to the Goodwill and buy some clothes, then he would come back here and put them in one of the rooms for safe keeping until Friday. He finished the day at three pm and had the owner sign his ticket so he could get paid, then rode the bus back.

He got his check and cashed it at the store, bought himself one pack of smokes for six bucks and 44 oz. can of malt liquor. There was still $51.00 and some change left. He started to go buy his new clothes and planned to just spend the night without eating, but he was hungry.

He went to the Bull Pen on Fourth to eat, it was a mistake. Bernie was there in front of the place holding a cardboard sign.

"Please help. No work, no food." Bernie dropped the sign and followed Roger into the restaurant.

"I ain't feeding you, Bernie," Roger said.

"I ain't ate nothing all fucking day, Roger, loan me ten until tomorrow."

"No, you can't work, and you can't pay me back."

"Come on, give me ten, man! I'm hungry."

"You smell like you been drinking all fucking day. I ain't giving you nothing."

Bernie just stood there behind him until he gave in like he always did. They ate and then had two drinks and he was down to eleven dollars, not enough to buy his clothes with. He bought another pack of smokes and one more 44-ounce drink, and then he was down to two dollars and some change. He left Bernie and headed back up the hill to the place under the bridge where he slept. He finished off his two cans of malt, smoked a few more cigarettes, and finally went to sleep.

He got his ticket the next morning and swore to himself, this time he was not going to spend the money. He was going to go get his check and then go directly to Goodwill and buy his new clothes. He was not going anywhere around Bernie, or anyone else who might try to talk him out of his money. There was a lot of time spent thinking about that. He knew better, but he was just too easy, or he somehow deep inside just didn't care that much about what happened to him. He was healthy and strong, didn't steal or beg like a lot of the men he knew did. He liked to work and show what he could do, but when it came to money he was way off the track. No matter how hard he tried, he never could save a dollar. Come Sunday he was broke, every Sunday come hell or high water, always broke.

He was on the job and working a half hour before any of the others arrived. "You can't start until I get here," the owner told him. "It's an insurance thing."

"I don't like to just stand around and wait," Roger answered.

The man said nothing, just gave him a look of warning by raising his eyebrows and looking down his thin nose.

"Come a little later tomorrow."

"You think it would be alright if I tossed my sleeping bag in one of the garages and just slept here?"

"Let me think about it, you have to go get your ticket every day, don't you?"

"Yeah, but I can get it at night and just come here. I wont be around the bars if I'm out here."

The man studied him a few seconds and said "Sure, just don't steal anything, we're already short on shovels around here." It was supposed to be a joke but he didn't get the humor of it.

He spent the day working and felt good when three o'clock came; he went and picked up his check, then cashed it at the store. He saw Bernie and ducked into an alley, then ran to the end of the block and went in the opposite direction. He didn't need him tonight, he bought a Coke instead of a 40-ounce, then went to Goodwill and bought his clothes, a complete set, including new socks and used shoes. He packed them into a plastic bag and tied it up so it was watertight, stopped and bought a hamburger at Wendy's, and caught the bus back out to the job. He sat and smoked most of a pack of cigarettes and fell asleep as soon as it was dark. He felt like he was halfway home. He had the clothes, and now he just needed the bus fare. He would have that tomorrow, then one more day 'til he was gone to California and into the sunshine.

He slept good and never woke up until he heard the men talking the next morning. He was still in his sleeping bag when they came into the garage to start work.

"You sleep here?" One of the electricians asked him.

"Yeah, I did." He answered.

"Man, you homeless guys are funny, No, weird is the word for it."

"I like being homeless." He answered, "I got no worries this way. Tomorrow I'm going back to California and while you're here working in the rain, I'll be sitting on the beach getting a tan".

"And be broke," the electrician returned.

"So? What do I need money for, buy a bunch of things I have to take care of?"

"Whatever turns your crank," the guy told him, and they walked off sort of laughing at him.

"Let them laugh!' he thought. He had stuff once or twice in his life but it was too much trouble to keep it, then you have to move it around if you move anywhere. It's better to just have a backpack and some money to eat on. He got up and started his digging on the sidewalk.

"So how much does it cost to go to California?" the electrician had walked up behind him.

"Why? You going to buy me a ticket?"

"I was thinking about it. How much you make working like you do?"

"About sixty a day."

"You know how much I make? Over two hundred."

"So?"

"So how much is a ticket?"

"About a hundred," he answered, then watched as the electrician took out his wallet and handed him a hundred dollar bill.

"Have a good trip home," he said, and walked off.

"Why you doing this?" Roger called.

"Hell if I know. Because you're homeless, and I'm not?"

"Well, thanks," he called but the guy never looked back at him, he watched him walk away and get into a new pickup and then drive off.

He thought for a moment and wondered why he had never had the urge to have a new truck or a new car, a house or family. He thought for a second he was selfish. It was just easy to have nothing. Want nothing and do as little as possible. He started to

17

leave the job but he didn't want to seem like a loser, so he just kept working and finished the day.

He went back and got his check, then cashed it. He went and took a shower at the mission and put on his new clothes. Packed his old ones in his backpack and walked to the bus depot. It was eight-fifty pm when the bus left for Los Angeles. He slept all the way to Portland, Oregon, then, when the bus stopped for a half hour, he started having second thoughts about leaving. He wanted to get off the bus and go have a drink. It was only midnight, so the bars were still open but he knew if he got off and had one drink he would still be here in the morning, broke and stuck in Portland for a long time. Instead he stayed on the bus and waited for it to leave again.

By the time he got to Medford, it was eight in the morning and he wanted a drink but forced himself to eat instead; he almost bought a bottle of wine but stopped himself and bought a quart of Coke instead. He sat in the seat on the bus and sipped the soda looking out of the window wishing they were in L.A.

In Redding, California, the driver announced that the bus in front of them had broken down and they were going to pick up the stranded passengers. A few minutes later, the bus stopped on the freeway and about forty more people got on. Every seat was now full and a woman sat next to him and she wanted to talk, but he didn't. He listened for a while then told her, "Lady, I'm really not interested in anything you got to say so please just don't talk to me, ok?"

"You're a rude person," she said and turned away from him.

He sat there trying to sleep for five more hours until the bus stopped in Sacramento and the lady got off. He got off the bus to buy a hamburger and a forty ouncer of malt liqueur. He carried it back on the bus in a sack and waited. It was now nearly five in the evening and he was finally in California. Three hours to San

Francisco and eight more to L.A., then he was home. Home in time to see the sunrise.

He slept all the way to San Francisco, then had to change busses there. It took an hour to change and they left for L.A., at nine-fifteen pm on Thursday.

It was six-eighteen when the bus parked at the terminal in L.A. He got off and gathered his pack and walked out of the bus depot and headed to catch his bus to Santa Clara, sixty-three miles south. He still had almost fifty dollars in his pocket and he was feeling pretty good about himself. He bought a hot dog, a bag of chips, and a forty ouncer, sat on the bench and waited for the bus to come.

It was about two in the morning when he laid down his pad and rolled his sleeping bag out in the same place he had laid it out for four years - under the tree behind the fence, under the on-ramp at 405. Some of the small things he had left there a year ago were still there, the small radio that didn't work and the cigar box with his shaving things were still under the tree. He found his pen light in the box and it still worked, the batteries were good. He was so happy to be home again. He took off his clothes and hung his socks on a branch of the tree. Sleep came in two minutes and didn't wake up until three in the afternoon.

It was sixty-eight degrees when he woke up. He spent the whole day just lying around under the tree, except for the few minutes he spent walking the two blocks to the store, buying food and walking back. Tomorrow he would go look for a used bike or find one abandoned somewhere and fix it. Then he would go look for things in dumpsters. He was home, he was happy.

Two police officers were driving by when the passenger said to the driver, "You smell that?"

"Maybe, what did you do?" he smiled.

19

"I didn't do nothing. I smell a dead body. Something is dead under the on-ramp over there."

"You look, I'll wait here," the driver answered. He sat in the car until the other officer motioned for him to come and look.

It was a man's body still in his sleeping bag, he had been shot twice in the back of the head while he was sleeping. The officer stood, looking down at the body that had been there for over a week.

"I remember this guy. He was here a couple years ago. I think his name is Roger something."

"I don't think it was robbery," the other officer answered.

"No, I think it was just another homeless guy getting shot in his sleep."

"Drugs?" the first asked.

"I doubt it. It's the same guys. Some of these guys just get a kick out of shooting these homeless people. They know no one cares about them and no one is going to come looking for them, so they just have to kill some poor son of a bitch that never done nothing to no one. He was probably sound asleep and never even felt it when it happened."

"Looks like two through the top of his head."

"Call a coroner," the first one told the second and then reached down and put the plastic tarp over Roger's body and walked back to the car waiting for the coroner to come and take the body away.

The Secret of Tonto Basin

A short story

Their language consisted more of hand motions than spoken words. Words were used, but they had only about a hundred different sounds to describe things with. The following is my opinion of what their language might have sounded like. This was formed by using a formatted derivative of the beginning of the Spanish language and removing all things that have come into being during the last three-thousand years. Even before the pyramids were being built the silent people of the Tonto Basin were going about their daily lives, the Aztecs were building their own pyramids in Mexico and the great Indian tribes of America were being formed. Nothing was named, no trees or animals had names, they were identified as:

Fauweer were animals that can be seen moving. *Youkie,* was trees and brush. Birds were named by imitating their sounds. Grass was called *Wieouki,* like the sound of the wind rubbing dry grass together. Water was called, *Auwaue.* The river - *Tonto.* The earth was called *Tonto.* A good place to live. Sun and fire was called, *Basin. Basin,* the light and the land around them. *Yatiee,* was fish.

The words arrived one at a time from sounds heard by the people who lived here. The quiet sound of water rippling from a brook. The sound of the wind rustling through the grass and the sound of branches rubbing against themselves.

The sound of a dying deer or a calling Elk. These words came slowly, one at a time throughout the thousands of years the people lived in their area, and still only about a hundred were ever spoken. The people were a silent group who spent their days gathering food or building houses on the cliffs and knolls, out of rocks and trees, away from bears, lions and other people who would come and take what they had built or stored.

Men were named, *Yeah hie*, and women were, *Yahie ie*. There were no names for possessions.

A home was named *Basin* as was the land, but spoken softer. There was no name for weather or rain except the name of the river, *Auwaua*; water, wet. There was no name for food, only the action of eating food, *Chanawie* - spoken with a hand to mouth motion. Hunting was never a spoken word only a hand motion as of throwing a spear or shooting an arrow.

It was a silent world these people lived in for over a thousand years, living in small groups of twenty or thirty. If there was an argument the one who was in the wrong was made to move away and he would take his friends and family with him and move to a different place on a nearby hill or cliff. A group would start building their house by stacking rocks in a circle and holding them together with mud and grass. Soon there would be another community with twenty or thirty people living there, then another and another potentially until there were over eighty-thousand people living as in what is now called the Tonto Basin in Northern Arizona.

This is a two-part story of one man, his descendants and his family, and their journey from Tonto Basin to the black hills of South Dakota where his tribes name would become, Black Feet. And all across America, creating different tribes, nations and many more. It is about his distant descendants as they travel back to Tonto Basin, and the treasure they found when they got here. It begins over one-thousand-six-hundred years ago and eight-hundred miles to the north on a day in spring.

The rain started in the night, raining hard all the night hours and then in the day it warmed and the snow melted in the mountains causing millions of gallons of water to run off the hills, melting the snow and creating even more water. The land began to erode and a huge slide of mud, earth, rocks and trees slid several miles down into the river canyon. Blocking it completely for five years, before a huge lake one hundred-thirty miles wide and three-hundred miles long filled and began to spill over the top of the earth dam. This began to slowly wash the fill down the river. Letting the water return to the basin fifty years later.

They were a small people, not much over five feet tall, and silent, they never spoke much, never danced and never learned to make music; there were no drums or flutes to play. They had no name and did not know they had no name. They were just there, why and how they were there, they did not think of. They were the same as the animals. Their days were spent gathering food, and building pots to store it.

Some gathered food, some made the pots, some made weapons. This was their life in the great Tonto Basin of Northern Arizona and so it was for over three-thousand years.

He had no name and he needed no name. Same as all the other men, "Yeah hie." His wife's name was the same as his but spoken only to others. She called him, "Eie ha," or "my husband," as did all the other women their own. He had no belongings, only his few robes, his bows, many arrows, and three long spears.

He was an arrow maker and a hunter. He built fish traps to put in the river, rabbit traps, and snares to catch wild pigs. He was the best hunter of the people living there. His days were spent hunting and his nights spent making arrow heads, scraping branches to make arrows, weaving sticks together to make fish traps. He braided rawhide into ropes for his snares, used hair from his head to tie fish traps. These things he traded to others for food and pots and things to decorate his home.

His woman was a pot maker and she spent her days gathering food, grinding beans, and gathering wood for the fire. Her evenings were spent squatting over a hole in the earth, making pots to store food in.

He had two children, one son, one girl, neither of whom had a name. There was not much need to call to each other because they were never far apart. To be alone meant to be killed by others or a beast of the wild. So they stayed close together and there was never a reason to call to each other.

He had stood on the bluff along with several hundred others and looked down at the river bed and saw there was no water in it. One day it was wet, the next morning it was no longer wet. Only dry round stones and dead fish were where the water had run. Fish were crowded into small pools fighting for what little water was left there. They stood looking and not understanding why the water had left. Had some huge beast drunk it all during the night? He did not know, but he did know he had to have water. For several nights and days he waited with a hundred others, by the river with his pots, waiting for the water to return, but it did not come. On the nineteenth day he took his woman and two children and began walking up the empty stream bed to look for water along with several thousand of his fellow tribesmen. Leaving their rock houses and grinding stones to be slowly taken away by time, becoming a ring of fallen stones a hundred years later. Found, still there, two-thousand years later.

This journey would take him thirty-five years and nine-hundred miles to the north; up what are now called the Salt and Colorado rivers, through the Grand Canyon. Continued by his descendants through the great Salt Lake Valley, through

Yellowstone Park, into the grasslands of Montana, east into South Dakota, south into Kansas, Nebraska, then back west into New Mexico, Arizona and up north into California, Oregon, and Washington. Finally east to the great ocean now called the Atlantic. The tribes divided and became many.

The sun was hot, the wind was hot and there was no water in the river bed or in the shallow pools where there used to be. The beasts were all moving out of the valley and going North, up into the cool trees traveling with the afternoon wind as if they knew where to go. So the people followed them searching for food and water as they traveled. Moving only one mile each day, or less. The first three months several thousand of the people died of thirst and hunger. He took his family and moved faster leaving the rest of his people behind to fend for themselves. People were starting to fight with each other for the little amount of food the women found or the small game the men killed each day.

He feared for his children, and now it was summer, the sun was hot and the days long. It was hard to travel and hunt at the same time. He hunted during the morning hours, rested in the afternoon and traveled at night.

By the time he reached the trees, more than half of the people had died. He found small places where there was water, and he saved it in several small bags made from the hanging bags of elk and deer, or the stomachs of wild pigs. He carried as much water with him as all four of them could carry, not wanting to run out. He was lucky in the fact that he was very good with his bow and throwing spears. He set his rabbit snares each night before he rested. They were not hungry or thirsty as they traveled.

They came across dead people who had traveled before them, and met with others who were not so friendly. He had seen bodies half-eaten by the wild beasts or people who were hungry;

he learned not to trust anyone during this time of hardship. He kept to himself and taught his children to hide at a slight signal from him.

In six months, he had moved about one-hundred-fifty miles north into the hills, and now about fifty others were following him - trusting his decisions and helping as a family. Then it began to snow, something he had never seen in his life. The weather turned cold and several people died, wet and freezing. He stopped moving and built a shelter out of the flat rocks along the bottom of the cliffs, carrying them far up in the wall of the canyon then stacking them under the overhanging ledges. Building a fire behind them, they were warm in the coldest days. He hunted the large elk and small rabbits to feed the people as the women gathered beans and seeds from the fir trees, picked wild wheat and stored it in the caves high up on the cliffs, behind the flat rocks so the mice and rabbits could not eat it.

Twenty-five years these people lived in the shelter under the cliffs, moving north only after a great flood came, carrying all the trees and the small animals away with the water, there was nothing left. All that had been was gone. The animals were gone for several months, no wheat grew and no rain fell. So again he had packed his family which numbered sixteen of his own children, and eighty others. They moved north into the great canyon with walls too high to see over. For three years, they traveled north through the canyon then up onto the flatlands of northern Arizona and into the canyons of what is now Utah. Here was found a huge lake where they built homes of stone and grass. They hunted, becoming prosperous again. It was here he died and his first son became leader of the clan, which now numbered nearly eighty. There the son became an old man and he died, leaving three sons and five girls. His sons died, their sons died and eight generations died as three hundred years passed. These people lived beside the great lake for three hundred years. Their language changed, words were added, and they called each other by names made from what they did or who they were and how they ran, after the birds of the sky and the beasts they killed.

They lived in houses made of rocks and dirt held together with grass, covered with skins over the top and they called these houses *Hoqies*, meaning a warm place to sleep. They lived by the great lake until it became small and too salty to drink the water of, and people began to die from the poison in the lake.

Some of them moved back south into the great valley of the sun and called themselves Apaches, Navaho, and Hopi. Their leader was a great thinker who spent time sitting on the rocks and looking down into the flatland. He taught his followers how to make ditches in the earth that water would run down from the hills, feeding the ground so plants would grow. They grew wheat, melons, and corn, and raised cattle. The clan grew to be over three million in number. Then the earth turned cold and all the plants froze and died. The water in the ditches froze and the people starved, dying in large numbers. Then it warmed and the water from the mountains was so much it covered the ground and people drowned in it. It then turned hot and no rain came for twenty years, and the people left the valley.

Some of them moved east into the lands of the tall grass, calling themselves Pawnee, while some called themselves Cherokee, and others called themselves Cheyenne. Some of them moved north up into the tall trees, becoming men who rode on horses and hunted the great Katonkahs; these called themselves Black Feet because their feet turned black from walking on the black stones of the ground. Others called themselves Sioux, they were known as the great people of the north. Some moved west and called themselves Abaquaha, hunters of the bear. Some were called the Willamette, men who fish from rocks. Some moved east and called themselves Flat Head and Eariqua. All the tribes were named with their own leaders. Some moved west, becoming breeders of great horses and their name was the Nez Perce. Some were called Umqua, they were makers of great boats and fished the sea.

It was his greatest descendant who first walked among the steaming waters of the great Yellowstone Valley and he named it, Yuka'ap'ie, land of steaming holes in the ground. He also called it Fanweer le O' Katonkah's, and Kati'O'jabna' meaning land of the fat bear beasts, and land of sweet grass and water.

They lived in the Yellowstone Valley, north in Montana and west in mountains called the Tetons (sharp points), for six hundred years and from the first of those with no name. Who had no name and needed no name, who left the place called Tonto Basin. There became eighty-five generations and four hundred nations scattered over sixteen million miles of mountains and flat lands.

The tribes were named, the men were all named, the women were all named, and the animals were all named. The spoken words of the tribes numbered more than a thousand. Their horses numbered thirty million. Buffaloes named Katonkahas numbered one-hundred-fifty-million. Beaver, foxes, bears, elk and deer numbered as many as the stars in the sky and blades of grass in the ground.

The tribes' homes were made from rocks, earth and grass - lodge poles and skins from beasts and earth, from the Katonkahas. Things were named differently by different tribes but all the descendants were called human beings and lived in respect for the land that gave them life. It was called Tonto, a good place to live.

There were fish in the rivers and wheat on the ground. Deer and elk walked among them and life was good for the ninety-second-generation grandson of the man who was not named and needed no name. This grandson's name was One Who Catches the Eagle. But there were no great names to be remembered, because the dead were not remembered or spoken of out of respect for them and the things they had done when they were alive. Only the living and the future was talked about.

Men did not talk of things they had done or things they would do. It was not a thing to do for fear of being laughed at. Men did not steal from others or lie, or use other men's wives. Nor did they brag in front of others for fear of being beaten and fed to the dogs, this was the worst thing that could happen to a human being.

This man who was of the ninety-second generation of he who had no name and needed no name, who was called One Who Catches the Eagle, was also called White Eagle by those who liked to joke about him and knew about when he was a young man; how he had caught a white goose and carried it home telling his father he had captured a white eagle, and wished to be named after it.

This man had a son who was a very brave young man. When on a hunting trip he snuck up on a very big sleeping male Katonkaha and then sat on him without waking it. He sat there with his arms folded on his chest to show how brave he was and was then called, One Who Sits on Sleeping Bulls or Sitting Bull. And he became the first great one to be remembered by others as was his father before him, but only after Sitting Bull was remembered.

Before Sitting Bull, a great uncle was named, and his name was not remembered, but he was a great trader of horses and he took his family and moved west into a great flat valley to breed his horses, then north into the great trees and started the Nez Perce tribe. His grandson began the Willamette tribe, and another the Moab tribe, and yet another started the Yakima tribe, all of whom were breeders of great horses and painted them, braiding their tails and washing them in the river.

Now the time has passed and a lot of things are remembered. Much time is taken away from the future by spending so much time remembering things we cannot change. The reason I remember the man who had no name and needed no name, all the things that needed no names, is that it was different then. I like to think of how it might have been had I been there to see it for myself, I would have had no name and needed no name, but I would have been me in the same body still. No one would have called to me, asking me to come to them. I could have done my day with others, slept without thinking of so many things I do each day.

But now the tribes of the human being are gone, they've been replaced by different names, things written on rocks and in books, images built into statues of things who look like human beings but are not alive, have no life in them, and make no difference to the world we live in.

I might have stood next to the man who was not named and helped him to bury one of his people. Maybe a child of a friend or the wife of my brother, helping to place the body into a grave with the head facing a morning sun so it could see the light of the world as it left this one and moved on to the next. I might have stood by him and wondered where the water had gone to from the river and helped pick up the fish left floundering on the rocks, drowning in the same air we need to live. What if I had been there?

Would I have been in the sun chipping at flint to make arrowheads, sat scraping on limbs to make arrows, and carried

30

the rocks to build my house? Would I have ever lived to be sixty-five years old, I don't think so.

Be that as it may, now the story of the man who had no name and needed no name and all his descendants begins.

Chapter One

Some of the ninety-third generation grandsons of the man who had no name, and needed no name, were called Sitting Bull, Cochiese and his brother Guronamo, Buffalo Hump and his brother Crazy Horse, all of whom were great warriors. As were many more of his grandsons of the ninety-third generation in the great Indian wars of the nineteenth century.

As time passed into the present, the tribes became no more, and they passed into history as did all other things of the past. The great warriors left sons, and these left sons through which all of the human beings became part of the present.

In the ninety-eighth generation of the man who had no name and needed no name, some were white, some were red, and some were mixed. From this mixed breed there came twin brothers, who were named White Cloud and Black Cloud. They became great warriors, fighting the white man. Both died of the red spots on their faces and were remembered by the white men but not the red men.

From the great horse breeders there was a man named Joseph by the white men, but named Leans Over by the red men. Joseph was the father of William Joseph who became a white man and lived in the city working as a teacher of children. William Joseph married and had two sons who were twins, the first was born and then a second, three minutes after his brother.

When he was about ten years old, the oldest of these twins had a dream and his brother had the same dream on the same night. This dream was of the man who had no name and needed no name. He was standing on the hill looking at the piles of stone left by himself and the eighty thousand others who had left the place called the Tonto Basin, he stood on the hill wearing his leather clothes and rabbit skin boots, holding his spear. Saying to the brothers, "Hear me brothers, this is a sacred place and it should be respected and not torn apart or divided, the graves of my ancestors should not be dug up, and their things should not be dug up. The silent people have lived here and died here and it should remain a silent place."

Then his spirit went into their minds and he took them on the same journey he, his sons, grandsons and great grandsons had traveled. He took them down into the Basin and they saw the people when they were all alive and working, they saw the river and the elk, and they saw the rock houses where they lived. He let them see the people leave the Basin and move north and die. They saw the dead bodies of thousands laying on the rocks, cooked by the sun. He took them into the great canyon when there was no water and showed them the houses made of flat rocks up in the cliffs, built when the ground was covered in deep snow and the people were warm behind their rocks, singing around a fire. He brought them up over the great cliffs to the great lake when there was no salt in it, and they saw the people living there along the great lake and saw them die from the salt in the water after the lake went away into the hot air. He took them into the great Yellowstone Valley and they saw the ancestors of his sons there. He took them north into the grasslands where they saw a million buffalo moving across the flatlands. Then they saw the same million buffalo dead with their skins gone, the meat of their bodies rotting in the sun. They could smell the stink and it made them remember.

He showed them some of the great slaughters the white man had perpetrated on the women and children of the human beings. He showed them the thousands of human beings laying and dying with the red spots on their faces. He showed them the human beings inside fences, being beaten by the white soldiers. The young girls who had been drug into the brush and made naked and raped and then killed by the soldiers guarding them. Some of them were less than women, only children, left there rotting on the ground. human beings being herded like cattle out into the open, and left there to starve because the white man had killed all the food. They had taken away their homes and sold the painted skins from the walls of them. He took them back to the Basin and left them there alone to find their own way back to where he had found them.

As he was leaving, the oldest brother called and asked, "What is your name? What should I call you?" And their ancestor turned and answered by saying, "I have no name and I need no name, because all things are from the earth, all things go back to the earth, and again nothing will have a name, nor will it need a name."

"Why did you show us these things?"

"It was better when things had no names and they belonged to no one and all things were shared by all. The earth fed the people and the people shared the earth, they died and their bodies fed the earth, it was equal to all."

"But why did you show us these things and not someone who is older?"

"Because you have seen it in your mind and you know it is real now. You have years to think about it and walk among these rocks and feel the presence of the silent people. Believe in them and learn respect for them, the earth and how it was, how it is, and how it will be."

The older brother woke up and was filled with wonder at what he had dreamed. The younger brother woke up, and he was scared of what he had dreamed. Both brothers were afraid to tell the other of the dream for several days.

Then the older brother said to his mother, while sitting at the table after she called him by his name, "I have no name and I do not ever want to be called by a name. I do not want to hear anything called by a name because all things come from the earth and all things return to the earth. Nothing is owned by people and should not be called by names." The younger brother knew why he had said this and he was more scared than before. He told his father and mother about the dream, told them his beloved brother had the same dream on the same night he had.

So the father and mother called the older brother to the table and asked about the dream, saying it was just a dream, and that quite often twins have the same dream because they are of the same seed.

But he answered sounding more like the parent than the child. He spoke in a soft slow voice leaning forward on the table with his hands together sounding like a teacher, saying, "What I have seen and the things I have seen, I know are real and I know they are real because I have not yet learned about them, but now I know them, and I have never seen them, but I know what they look like and I have been there. I saw the people in the Basin and I saw the stone houses and the fish hanging on poles and the women making pots in holes in the ground and children gathering sticks and grass for fires. I saw them leave when the river went dry and I watched them die and their bodies cooked by the sun on the rocks, I have seen the great Grand Canyon when there was no water in the bottom of it, and I saw the sun shining on the tall cliffs above it, I have seen the houses in the cliffs built of flat stones. I saw the Great Salt Lake when it was a hundred miles across and three hundred miles long, with no salt in it. I saw the houses where the people lived beside it and I saw them die from drinking the salt after the water went up into the air. I saw the great green valley where the hot water sprays up into the sky each day. Great bears with humps on their backs and a thousand tee-pees along the banks of the river. And children were fishing and horses were running free. And I saw the creation of the great Indian nations, the people were called human beings, and that is the only name I wish to be called. They numbered over four hundred nations and three thousand tribes among them. The human beings were more than the white beings. And I saw the great creation of the northern tribes and they numbered a million in the great grasslands of the north. I was shown the destruction of it by the white man because of his greed and sickness. I saw fifty thousand human beings, children, dying from the red spots on their faces, I saw them put into fences like cattle, and I saw them beaten by white soldiers, young girls drug into the brush and left there to die naked and beaten. I saw them on the prairie starving, being herded like sheep out to where there was no food or shelter to die in the winter because the white man had killed all their food and took away their tee-pees, selling the painted skins. And I saw a million buffalo, dead, with no skin, rotting in the sun, I smelled them rotting. And I can smell them now as I sit here telling you what I have seen."

"I learned the names of the great leaders of the tribes, and I could tell you their names but I will not speak names any longer. I could also tell you why they were named, but I won't".

"I know of the great horse breeders in the north whose horses have gray spots on their rumps, and they have a name but I will not speak it. I know he is of my own blood and your father's blood and his father's blood and he is my great, great, great grandfather.

"And I have learned how to make arrowheads, arrows, and to start a fire from nothing. In one night, I have learned all these things I need to know for the rest of my life and what my life is about and my brother's life is about. I am only ten years old and I know all of these things to be the truth. I have seen it and I believe, I know they are real and I don't want to be a part of this world, I want to be in a different world, the silent world of the human beings, where things are not named and have no need to be named and nothing belongs to no one and all things are shared by all." At that he folded his arms and stopped talking.

Then the mother took the youngest twin into a different room and gave him a paper and said, "draw me a picture of what you have seen." And the father gave the older one a paper and said, "draw me a picture of what you have seen."

And both twins drew a picture of a small man with long black hair, greased, and tied in the back with a strip of rawhide and held with small stones, standing on a large rock, holding a spear. He was wearing skins and boots made of rabbit fur with the ears on the sides. There were round houses made of stones and poles with fish hanging on them and meat drying on stones with women grinding beans on flat rocks and children carrying sticks and grass. Both pictures were exactly the same in every detail.

The parents tore the pictures up and burned them, telling the boys to never speak of this again because people would think them crazy and laugh at them. Still they tried not to call the oldest one by his name, and tried not to speak names in his presence. And he became one of the silent ones, speaking only when he had to and then saying as little as possible. He became a collector of things, arrowheads and small stones with holes in them and polished stones and grinding stones and throwing stones and he knew the use of each of them without asking anyone.

He grew into a man and his brother grew into the same man, tall and thin and healthy from walking and searching the ground and hills for things from the past, and they were educated and went to college and married two sisters who looked alike, and they lived in different houses on different streets but always knew what the other was doing or thinking. And after hearing them talk about the man who had no name and needed no name, and watching them do the same thing at the same time even though they were not together, the sisters became afraid and thought them to be strange and maybe insane and left them after only a few months.

And it was on the night of their thirty-third birthday the man who had no name and needed no name returned to them in a dream. He was standing on the rock above the river and he pointed with his spear to a distant place on the side of the mountain across the basin and told them, "There is where you must go, I cannot take you there because I have never been there, and I can go only where I have been and it was there before me, and it was there before my father and his father and his father and before even the first word was spoken. And the people who lived there were there even when the ground was covered with ice and snow and they watched and saw what was happening down here. And they have things there you must see to become who you are." And he took his spear and placed in on the ground and piled stones around it so it was pointing to the place on the mountain and he said, "There is a huge cave there on the side of the cliff and when you find it you will see where trees were put into the side of the cliff to climb up on, and you will have to replace them before you can climb up there. It will not be an easy thing to do, but you must do it."

"Believe what I say. When you awake and come here, this spear will still be here and you will know it is real when you touch it and it will be one thousand six hundred years old and still be here as you see it, take it and keep it for yourself but first mark the place it is pointing to because that is where you must go to find what it is you need to find." And he went away into the air.

Both brothers woke up and called the other on the phone at the same time and both phones were busy and each time they tried the phone was busy because they did things the same, and one dialed faster than the other and the phone rang and was answered by the older of the two and he said, "Meet me in fifteen minutes."

They met and packed thing into their truck and drove to the place below the river and then walked into the place where the man with no name and needed no name had stood, and there in the stones was the spear pointing to a distant place on the side of the mountain and to a cliff they had seen but never been to.

The oldest of the two reached out and touched the spear to see if it was real and it was, and the younger of the two touched it and he knew it was real, then the older one took his camera then sat behind it and aimed it along the shaft of the spear and made pictures of where the spear was pointing and then marked the place with a straight limb from a tree and they left to prepare themselves for the trip to the place on the side of the mountain. They wrapped the spear in a blanket and put it in one of the rooms of their house where other things from the past were kept and saved it.

They spent several days looking At maps and pictures of the area and finally pin-pointed the exact spot on the mountain where they had to go. It would not be a easy climb but they figured they could do it and had to do it. They bought rope and spikes and pulleys and things to climb the cliff with and after fourteen days they left and drove back to the place where they had found the spear and then left their truck and began the long walk across the Basin and up to the other side and even past that. Six days it took them to walk to the place in the picture and it was three hundred feet above where they stood. They could see where the tree branches had been placed into the side of the cliff and created a sort of ladder the people had climbed up to the cave on, it took them only a few minutes to decide they could not climb it with ropes and even if they went to the top and tried to lower themselves down it would be nearly impossible. It was several hundred feet to the top of the cliff above the cave and then straight down. They did not have enough rope to do that.

They camped at the bottom of the cliff for two days and nights trying to figure a way up to the cave and finally decided it was as the man had said, they would have to replace the tree limbs in the side of the rock wall and make their way up on them. Two more days they camped and made a list of things they would need. Saws and axes and harness and pins to drive into the face of the wall in case one of them should happen to slip and fall. They sat and looked at the wall through a pair of binoculars and counted one hundred four places where the branches had been placed into the rocks at a forty-five degree angle. They would have to dig out the rotten remains of the branches and then replace them, one at a time as they made their way to the top, and there were no trees nearby. They almost decided to give up the whole idea but couldn't do it. They would have to go back and buy supplies and food and bring posts to replace the branches. It was becoming almost too much to consider.

On the fifth day, they started back across the Basin to buy the things they needed. They had figured it would take them at least two months to replace all the branches in the face of the cliff and there was weather to consider, and the forest service, and money and food, and how to get the things they needed all the way up here. It was getting into thousands of dollars and they hadn't even started yet.

They would have to make three or four camps and bring the things to the first one, then the second, and third until they had enough supplies and material to make the climb to the cave. They would need to buy mules to pack the things in on and then they would have to carry them on their own backs for the last fifteen miles because it was too rough for even mules. They finally walked back to where they had left their truck and it had been stripped of every useable part, the tires and wheels were gone, the motor and transmission was gone, even the doors were gone off of it. They were stranded fifty miles from the main highway. They camped next to what was left of the truck and in the morning, they started walking back, not feeling good about even coming in here.

The younger ask the older, "We do have insurance, don't we?"

And he replied, "No."

"I knew that," returned the younger of the two.

It took them sixteen hours of steady walking to reach the highway, then they caught a ride home, exhausted, seventeen days after they had left and were no nearer than before they had left. It had been thirty days, a whole month since they had had the dream.

Both men went straight into the room and looked to see if the spear was still there or had it all been just a dream. It was there, wrapped in the blanket. They felt better. but now they had to explain where they had been and why they had not been at work and people asked them questions they did not want to answer. They decided it was best if they just quit their jobs and sold one of the houses to raise the money for the project. The younger of the two put his house up for sale and moved in with the older of the two and when it was sold a month later they began to buy the supplies they needed. The list is too much to tell, but they began taking things up into the basin and storing them in a small cave they knew about not far from the river.

It took them five months and many trips to carry all the posts and things they needed to the cave and then it was winter and they would have to wait until spring to start the trip. It had been fifteen months since they had the dream.

In April, they left their house and rented three pack mules, then had them trucked to the place by the river. They knew nothing about packing mules and had a very difficult time at first because the packs would fall off and things would fall off the packs and the mules did not do as they were told to do. It took almost a month to carry the supplies to the first camp and they learned that a mule will eat a lot more than they had thought. They had to make repeated trips back and buy grain and hay for the mules to eat, and then it took them three weeks to the second, and three weeks to the third. They returned the mules to the river and drove back and asked the man who had brought them to come and get them. He was not pleased with the condition of the mules and told them so in not too few words.

It was July and very hot when they packed the first of thirty loads each onto their backs and began hiking the fifteen miles to the base of the cliff. They made one trip every two days and it was late August before they had the things they needed located at the base of the cliff. Now came the task of replacing the branches into the side of the cliff.

It took only three branches to realize it would not be easy. It took them a day to dig out the first stump and replace it with a post they had carried in, and then it was so loose they had to pack something around it to hold it in place. They realized all the holes were larger than the posts they had brought and they had to find something to secure them into the side of the cliff. They accomplished this by mixing small stones and mud and grass and then chinking it in around the post and letting it dry, then tying a line around the outer end of the post and securing it into the face of the cliff with a pin. It started to snow in October and they had secured only eleven posts into the cliff and though up twenty-five feet, they had to leave until springtime again. It had been nineteen months and over twenty-one thousand dollars and they were only twenty five feet closer to the cave than when they had the dream.

In March they returned and again started the task of digging out the rotten stumps and replacing them with new posts and chinking the mud, rocks, and grass in around them, then securing them with lines held into the cliff wall with the metal pins. They worked each day and managed to secure one post each day unless something went wrong. But the higher they got, the more difficult it was. First, they had to sit on the new post and then dig out the old stump, then pull the new post up by a rope and then the mud and rocks in a small bucket and chink it into place and tie it off until the mud hardened, then let it dry for a day before stepping on it. By the end of June, they were one hundred thirty feet up the side of the cliff and it took three days to replace one post. By the end of July, they were one hundred sixty feet up and out of supplies. They had to stop and return to their home and then bring more food and supplies in to the cliff base. They waited until spring.

It had been over two years and now the cost was over fifty thousand dollars and the older brother put his house up for sale and then bought a small trailer and they lived in it in the backyard of a friend who thought them both to be insane.

In February, it rained and in March, it rained and in April, it rained and in May, they went back to the cliff taking in a new supply of food and other things, and then started over, replacing the posts, one every three or four days. The hotter the weather, the quicker the mud set and got hard. It started snowing in October and they were only fifty feet and twelve posts from the entrance of the cave. They had to stop again and wait for the spring to come. It was now over three years since they had the dream. Both houses were gone. Their furniture was gone and their truck was gone, they had almost no money left and spent the four months waiting for spring by eating noodles and food from the food bank in town. They were unkempt and dirty and their clothes were worn out and needed patching, their boots were worn out and people thought them both to be going completely insane. Some thought they had a gold mine or something and just weren't telling anyone about it. Some thought they were burying all the gold and when they got enough they would just go away and spend it all somewhere. But most people thought they were just crazy in the head, something from them being so much alike.

In April of the fourth year, they returned and again began the task of climbing up to the cave, one post every four days, and in May, the oldest brother climbed up and stood up and walked into the cave and never came back out.

The younger of the two sat and waited for several hours and was afraid to climb up into the cave for fear he might not ever come back out. Was it full of ghosts from the past? He waited for one day and one night then when his brother never returned, he started to climb up the posts one at a time slowly, until he had reached the entrance to the cave and he walked in. The cave had nothing in it, it was empty, and his brother was not there.

He searched the cave from front to the back and there was nothing in it. No sign of anyone ever having been in it, but he stayed there for two days without leaving or eating and tried to feel where his brother had gone to. For the first time in his life, he was without his brother and he felt completely alone and he was afraid to leave thinking he would be alone for the rest of his life. What had happened to them? Now they had nothing, no houses, no wives, no money, and now he had no brother. He was terrified and he sat in the cave for three days and waited without sleeping or eating and had no water and he was getting weak and knew he had to climb back down to the camp. He left the cave and slowly climbed back down, nearly falling several times, and finally reached their camp, He ate and drank then slept and stayed there for eleven days, and when he woke up, his brother was standing over him looking at him smiling.

He jumped up and stood looking at his brother and asked, "My God! Where were you?"

"I was there, I could see you".

"Where? I looked all over there's nothing in there".

"Not in there, on the other side".

"What other side?"

"In the other world. On the other side of the wall.

"What are you talking about?"

"I was there, with the silent people, in the valley where the dead go".

"Are you crazy or something? I was there, there's nothing in there! Where were you?"

"Believe me, I was there, I saw you sitting on the floor waiting for me to come back".

"Then why didn't you?"

"I didn't want to."

And he looked at his brother and cried, "My God! You're going back, aren't you?"

"It's where I belong, and where I should have been, I should never have been born in this world".

"What about me?" he cried, "If you're going, I want to go too."

"You can't."

"Why not?"

"They said you can't go there"

"Why not? If you do, why can't I?"

"I don't know," he answered.

"Are we dead?" asked the younger one.

"No, we're not dead, touch me, I'm not dead!"

"I don't want to touch you! You're scaring the hell out of me! Where were you?"

"I was there, in the cave just a few feet away from you, but a thousand years away from you".

"You're really scaring the hell out of me," said the younger one.

Then the older of the two said, "Call me by my name". And the younger one tried and could not remember his own brother's name.

"I can't think of it," he cried.

"It's because now I have no name and I need no name. I am part of the earth and I came from the earth and now I can go back to the earth".

"Stop it!" The younger one cried and tried to grab his brother but he stepped back and said, "Thank you for helping me come here".

Then he turned and began walking up the posts stepping from one to the next until he was at the top and he stepped into the cave and was gone.

The younger of the two stayed in the camp for sixteen days and was afraid to climb back up into the cave. Then it started raining and he watched the rain against the side of the cliff and one by one the posts became loose and fell to the ground. In two days, they were gone from the cliff and laying on the ground. He packed some things and began his walk back to his world alone. Leaving his brother in his.

The Sailor

He was much too short to be called a country bumpkin, but he was from somewhere back in the hills of Tennessee. Not very well educated and his vocabulary was somewhat limited. He sort of talked out of the side of his mouth using slang words that he had to explain what they meant when he used them. They were the cause of a lot of the ridicule he received during the time I knew him, which amounted to a month or two over two years. I can't tell you his name because it just wouldn't be fair if I did, but I can tell you this. I never knew a man who tried harder to succeed than he did.

He was a small man, just barely big enough to get into the Navy, 5'2" and 1/8" and he weighed in at 126 pounds, one and a half pounds over the limit. He sort of took to me I guess because I was kind of a misfit myself, maybe not as much as he was because I was larger and could take care of myself in a scrap or a all-out fist fight if I had to (I had three older brothers) and a couple time I did because of someone picking on him. He just wasn't a fighter. He was quiet and shy and would do about anything anyone asked him to do, be it right or wrong.

If I had to describe him, I would say he was a small Ickabod Crane as described in the tale of the headless horseman. Small and thin with thin tight lips and ears that seemed to stick out too far, his neck was long, skinny and his Adam's apple protruded in a unsightly way so as to make you look at it instead of his face when he talked to you because it moved up and down as he spoke out the side of his mouth with that all-too-well-known Tennessee drawl. Even the smallest size of clothes were too big for him and they hung loose on his small frame so as to make him look sloppy all the time. Even the smallest t-shirt hung loose around his neck. His eyes were large and I don't really know if I ever saw him blink. They were sad eyes, filled with fear and looking away from whoever he was talking to. He spoke only when spoken to and he never started a conversation that I can remember. He would just stand a foot or two behind everyone else and wait for someone to speak to him, and if no one did, he just remained silent.

His only purpose in life and the reason he joined the Navy was to save three thousand dollars so he could buy a piece of land back where he came from and marry his childhood sweetheart, who he described as the most wonderful girl in the world, who also happened to be his second cousin, removed by a divorce. But after seeing her picture in the door of his locker, she looked more like a twin sister than a second cousin to me, the only difference being she had long braided brown hair. She was standing in front of a small clapboard house with a stone foundation and a sagging front porch held up by three wooden posts. She was wearing a simple print dress and holding a hound dog in her arms. He bragged about the hound dog, saying it was a good coon'er. Both were named Mary Lue. I would guess the dog was named after the woman, anyway, I hope that was the case.

Not a single day would pass without him writing her a letter and him asking me to look up words in the dictionary for him. And she wrote him back every day. Most letters he read to me read almost the same word for word.

"Hey there, miss you a bunch. Didn't do much today but the weather was all right down here. We're expecting a good rain tonight, Paw says it good for the crop. Maw's cooking (whatever she was cooking) and she would name her seven brothers and two sisters and tell what they were doing, then say the family is

48

proud of him and she was saving the money he was sending
home except for the small amount she was paying on the land
and she would tell him how much she paid and how much was
owed on it still and how much she had paid for the stamps and
envelopes and how much she had saved in her drawer then sign
it,

   I'm waiting for you to come home.
   Mary Lue

   In one letter, she told him, '*We got more money than anyone*
in the whole darn valley--$931.00'.

   But it was without fail if six days passed, he got six letters,
and he sent six letters home with money in them. Sometimes
three dollars, and sometimes more, but he sent every penny he
earned home in those letters. He shined shoes and did laundry for
the other sailors on the ship and even bought himself an iron and
earned money keeping the men's uniforms ironed and pressed. I
admired him for doing what he was doing and how hard he was
working, never leaving the ship when we were in a port of call.

   I always felt guilty and still do to this day even after forty
years have passed, because I never enjoyed looking at him, and
tried not to look directly at him when we were together talking or
writing his letters. I guess I sort of thought of him as an oddity or
maybe just ugly on the outside to look at, but I thought he was a
great man with great determination on the inside.

   We both had less than a year to go when he told me he had
the land paid for, $2,500.00, and they had $1,100.00 saved to get
married on. He was so happy he beamed and for the first time I
saw a shining in his big open eyes and a smile on his lips.

   "I'm a proud hillbilly," he told me.

"You should be, you worked hard enough to get it," I answered, thinking I had not saved even one dollar during my thirty one months on the ship.

We were in Japan, the last leg of our West Pac (Western Pacific duty).

In six months, we would return to the U. S. and remain there until our enlistments were up when it happened.

A guy from Montana. A man twice the size of him sat down at the table and started asking him questions, more or less making fun of him because he had never had sex and was saving himself for marriage.

"That's just stupid," the man told him.

"How is so stupid?"

"She's just going to divorce you cause you won't know how to keep her happy."

"No, she won't," he returned.

Don't you know anything about women?"

"Guess not too much."

"Why do you think most women get a divorce after two or three years?"

"I don't know," he looked somewhat puzzled and frightened.

I sat and listened and wanted to tell the man to shut his mouth, but I didn't want to get into a fight on the ship and get busted or put in the brig, so I said nothing as he talked and talked and scared my friend half out of his mind, telling him he had better go ashore and have sex with a woman so he would know what he was doing on his wedding night.

"Hell, you ain't even seen a naked woman have you?" he teased, then went into detail about the parts of a woman. Then someone else came and joined in and then someone else and pretty soon there were about eight or nine men telling him he should go ashore and find out about sex and finally they took up a collection for him and even thought I tried to talk him out of it, I was badly outnumbered and off he went, only to return several hours later half drunk and crying.

"I cheated on her," he cried. It was more of a sob than just crying, "And I cheated myself, I let them fellows talk me into it, and I cheated her out of the wedding night".

"Just don't ever talk about it. Don't tell her," I said.

"I got to, if I don't I'm just a cheater and then a liar on top of it. I'm not fit to even marry her now," the tears were running down his thin cheekbones and he held his face in his hands and said, "I got to, I got to tell her or I won't ever be able to face her, as soon as she looks at me she'll know I did the wrong thing," and he sobbed harder.

I tried to stop him. I tried to explain it wouldn't do him any good to tell her, just hurt her, and it was better if he never said anything about it, but he wouldn't listen and I sat on my bunk and watched as he cried and wrote her the letter telling what he had done.

He received five letters, and then none came for almost two weeks and he knew she had gotten the letter. "She's done with me," he said, "She read that letter and she's done with me."

"Maybe not. Maybe she's just thinking about it and she'll write you and tell you she understands why you did it," then two days later, he got the letter from her.

"I understand why you did it,' she wrote, 'I thought about it and I know you did it just because you wanted to make sure I would be satisfied. I showed the letter to Joe Bob and he told me it was the right thing for you to do and that I should do it too so you wouldn't feel so guilty about doing it and I would know something about it too. I went to the show with him on Saturday night and then we did it in his truck. It wasn't anything what I

51

thought it was going to be, it was very pleasant and felt really good, I don't see too much wrong with us doing it with other people. I've done it with Joe Bob and his brother, Raymond, and it was not bad at all. I'm not mad at you for doing it. I think it is fun.'

Then the letter returned to the standard text about her saving money and the rain and her brothers and sisters and she closed the letter with,

'I got to go now, I been asked to go to the dance with Raymond and his cousin. You take care and write me back, Ok? Don't worry, I'm not mad at all, it was a good idea.'

I sat on my bunk and watched his sad face and he read and reread the letter about ten times, then handed it to me.

"I don't guess I even want her now," he said.

"Why not? It don't change nothing, you'll be home soon and it'll be just like it was when you left, you got the land and money saved. So you both did it, so what?"

It didn't seem to console him much; he sat there for several hours reading the letter then wadded it up and threw it in the trash can. I took it back out and straightened it out then put it back in the envelope for him and laid it on his bunk.

But no letter came the next day or the day after and none came for a week then she wrote,

"Don't be mad at me, but I spent some of the money on buying new clothes. I got a job as a waitress at the Silver Bar. Raymond is the bartender there, now so I ride to work with him. I made almost thirty dollars last night in tips.'

"I really like working there, people are so nice to me, everyone is asking me to go out with them after work but I only go with Raymond, then I go home.'

"I have to go to work now. Write me.'

Then five weeks passed and he got another letter.

*"Dear ******,*

"I'm writing to tell you I have to get married. It's Paul. You know, from the sawmill. I got pregnant, I didn't know that could happen, but it did, and now I have to get married to him right away or everyone will know what I been doing. I hope you're not too mad at me because I had to use most of the money to buy a wedding gown and things and Paul needed a new suit and a pair of low-cut shoes to get married in. Everyone says second cousins shouldn't get married anyway, so I don't think I'm doing the wrong thing.

"We're getting married this weekend at the church in Troy town so I guess we'll be moving to Nashville. Paul wants to play his Banjo there and maybe make some records.

"I hope I get to see you when you come back to Tennessee, I'm sure someone will know where we are and Paw says you'll find a nice girl to marry with after you come home. As least you still got your land you bought so you can build a house on it.

"I have to go now, see you soon,
Mary

I couldn't believe what I was reading and he sat there crying for three days. He cried when he was eating and when he was walking and laying on his bunk. Then on the fifth day we couldn't find him anywhere on the ship. We searched and a Man Overboard drill was called and every compartment on the ship was searched. It was decided maybe he jumped overboard and killed himself. That night I found a note under the pillow on my bunk.

"I guess we never know what God's going to do with us, do we? Thanks for being my friend.

And he was gone? When they opened his locker, we saw he had cut the hound dog out of the picture of her standing in front of the house but left the picture of her pasted to the door.

2007

We, us, you, me, them, those guys, men, women, girls, boys, we all do it. We spend our money foolishly. It's a joke, an insult, to the rest of the world and all the people who are starving and living in fields without anything, including food.

Here, the police are against the rest of the population and their only real function it to collect more money to get stronger so they can collect more money to get stronger. They police themselves and so they don't police themselves just make excuses for each other's wrongdoings.

The politicians are all for the party and not for the people, (Republicans). Russia is a red state, Cuba is a red state, China is a red state. North Korea is a red state. And the Republican party here in the US represents itself as a red state. Does that tell you anything??

The news media is now all for itself. It twists everything to make it sound worse than it is and make the story last as long as it can so they can get in as many commercials as possible during the shows, and they are shows.. not newscasts like they used to be.

All the best songs have been written.

All the best singers have died.

All the real actors have passed on.

Real talent is a thing of the past.

There are no real dances, just a bunch of gyrations.

Everything worth doing has already been done.

What happened to the people who used to dress up in nice-looking matching clothes and stand on a stage and play music?

A few years ago, I went to the local dump to dispose of a few things and as I was emptying the truck, I happened to see a few books lying on the trash heap and I picked them up. One of them was a small red book about two inches by two inches and only thirty one pages thick.

The cover read:

The Constitution of the
United Soviet States of Russia
1949

Inside there were maybe four or five laws on each page; some had one and some had two. I don't remember them all but I remember a few of them.

Every person is born and evaluated equal.

Every person is responsible for his fellow men in a equal manner as he is for him or herself.

Every person is responsible for his or her parents as long as they are alive.

There were more. And if I remember right there were 67 laws total, when we had 16,000 federal laws here. But I don't remember them word for word; I do remember all of those laws were deemed communistic by the government, or at least by the Republican party in the government. We were at war with Russia then, a cold war, which amounted to a lot of people telling things to a lot of different people ... just minding other people's business instead of their own.

But... You know the law that I saw that stuck with me more than any other law I've ever read in this country or in Russia is

 # 33 If you don't work, you don't eat. I like that one.

I think they should make every drug addict and every alcoholic on SSI come to the office and take a test before they get their check at the first of the month. If they test dirty.....no money!!

Mama's Biscuits

He stood, as he did each winter morning from about five until six, beside the wood heating stove in the living room in front of the window, watching the sun rise in the east. He enjoyed watching the rays as first one bolt of light then another and another sprang like javelins being thrown by some long-ago warrior through the tree tops and then across the field and down through the pasture and finally making tiny little crystals out of the dew on the grass in the front yard.

His coffee cup, a big old white mug he had had for as long as he could remember, was empty and he sat it on top of the heater stove on the warming plate and rubbed his side where his overalls were starting to get too hot, then he moved away, around the back to stand on the other side of the stove.

It was an old house when he had bought the farm for three hundred dollars down a week after he left the service and a month after he turned twenty-seven years old. He had been on it working every day for the last 28 years. The outside of the barn was unpainted and looked rustic as well it was, but the house he had repainted this summer just to have something to do. It too was old but the inside was spotlessly clean with wallpaper on the walls of every room except the kitchen, which was open to the living room through a large archway near the heater stove where a large braided oval rug had laid for the past twenty-two years and now had a path worn through the center of it. The kitchen was white, painted with enamel paint long before and had been scrubbed so many times the paint was worn off where the handles were and where washing had taken place a million times. The huge oak table in the center was the same, showing wear at each setting in front of the five chairs of which three now sat empty with no place mat on the table.

He stood looking out the window in the living room, watching the sun rise and glancing at his wife making biscuits in the kitchen as she had done every morning for the last twenty-six or more years. Kneading the dough and adding flour as needed, then rolling it over again and kneading it into shape. He watched her cover the dough with a towel and move it to the kitchen stove and check her fire, then add two pieces of wood and close the lid.

He could feel the heat of the heater stove on his backside now and moved away and rubbed his butt trying to cool his overheated coveralls. He had made up his mind that this summer he was going to have electric heat put into the house and buy his wife an electric stove, because the thought of cutting the fifteen cords of wood by himself was too much to think about at his age. Not that he couldn't still do it, but it seemed not too practical now when everyone around him had electric heat or oil.

Wood was stacked along the north side of the house in a long row. His two boys had made sure there was enough to last all winter and he would not have to cut any before they had left. He was in his late fifties now and he felt it, a little more each day, his arms ached from not working all winter and he was stiff when he got up in the morning and had to walk around just to loosen up his legs. They had gotten a late start with their marriage, he was thirty-nine and she was thirty-seven. She was the smart one in the family and kept the money and paid the bills, so he was glad she had decided to marry him. She in fact had been the one who asked him, knowing he would never have the nerve to ask her. He regretted that now, wishing they had started earlier in life, so they would have more time together through the late years.

He had gained a lot of weight during the winter. He didn't know how much, but too much, he thought. His coveralls were tight in his crotch and he had to let the shoulder straps out as far as they would go this morning and the two buttons on the sides were no longer able to reach the buttonholes so they hung open.

"You think those mules feel as stiff as I do?" he asked, looking into the kitchen.

"It's too early to start plowing, ain't it, Bob?" she answered.

"I was thinking about pulling out those three stumps while the ground is still soft."

"You want some more coffee?"

He heard what she had said but his mind was thinking about the mules standing in the barn and they would be hard to handle after standing around and not working for three months.

"Well? Do you or don't you?"

He looked back into the kitchen. His wife was standing holding the coffeepot in her hand ready to pour. Then he glanced out through the window at the two dogs laying by the wood pile waiting for his sons to come out of the house and start the days work.

"Yeah, ya I do," he answered and walked into the kitchen holding his cup in his hand.

"We got any honey left?" he asked.

"A dab. We got a dab left, maybe you could get some when you go to town. You need to get a haircut anyway." She sat the honey jar on the table in front of him.

"I'm getting fat," he said as he dropped a half spoonful of honey into the coffee and stirred it, then walked back to look out of the window. He felt himself inside his coveralls and said "I think I grew a little too much this winter from not working, I should have kept more of the livestock so I'd have something to do."

"You do enough, Bob," she sort of laughed. "You've worked hard all your life."

He didn't answer, he was thinking about the boys, gone off to college. The dogs had moved to just in front of the porch and were laying side by side in the sun, the younger one with its head on the other's side as it did each morning, waiting.

He looked at the field, then beyond it past the pasture and at the hill, he could see the three stumps and knew he would never pull them out, there was no need to do it now. But he needed to take the mules out and let them walk so they didn't get the gout from standing in the barn.

He looked at his wife rolling the biscuits around on the table and then tossing them from hand to hand shaping them and then placing them on the baking tray side by side. He wondered how it felt to be fat all the time. She was plump when they got married and she had put on a lot of weight after their daughter was born and she never lost it. She seemed to gain a bit each year, and he wondered if his wife had gotten so used to it didn't bother her any longer. Did she know her side of the bed was all sagged down and her side of the couch was sagged down from her weight? He thought about the girls he had known in high school, all of them! He sort of laughed, they're all fat now. All of them except Ima Shurefield who had thirteen kids during nineteen years of marriage, seven boys and six girls. He wondered how Jake was going to feed them all when they became teenagers, God help him, his place was smaller than this one.

He had been giving three gallons of extra milk to them every day since the boys had gone last September and she was still as thin and shapely as she was in high school. It must have been from working so hard raising all of those kids. But he enjoyed giving them the free milk, he enjoyed that, and looked forward to the boys coming to get it every day. One or more of the kids came every afternoon and carried the milk back home. He was glad to help them. The Shurefields were good people and the kids were all good workers, happy and always together.

His three children were good too, the best in the county, the best in school and the best in sports, and always helping without being asked to help. They learned that from their mother, that's how she was, always doing something a little extra to make things go right and make you feel good.

"Did you like raising our kids?" he asked.

"What!" She looked surprised and stood there holding the tray of biscuits in her hand and the oven door half open in her other one.

"Why in God's name would you ask me that? You know I loved every minute of it, Bob." She slid the tray into the oven and closed the door. "All children leave, Bob, it's part of life. Thank God you worked hard so they could get a good education. They'll be home soon for the summer."

For the first time in his life, he had a bank account and two credit cards, every bill was paid and the farm was paid off, as was his truck and the rest of the machinery on the farm.

His daughter was the first to be born and a year and one month later, the twin boys. The girl had gotten married last summer and moved to Seattle, the boys both went away to collage a month later, and he missed them. He missed then at breakfast, he missed them fighting over the last couple of sweet cream biscuits, or the last ear of fresh corn; it had become a sort of game around the table.

He thought about buying a tractor and wondered how it would feel to plow all five fields in just a few days instead of the month it took with the mules.

He gave up the idea. If the boys wanted a tractor they could buy one when they came home, if they ever did.

"Maybe I'll just turn the whole place into pasture and raise beef," he said.

"Were you talking to me or yourself?" his wife asked.

"Both, I guess," he answered.

"Ready?" she asked, removing the tray of hot biscuits from the oven and dumping them into a large woven basket on the table she had lined with a white towel.

"Why did you make so many?" he asked.

"I don't know," she answered, looking at the two sixteen biscuits in the basket.

He came to realize why he had gained so much weight in the last ten months. All three kids had left and she still made the same number of biscuits each morning and he ate almost all of them with honey and butter on them plus the rest of his breakfast, lunch, and dinner. That's why they were out of honey and he had gained so much weight.

"Maybe you should start using a smaller pan."

"I don't think I have a smaller one, Bob," she answered, realizing there were way too many biscuits on the table for two people.

"Maybe I should get you a smaller pan."

"You could buy me one when you go to get your hair cut."

"It'd be smart if I did," he said, taking the first biscuit and spreading butter, then honey on it.

She watched him as he ate the biscuits and said, "You don't have to eat them all, Bob."

"You do make good biscuits, Alice," he said and looked across the table at her and watched her eyes go from one empty chair to the next and then he watched the tears start to run down her face making little trails as they ran through the flour dust gathered on her cheeks. For nineteen years those chairs had been sat on and now all three were setting empty.

"We got them all at one time and lost them all at one time." she cried softly.

They had not tried to stop having children; they just never had any more. Katy had gotten married in August and the boys had left in September for college in Colorado. He looked at the three chairs and then out through the window at the empty pen by the barn where there had always been at least thirty head of prime beef stock this time of year but he had sold them all off to pay for the boys' college and now the pen was empty. The fields were empty and his house felt empty and so did his insides. His belly felt full and he felt empty. Even the honey jar was empty now. He could never remember the honey jar being empty, it was the first time he had really looked at the empty chairs or felt the emptiness of the house, no chairs scraping on the floor and no kids fighting for the last biscuit.

"Son of a bitch!" he uttered.

"What did you say, Bob?" she looked astonished.

"Son of a bitch!" he repeated.

"Why on earth would you say that?" she asked.

"I just felt like it, son of a bitch!" He said it louder.

"Well, what are you son of a bitching about?" She looked at him.

He thought about his mules and the stumps he knew he would never pull out.

He thought about the two dogs laying out there waiting for the boys to come out, one was seventeen years old and walked with a limp in her hind leg; she would be gone soon too.

He looked at the now-dry streaks down his wife's cheek from her crying.

He thought about how fat he had gotten and how lazy he had become since he sold off everything.

He thought about all the time he had stood leaning on the fence by his barn and watched the herd of beef he had raised. Ninety-six had been loaded into trucks and hauled away in one weekend.

He looked at the empty honey jar and said, "Son of a bitch, you sure do make good biscuits, Alice."

"I been making them the same way ever since we been married."

He looked at her face and saw the wrinkles for the first time and the age in her eyes and flour on her dress and thought it looked so natural on her. He'd seen her more times with flour on her than without flour on her.

"Was something wrong with them this time?" she asked.

"Don't make so many biscuits, Alice."

He looked at her and the tears were running down her face again making little white balls as they gathered the flour dust.

"I'm sorry," she said.

He got up and slid his chair back, then walked around and kissed Alice on her lips and said, "I'm going to town to buy a bull and two heifers and a tractor and a smaller pan."

He walked out of the house, heading for the barn. The two dogs sat up and waited for the boys to come out of the house. When they didn't, the dogs got up and followed him out to the barn.

Brownstone

He wasn't a small man. Just short of stature and thin. His hair was a sort of brownish red in color and his nose was a thing he wished he had never seen. Not large but just unattractive. It seemed to point up, exposing his nostrils. And his eyes were his worst enemy, small and clouded from so many nights of reading by a dim light. Now he had to wear thick glasses that he hated and he had every intention of getting contact lenses but couldn't make himself pay out the money.

Money was one thing he was good at. He saved exactly sixty eight percent of what he earned. He had lived in the same two rooms ever since he came to New York. In three more months it would be twenty-five years. In two more months he will have sat at the same desk for twenty-five years and rode the same numbered bus twice a day, five days a week, for twenty-five years.

He even thought of himself as being a little too cheap, but he had a dream of going off to Oregon and finding a cabin in the tall fir trees and spending his last years there, cutting his own wood and growing a garden. It was Friday and he was on his way home. Sitting in the right-side seat next to the back of the bus where he always sat. He liked to sit by the window, but the seat was taken already. He didn't know this man, some of them he knew and spoke to, but not tonight. He sat and waited as the bus turned the last corner and he got off, then, as he done each Friday, he stopped at the bank and put his check into his savings account. Took out the exact amount of change to pay for his bus rides the next week and stopped at the restaurant and had his once-a-week Rueben sandwich and potato salad. Paid the waitress and left for home two blocks away. He sat on his one chair and removed the rubber slipcovers off of his shoes. The covers cost six dollars and shoes cost thirty, so he put the covers on every time he left the room so as not to wear out his shoes. He looked out of his one barred tiny window which was even with the sidewalk and just before the railing leading down into the row of basement apartments to see if anyone had left any donations at the mission across the street. He used to stand and look up through the window and try to see up under women's skirts as they walked past, but not anymore, he grew tired of it after several years of failing to see anything. These days, at various times of the month he could go over and look through the bags and find good clothes. At times he had found clothes nice enough to sell on the street a few blocks away where people sold things on the weekends. Several times during the years he had made as much as fifty dollars selling a few things. But he had to be careful because he had gotten caught once before and fined. He saw no bags on the steps and set to doing his bus change, placing three quarters and one dime into ten separate stacks and then placing scotch tape around them, making ten separate bundles of change, two for each day of the work week.

He sat on the side of his bed and thought to himself, "I should do something this weekend" but then as always, he thought about the money and dismissed the idea. He looked out the window again hoping for a bag of clothes to appear on the steps of the Mission. It didn't happen, but something else did.

He saw the legs as they passed by the window. Four were female and two belonged to the super who knocked on his door as he passed.

"Charles! I'm renting the apartment next to you so don't get all excited if you hear people over there. Charles? Did you hear me? Are you in there?"

"He's always in there," the super told whoever it was with him. He opened his door and looked at the two women. One was about his age and the other one was a small teenage girl with long dirty-looking straight hair. She looked at him and smiled through badly-decayed front teeth. He closed the door without looking at the woman's face.

"He's sort of a hermit," the super said, then added, "He's got tons of money in the bank and he's too cheap to spend a penny of it."

He heard the woman answer, "Oh. That's nice to know. He has money, Mindy".

He spent most of the weekend listening through the wall and watching their legs go up and down the stairs past his window. He even tried to look up their skirts as they passed and managed to catch a quick glance of the teenager's white panties under the short skirt she was wearing.

It was Sunday evening when the girl knocked on his door.

"I'e Mister, you got a telly?"

"A What?" he asked.

"A telly. You know, a TV, me mum's gone off to somewhere and I got nothing to do. Can I watch your telly?"

"What?" he stammered, looking at the girl's almost open man's white shirt hanging loose around her. She had no lower garment on that he could see.

She looked at his eyes looking at her bare legs and laughed.

"Don't worry, I got me drawers on." She lifted the shirttail to show him her panties, and then let it drop.

"I don't think so," he answered, and tried to close the door.

"Come on, Mister, she'll be gone who knows how long ,maybe all night, if I know her. You do got a TV don't you?"

"Yes, but..."

67

"Oh, I been with men before," she laughed and walked past him into the small apartment.

"A bit tiny, ain't it?" she said.

"It's all right. It fits me".

"I could too," she smiled and sat on the bed, then raised and folded her legs. "What you watching?"

"What?" he answered, looking at her crotch completely exposed. He could even see the hair through the light material of her panties.

"You better go," he said, and opened the door, then held it open.

"Want I should go put on more clothes? Most men don't," she smiled, showing her decayed teeth.

"Go!" He demanded. "Please just leave!"

"You're no fun at all," she answered, then added, "Bet you never even bumped a girl, 'ave ya?"

"No! Whatever that means," he said as she walked past, then stopped and opened the front of her shirt and showed him her small, but very developed, breasts, then told him "Just knock on the wall and I'll come back if you want to play a little with them, I won't charge you nothing if you don't tell me mum I didn't."

He was scared half to death and shaking as he motioned with his hand for her to go past him and into the hallway. "Goodbye," he said and closed the door and wished he hadn't ever opened it. He sat on the bed next to the wall and watched the TV with the sound turned as low as it would go so he could still hear it for three hours trying to hear what she was doing through the wall. He was watching the TV but his mind was seeing her small round breasts and the large protruding nipples.

He heard her leave and walk by his door. He watched for her legs to pass by the window but as he watched she leaned over and looked in at him. It startled both of them and she left up the

68

stairs and he went into the bathroom and sat there for several minutes. Then locked his door and leaned a chair against it.

In the morning before leaving for work, he locked all of his valuables in the small storage room down the hall, put on his coveralls so his suit wouldn't get dirty from the grime of the streets, then his rubbers over his shoes, and went off to his bus stop. He stood waiting for the bus and saw the girl standing on the stairs looking at him. He was sure she was going to try to rob his apartment as soon as he was out of sight. Then he saw it, partly stick under the leg of the bench. A picture. He reached down and picked it up then looked at the woman and two children in the photo. They were on a ski slope standing next to each other waving at whoever was taking the picture. It was a very colorful picture and it looked as though it might have been taken in Oregon or somewhere in Colorado maybe. The background was filled with huge green trees and snow-covered slopes.

"Oh! Let me see," a lady said and looked over his arm at the picture.

"Lovely. They're just lovely. I bet you miss them, don't you?"

"What?" he returned and looked to see who had said it.

"Your family. They're lovely," she said, then asked, "Are they on vacation without you?"

"Huh", he stammered for a second, but something about the snow and the fir trees in the background and the color of their ski clothes and them standing like they could be waving at him as well as anyone, and he answered, "Yes, I couldn't got off work, so they went without me."

"She's very pretty. Your wife I mean" the lady told him.

"Yes, yes she is," he answered and put the picture in his pocket and took out one of the packets of coins for the bus. He took the tape off them, then stuck the scotch tape on the light pole next to the bench as the bus arrived. The girl was still standing on the stairs looking down the street as the bus went past. He guessed he had been wrong and she was looking for her mother to return. She was still standing there when he arrived home at six in the evening.

He tried to step past her and down the stairs but she asked him, "You got any food? Me mum's not come home and I got no money."

He started to just go on into his apartment but she asked him, "Please, Mister, I ain't ate nothing for two days. I'm awful hungry. Just some bread would do me fine if you got some".

"Where is she? Your mom?" he asked, looking at her thin face, then down at the swelling in the front of her dress. He saw her sort of smile as she answered, "I don't know, she just goes off for a few days at a time. She don't tell me nothing."

"All I have is some lunch meat and soup, I can't cook in my apartment".

"Anything," she answered then said, "Thanks ever so much, Mister."

"You from England?" he asked.

"London, but we had to leave 'cause me mum was getting arrested and I had to go to the girls' dorm until I was eighteen".

"What did she do?" She followed him down the stairs and into the hall.

She's a 'ore. I'm one too! but me mum don't let me do just anyone. She has to pick them out for me so she can put the pinch on them when they learn I'm only fifteen."

"Don't talk any more, OK?" He looked back at her as he opened the door then stood looking to see if anything had been moved. It hadn't as well as he could see, and he let her into his room then showed her the small refrigerator and things to make a

70

sandwich. He got a container of pre-made soup and sat it in the microwave, then took off his coveralls and his slippers. He took the picture he had found and laid it on the dresser.

"What you wear that oversuit for?" she asked.

"It protects my suit from the smog and scum on the street. Clothes cost money and I don't have much," he answered, trying to detour her from asking him for money.

He watched as she buttered the bread and then put one slice of lunch meat on it and turned to him, "Can I have two slices?

"Have as many as you want," he answered and she put three slices of the meat on the bread then cheese and onion and pickles and catsup and mustard then salt and pepper. She turned and looked at him again, "Maybe a glass of milk? You got a whole jug in here."

He took one of his three glasses and rinsed it out then handed it to her. Then took the container of soup out and handed it to her.

"You got me a whole dinner going here," she smiled and he sort of wished her teeth were better to look at.

She sat at his small table and ate the food, then wiped off the table and cleaned the glass, then sat it back on the shelf where he had gotten it. She looked at the picture on the counter and then picked it up and looked at it for a long time, then laid it back down.

"Wish that was me in that picture," she looked at him, "They don't live here with you, do they?"

"No," he answered.

"You got a nice house out there in the country, do ya?"

He didn't answer her.

"Must be hard on you, you living here and your wife and children living out away like that, bet you go and see them a lot, huh?"

"Not too often," he answered.

"I was gonna ask you if you wanted a hump but I guess if you got a wife and kids like that you wouldn't do it anyway. Oh, I wasn't gonna ask you to pay me anything. You feeding me like you did. I was real hungry but I'm not now," she smiled again.

He thought to himself how sad and hard her life must be, he thought about the hookers on Sixteenth Street he passed every day on the bus and them walking around almost naked trying to find some man to give them some money.

"You want to watch the TV for a while until your mom comes back?"

"It's ok with you?"

"Yeah, it's ok," he answered then sat on the bed and turned on the TV, she sat beside him with her hands on her lap and watched the TV for a while and then got up and looked at the picture again.

"Where is it you house is?" she asked.

"Oregon," he answered. "It's out in Oregon."

"That's above California. I been looking at the map. I want to go to California when I'm eighteen and get a job there. I need to fix my mouth. My teeth aren't too good."

"I noticed," he answered.

"Ugly, ain't they?" she said.

"Not really, they just need to be fixed."

"They're ugly, I know they are," she answered and carefully put the picture back like it was crystal and might break if she dropped it.

"Wish it was me in that picture," she said again, then sat back down next to him.

"I wish it had been me, taking the picture," he thought and glanced at her uncovered legs.

"You sure got a nice family," she said softly then said. "I might have had a dad like you if me mum wasn't a 'ore like she is".

He looked at her face and saw she was crying.

"Why don't you go to the shelter and ask them to help you? They have schools where you can live and go to school there and even get paid for doing it".

"Where's such a thing like that?"

"Go ask a policeman, and tell him you don't know where your mom is and you don't have a place to live and he'll take you to child services and they'll find a home for you to live and send you to school and even fix your teeth for you".

"How do you know about that?" she asked, looking again at the picture then carefully laying it back down. She turned and smiled at him.

"Maybe I could go and live with your family. I could work and pay something".

He almost said the picture wasn't really his family but he couldn't. Something inside him felt proud for the first time since he could remember. Even if it wasn't real she thought it was and the lady at the bus stop thought it was.

"I don't think that is possible right now," he answered. "I'd have to talk to my wife about it and... I don't think so, I think child services is better for you."

"It's just like a dream," she said, then asked "Is it a big house?"

"Pretty big," he answered.

"Do you have a picture of it?"

"No, no I don't."

She looked disappointed and said, "If me mum don't come back by tomorrow I have to leave. She only paid for three days.

She was supposed to pay more yesterday but she never came back."

"I don't have any money," he said.

"But, maybe I could stay with you until she comes back?" Then she added, "I don't think she is coming back."

"She wouldn't just leave you!"

"She did before, but this time I don't think she's ever coming back."

Part of him wanted to just tell her to leave and never come back but the other part wanted to help her somehow. It was the first time he ever felt like he could, or even wanted to, help anyone. In fact it was the first time he had ever talked to anyone this much who didn't work at his office that he could remember.

"I have to eat something," he said.

"I'm not hungry now," she answered quickly.

"You could eat a piece of pie or something, can't you?"

She smiled with her mouth closed to hide her teeth and answered, "Sure, Mister I can always eat pie".

"I'm going down the street. Come on," he said and opened the door for her.

"You're going to take your picture, aren't you?" she said, and handed him the picture. He took it and put it in his pocket, then locked his door and followed her up the stairs. They walked the block and a half to a small restaurant where he ate once or twice a week.

He ordered the special and a piece of apple pie for her. When the waitress brought the food, the girl asked her, "Have you seen his family?"

"His family? I didn't even know you had a family, Chuck," she looked surprised.

"They don't live with me," he answered.

"You're divorced?" she returned.

74

"No, they just live out of town."

"Where out of town?"

"In Oregon."

"That's out of town!" She laughed. "So why do they live there and you live here?"

"Show her the picture. It's like a dream," the girl said.

He took the picture out of his pocket and showed it to the waitress.

"They're in Oregon and you're here? You're nuts!" she said.

"I make a lot more money here, we're buying a house," he said.

"So you're living here, and buying a house there? So you're not really so cheap, just sending all your money home?"

"Something like that".

The waitress leaned over and kissed him on the cheek. "I apologize for every bad thing I said and thought about you for the past five years, Chuck." She walked away and asked the other waitress, "Did you know Chuck had a wife and kids out in Oregon? He's buying a house there."

The other waitress looked at him and shook her head no.

"Unbelievable," the first one said, and went off into the kitchen.

He remembered the feeling from when he had made a good play on the baseball team in junior high; it was pride, something he hadn't felt for a long time. Now twice in less than three hours he felt pride. He smiled at the girl across the small table from him.

"You want another piece of pie? With ice cream on it?"

"Yes!" she chirped then said, "Thank you."

They finished eating and walked back to his small apartment and he told her she had better go back to her own place and wait for her mother.

"If she don't come back will you take me to the ... What is it?"

"Child protective services."

"Will you take me there?"

"Ask me tomorrow," he answered and closed the door, then sort of wished he had let her stay and watch TV with him.

He took off his overcoat and removed the picture from his pocket and sat it standing against the base of the lamp. He finished that and cleaned his shoes and rinsed out his five pair of socks and underwear then hung then up over the heat radiator to dry. He wiped down the small counter and the bathroom with a towel he had gotten from across the street and rinsed it out then laid it on the radiator. His chores were done. All he had left was to shower and watch TV.

He sat there looking at the picture, at the woman's blond hair and the red and white suit she was wearing, the white stocking cap with a blue ball on the top of it, the children's snowsuits and their smiling faces, then at the snow on the slope and the green tall trees and he thought, "I should have a family like that. Why don't I? Why do I stay here? I have enough money saved to go anywhere. I'm afraid, I think, I'm afraid to try and move away. At least I'm safe here."

He spent two hours watching the TV but spent more time looking at the picture than he did the TV.

He had just gone to bed when he heard the landlord next door talking to the girl. He leaned against the wall and listened to the man tell her she had to leave.

"Can't I stay until the morning?" she begged.

"No! You have to leave now, I can't have a teenager staying here by herself," he told her.

A minute later he heard her knock on his door. He wasn't going to let her in but he relented and opened the door for her.

"He threw me out," she said.

"I heard him," he answered.

"I don't have a coat," she said.

He didn't answer her, just looked at her wondering what to say or do.

"But it's raining out there!" she was almost crying.

He watched in shock as the girl laid down on the floor in the corner and said, "I'll just sleep here, OK? OK?"

"You can sleep on the bed but on top of the covers," he told her.

"I'll be real still," she said and climbed onto the bed and laid against the wall with her back to him. He got under the covers and turned off the lights.

"Mister," she said softly.

"What?"

"I wish I was your daughter."

"Go to sleep," he answered.

"Mister?"

"What?"

"Do you have a blanket? I'm kinda cold."

He took his top blanket and folded it over on top of her, covering her up, then slid one of his pillows over to her then said, "Go to sleep."

She was asleep in a few seconds, breathing softly. He turned over and looked at the side of her face in the dim light from the small window. She looked very small laying there and that made him feel bigger, bigger and proud and satisfied that he was doing something for someone. He hadn't done anything for anyone in twenty-five years. In fact, he used to enjoy closing doors just as people were getting ready to follow him through, and he had never spent any money on anyone. He had spent seven dollars on this girl and he didn't even know her. He laid there for several hours, sleeping only in short naps, because he woke up each time she moved. He was awake and out of bed at four in the morning. He made coffee and sat there looking at the TV with the sound turned down. The girl just kept sleeping until it was noon and he woke her up.

They always had a free breakfast at the mission across the street and he thought maybe they might help the girl so he took her over there.

The lady at the door said to him, "You're the guy who steals our donations, ain't you?"

"No! Not me! You're mistaken!" he answered.

"You look like him," she returned.

"I'm not him!" he stammered.

"You live over there in the basement don't you?" she asked.

"Yes, but I'm not him."

"Yes, you are! We got no food for you. Thief!" she said.

"I didn't come to eat, I came to see if you could help this girl, she has no place to live and her mother left her."

"You help her! Do something right for once in your miserable life! Thief!" she said again and pointed for him to leave. "Don't come here asking for help from us. I know all about you and so does everyone else around here, all you want is something for nothing."

"He's just trying to help me," the girl told her.

"You can come in but he can't," the woman said and then asked, "Did he do anything to you honey?"

"You mean like give me a good bump? No, I asked him if he wanted one but he has a family so he couldn't."

"What family?" the woman sneered.

"In Oregon," the girl answered, "He's buying a house there so he sends all his money to his family."

The woman looked at her, then back at him.

"Please, I need help, I don't even have a coat," the girl told her.

"Where have you been living?"

"Nowhere," she answered, "Me mum is gone and I don't think she's coming back."

The woman looked disgustedly at him and said, "Well, bring her in," and she stepped aside and let them into the mission.

"Grummie old hag, ain't she?" the girl whispered.

They were led to the main room and to the large table, but no food was brought to them.

"Where's the food?" the girl asked.

"I think they have a prayer first then they give the food," he told her, but then in a few moments, a sister came and asked the girl to follow her. She never came back.

He sat and waited for a half hour and another woman told him the girl had been taken to a different place where she could stay. He got up and left the mission and went back home. He felt a sense of loneliness he had not felt before and didn't even know it was in him to feel. He sat on his bed and looked at the picture leaning against the base of the lamp and had a strong urge to just pack everything and leave the city and go and try to find a life in Oregon, but it passed in a few seconds and he turned on the TV then sat and watched it until he fell asleep and slept most of Sunday.

He woke up Monday morning and got ready to go to his work, then just as he was about to leave he saw the picture on the counter, and he took it and put it in his coat pocket. Why? He didn't know, he was just sort of attached to it for some strange reason. Then when he got to the bus stop, he stood there untaping his change and sticking the tape to the lamp post where there were hundreds of other pieces he had stuck there during the past years. He stood there looking up and down the street at the buildings and the cars all covered with a light film of brown smog. He took out the picture and looked at it. The white clean snow and the clear blue sky and the tall green trees. Again he wanted to just go back to his apartment and pack his things and leave for Oregon or somewhere where the air was clean and he could feel good.

"How's your family?" a voice said behind him.

He turned and it was the woman from last Thursday when he had found the picture.

"Oh! They're fine," he answered, feeling the picture in his pocket. "I was just thinking about moving out there with them."

"You should you know," she answered, "Money isn't everything."

The bus arrived and he took his normal seat second from the rear of the bus, but then changed his mind and moved forward one seat from the front.

"You alright?" the driver asked him.

"Yes, I'm fine, thank you," he answered.

The driver looked surprised and drove on glancing in his mirror several times, looking at him. He had never sat anywhere but in the back before in all the years he had been riding the bus. When he got off and told the driver, "You have a nice day and be careful ok?"

"Yeah, sure, thanks," answered the driver, wondering what had happened to him to make such a change in him all of a sudden.

He walked the two blocks to work and took his place at his desk, then turned his chair around and looked at everyone in the office. "Good morning," he said and everyone looked in his direction. Some of them even stood up to make sure it was him who had said it. He had never said a word to any of them before, unless he was asked something and never had he said, "Good morning."

The lady who sat behind him asked him, "Are you all right?"

"I'm fine," he answered, "Why wouldn't I be?"

"I just never heard you say 'good morning' before."

He smiled and told her, "Things have changed in my life."

"Well, good," she returned and turned back around.

"Don't you want to know about it?" he said over his shoulder.

"No, not really," she answered.

He didn't return a answer. He just sat there and took the picture out of his pocket and sat it on his desk.

It took a few minutes before the first person saw it and asked, "Who are they?"

"Oh!" he said, "That's my family in Oregon, I'm moving out there to be with them soon."

"How soon?" the man returned, not believing he had a family.

"I don't know exactly, but soon," he answered.

"What part of Oregon? My brother lives out there."

"Eleven miles west of Bend," he answered. One thing he did know was all about the state of Oregon. He had studied it for years and knew every town by memory.

"Nice area," the man answered, "My brother lives in Portland."

"Oh, OK," he said and turned away from the man, not wanting to push the conversation so far he might get caught up in a lie.

"Why don't you have it in a frame?" the man asked.

"Because I just got it and haven't had a chance to buy one."

"That makes sense, I guess." The man looked around, smiling at the joke he thought was taking place.

Then another person came and looked at it and then another and another until almost everyone in the office had looked at it. Some of them made remarks and some of them remained silent.

There was a silent curiosity about the office all day long. People kept looking at him and smiling.

He didn't know if they believed him or if they were laughing at him. But then he thought it really doesn't matter what they think, what matters is he felt good about himself for the first time in his life. He decided to stop and buy a frame for the picture on the way home and tomorrow he would set it on his desk and leave it there. No, he would make a copy of it and keep one at home too.

He left work and walked to the bus stop. He stood there unwrapping his bus change and stuck the tape on the light post. Then a hand was on his shoulder. He turned and looked into the face of a police officer.

"You're the guy, huh? I been wondering who was sticking the tape on this pole. Clean it off!"

"What?" he stammered.

"You're defacing city property. Clean that tape off of there!"

It took him almost a half hour to pick all the tape off of the pole as the police officer stood there beside him watching and others walked by laughing at him and making remarks. He got on the bus, not feeling as good as he had but he told himself he never should have done that in the first place and decided to clean the other pole when he got there. Then he saw her, the girl, she was on the street with the other hookers wearing a short skirt and some kind of stretch top. She saw him through the bus window and waved as she smiled at him. He was disappointed to say the very least.

Then the last straw. When he went into the drug store to buy the frame he showed the picture to the woman so she could find a frame of the right size.

The woman grabbed the picture and asked, "Where did you get this?"

"It's a picture of my family in Oregon."

"You some kind of a nut cake? That's my sister and her kids. I lost that picture a few days ago, what did you do, pick it up?"

He turned and walked out of the drug store. He walked down the street looking at the buildings and the trash on the sidewalk. The people all talking and hurrying along pushing by each other. He walked the two blocks to the restaurant and sat at a table.

"So how is your family?" the waitress asked.

"Fine," he answered.

"It was all a big fat lie, wasn't it? I knew it was a lie," she laughed.

"I'd like to eat something," he said softly.

"What?"

"I don't care," he answered.

She walked off, writing on her pad. He sat there looking at the brown tile on the floor, then at her brown shoes and at her brown skirt, the brown counter and the brown table, then out the window at the brownstone buildings lining the street. Even the plate had a brown ring around the rim of it.

"Is brown the easiest color to make?" he wondered.

The waitress brought him a dish of hot roast beef and a bowl of corn.

She looked down at him and sort of laughed then walked away.

"Brown must be the ugliest color in the world," he muttered. He sat there and ate his dinner then went home and sat on his bed and watched TV. "I'll show them all," he said.

Tomorrow he would just go buy a car and pack his things then go to Oregon... If he got enough nerve to leave.

My Creek

It was in the late summer, more in the fall because the reason I had gone there was to see the maple and oak trees turning their pretty golden color and to see the squirrels bustling around gathering acorns from the oak trees. I was quite surprised to find myself driving on a paved two-lane road which was when I had last seen it, a narrow graveled road with ruts and chuck holes large enough to drop a small piano in and drive over.

It was a rainy day as it almost always is that time of year in the Willamette Valley, rain I used to hate on a daily basis when it came time to do the chores on the farm.

Today, as I sat warm and comfortable in my car, I liked it, I missed it, as I had missed the farm for so many years.

Sometimes in my dreams I could still smell the barn and the scent of the cows when it rained.

I still remember the rainy times we spent there as kids doing nothing or playing games, building forts up in the hay loft from the bales of clover hay. We built tunnels through the bales and used our imaginations to create adventures.

I knew I was in for a big disappointment when I drove past the Smith farm which used to have a white rail fence around it with several work horses in the field by the road. Now, there in the field there was a large sign.

Homes by Marion
A gated community

The rail fence had been replaced by a eight-foot high block and rod iron fence with a massive rail gate and a security building with a guard in it making sure no unwanted persons were allowed in.

My second disappointment was the covered wooden bridge that used to stand a few hundred yards past the farm to let us across the creek. It too was gone and a concrete flat bridge had taken its place.

It was a wonderful bridge with a wooden deck and windows where we all used to jump off into the creek below during the summer months. I was small when it was built by all the men in the valley to replace the old one and can still see most of them in my mind. All our friends and neighbors chopped trees and cut timbers and sawed lumber to build the bridge in 1936; it was a house you could drive through. And as a child of five, I sat on the new-cut oak rails watching as about fifty people played music and danced inside the structure the night it was completed.

A long table was made of three long boards laid from side to side of the bridge on the railing and white bed sheets covered them. Food was stacked from one side to the other. More than a hundred people could have eaten in one night.

Cars, trucks, and horses were everywhere, all taking turns crossing the bridge and then coming back across it until it was closed off by the table.

I listened to the men talk about how maybe they should have made the windows more decorative. Maybe put five logs across the creek instead of only four to hold the cars and trucks crossing the creek. I remember Mr. Jurardon saying, "With those solid oak beams, it will be here a hundred years from now." And I remember the sign on both ends of it that Mr. Jackson's daughter Charlotte had painted, saying, "Mill Creek Bridge, built Sept. 1936."

How long had it been gone? I still have no idea. But I do have a picture of it somewhere. A Kodak. with me and my brothers standing on the outside rail just before we all jumped into the creek below.

I drove further up the road and around the large hill which blocked most of the valley from sight until you rounded the top, then down below was thirty-five hundred acres evenly divided into eight farms, and the creek making a snake-like journey from one farm to the next and passing through all eight as it zigzagged from one end of the valley to the other and away to wherever it went. Now I know it just goes about ten more miles and emptied into the river, but then it didn't matter where it went after we had our use of it.

I stopped at the top of the hill and looked down, not believing my eyes as I saw several hundred houses all lined up in rows with paved streets. I could see where each farm had been divided as it was sold and the boundaries, which used to be fence lines, were now the streets creating the outlines of the shape of the developments. The farms seemed to still be there but instead of corn, wheat, beans, hay, cattle, horses, and pigs, houses had somehow grown. I looked across the valley to where our farm used to be and it also had not escaped the growth, but I could see where the house and barn used to stand and traced a trail through the winding paved streets to get to where it used to be. I drove down the hill past trees I remembered walking by on my way to and home from school. I remembered climbing in and collecting mistletoe at Christmas time. Somehow they had survived. A few, only a few of hundreds. The leaves, the billions of beautiful amber, white, and gold leaves we used to walk through almost knee deep and play in, were now nothing more than a nuisance to the people who had taken over the valley, nothing more than hundreds of eyesores to be blown away with a power blower. I saw several being used as I drove slowly through the houses this Saturday morning.

I looked up in the few trees that were left for squirrels. I saw none where there used to be hundreds leaping from limb to limb.

I heard not one bird singing, not one robin red-breast scratching for worms. No crows and no field mice, and I thought, "There's not much to sing about here now."

It seemed to me that the Chinese ring-necked pheasants had been replaced by toys scattered on lawns and a street light had been put down in every gopher's hole. But where was the creek? I saw no sign of it. How could they have done away with the entire creek? There was nowhere for it to have gone. Then I passed over what seemed to be a bridge, but was just a short rail on the right side of the street and a large valve fenced in with a sign on the gate: "Mill Creek Water Supply." They had buried the entire creek? Yes, they had, inside a large concrete conduit.

My wonderful creek where me and Tom and Bill and Joe and seventy others had swum and fished for trout all of our young lives. The creek where we all had laid on the grassy bank and talked about girls and horses and chewed on the sweet stems of valley grass. The creek where beaver after beaver had tried to make a home there only to be driven away by the farmers because they flooded the flat land and stopped off the water supply. The creek that had fed us all, our horses and cattle and watered our pastures, our crops, and gardens. The hundreds of trees that had lined its banks, even the one with our rope swing I had swung out over the swimming hole a thousand times and dropped into the clean fresh water was gone. Now the farmers had also been driven off unless their children were living in one of the two-story houses.

As I drove around one of the streets, I came to a large lake that was not there when I was growing up and it was quite plain to see where they had dug hundreds of yards of dirt out and filled in other places to make the streets winding through the valley completely flat. The lake was an ugly eyesore to me, more of a concrete pond than what the sign said: "Lands fill Lake" with a larger sign just above it saying:

"Keep Out - Trespassers will be prosecuted"

But there were three small red and white striped flat-bottom boats with paddlewheels on them you could paddle around in. It was as though someone had the right to go on the water but not just anybody. I thought, "Why would they want to?"

It had stopped raining as I turned my car around and drove away back up and around the hill. The sun was shining and I looked back over the hill to the east where a thousand times before as I was growing up and still a child, I had seen the rainbow stretching from one end of the valley to the other. We all as kids had searched for the pot of gold. I would guess that whoever developed the valley found it.

There was no rainbow this day and I wondered if God felt as bad inside as I did at this moment because of what man had done to his valley, and to my creek.

News

You know what the main problem in this country is? Besides fat and lazy, and no morals? And silliness and the Hollywood syndrome and greed and stupid people making stupid laws??

I always talk about silly, silly this and silly that! Too much talk and not enough action!!

When I was a young man, the news came on and it was one half hour long with no commercials.

A man would come on the TV and say, "Good evening, I am so-and-so and this is your evening news." And then he would tell you what was going on and had gone on during the past day or few days if the story was more than one day long. And there were a lot of things they didn't tell you because there are a lot of things people don't need to hear..

Like schoolyard shootings, people don't need to know about them... out of sight, out of mind!!

Teenage drop outs... Teenage pregnancies and things like that. If they don't hear about them, they're less likely to do them.

And when the program ended, the man would say, "And that is the new for this day *****, 1959. Thank you for watching and I hope to see you tomorrow night at this time."

Now every TV station had about fifty TV sets on the wall and about fifteen people watching them so they know exactly what's going on on all the other channels every minute. So if something comes on they can switch the TV to the monitor in front of the newsperson and it becomes ACTION NEWS!!! Right after this commercial message from your local butt doctor!!!

Out of the news hour you have, eleven minutes of them telling about what they're going to tell you when they came back, eight to twelve minutes of them repeating the first part of what they're going to tell you, and twenty-six minutes of commercials for a total of 45 minutes and fifteen minutes of real-time news that is on fifteen channels at the same time and repeated over and over on every newscast on every channel.

That's silliness!!

Then there are the interviews!! They let the person talk for about three seconds and then cut them off and tell you what the person said in their own words, and then of course turn it and twist it to make themselves sound as though they know more about it than the person telling it in the first person, so it becomes news or hearsay that they regard as news. I call it *gossip* but they call it *news...*

Then there are the Sports. Pre-game. Game. Post-game. Game records. Game players. MVP. Most bloopers. Play of the game. Best play of the game. Worst play of the game. Worst player of the game. And on and on it goes forever, talk, talk, talk, and they show the same play fifty-seven times over and over and over. Holy hell, if you saw it once you saw it. Holy hell if you saw it once you saw it. Holy hell if you saw it once you saw it... how stupid are we???

But it doesn't cost anything to show it over and over and it takes time, and time sells products. Right? Right? Right? Right? Right?

And then there are the women... Why doesn't a female football expert look like a football expert instead of a bathing suit model???

All female newswomen look the same now except maybe three or four of them. Long faces, long blond (bleached) hair, and you can watch them reading from the monitor so you know they didn't write any of it, or research any of it, they just sit in a room, get their faces painted and their hair sprayed so it doesn't move when they shake their head "No" or "Yes."

So, do we ever really see the truth? I mean the real truth as it happened? I don't think that happens very often, it's just another small part of the big drain. You know, the moral drain. The welfare drain. The extended overseas drain. The War drain. The housing drain. And you know where drains lead to, don't you?? Right down the sewer??????

Six years from now, I'm going to read this again, I wrote it six years ago and just found it. I wrote it on January 16, 2000, and I have to put this in... George Bush?? Boy, are we in for it now???

Benny

Sometimes when writing a story, I seem to get so involved in just telling the story. I forget about whoever might read it someday, and I leave out things. I was never taught how to write a story. So, I have always just sort of sat down and let it come to me as it happened on the keyboard until I came to an end.

This time, I have decided to take a little extra time and build the story instead of just writing it; because it is one of the funniest memories of my childhood days on the farm. How many days I spent looking at him or laughing when I did, I could never count.

My mother was born and raised on a small farm in northern Nebraska, one of eight children. My father, on a small farm in southern Kansas, near the Nebraskan border, the last of thirteen children. That is where they met and got married, my father at the age of seventeen, and my mother at the age of thirteen, which, at that time and place was completely acceptable. Girls ate food and didn't bring any home, so the idea was to let them marry as soon as possible and get them out of the house (according to my grandfather). At the age of twenty-one and seventeen, they left Kansas with two other families together totaling a number of 11, counting the children, in a 1933 Ford pickup, they left, as did many other families, and moved to Oregon, stopping to have "seventeen or seventy-five," I'm not sure, flat tires, the first five days. Then, as my father and friends, who traveled with them, said "fifty more," during the next two weeks it took them to travel the sixteen hundred or so miles to the valley where I grew up.

It was a wonderful place. Lots of big green trees, green soft grass, and a creek that came from the mountains a few miles away and ran through the lower pasture under several large oak and fir trees, and then ran into a river sixteen miles downstream from the farm. Lots and lots of large trout were caught in that creek by me during my younger years.

I began school in a one-room schoolhouse, and yes, we did walk to school, one and one half miles if we went around the road and three quarters of a mile if we walked up and over the wooded hill. Which we did, if the weather permitted us to, but too often, it didn't, so we walked with several other kids from the small valley along the gravel road, mostly having a lot of fun going to and from the school, but as soon as we were back home, the work came first.

It was 1951 and I was then in the third grade at Pratt School. It was November and maybe three weeks before Thanksgiving. To tell the honest truth I don't remember what month it was, but I do remember there were no leaves on the trees when someone unknown to me gave to the school eight small turkeys which were kept in a wooden box in the corner of the room then given away to us by our teacher, Mrs. Twialla Cole.

Who got the turkeys depended on who could find the most pine cones during the recess time and lunch hour of the school day. The pine cones were to be used as decorations for Christmas and we later painted them then put shiny sprinkles on them and then strung them along the walls as though they were Christmas tree lights. As I remember, they were quite nice looking hanging along the walls with our handmade Christmas cards hanging under them and strings of popcorn wound around the string holding the cones up.

I was nine years old then and a very fast runner, so, during recess and lunch time I would run the few hundred yards up on the hill, which was covered with fir and pine trees and gather pine cones, as many as I could carry, and that might have been maybe a dozen or so. Anyway, I came in second as the best pine cone finder in Pratt School during the year of 1951, and I think that was as close to winning a first place as I have ever come in my life. I got my name placed second to the top on the card that read, "These pine cones were found by, ... and then the number of cones that had been found by whoever found them. Mine had the number 84 behind my name and I was proud of myself. A few days later, Mrs. Cole carried into the school several arm loads of newspapers, magazines, and other papers, along with string and paper clips and several gallon cans of different colored paint. Then during recess and lunch time the boys would spread out the papers on the floor of the shed behind the schoolhouse and then after straightening out one end of a paper clip, insert it into the top of the pine cone and dip them into one of the cans of paint and hang it on the string to dry.

At the same time, the girls cut the paper into strips and made paper chains from them, then painted the paper chains with watercolors. That was how we made our decoration back then. Maybe children still do that, I don't know. I hope some of them do. If they don't, I think they should, at least in the smaller schools if there are any small schools left.

However, I had second choice of a turkey and I, of course chose the second biggest one as the biggest one had already been taken by a boy named Skeeter. I proudly carried it home in my coat pocket, which after putting my hand in my pocket, I found to be a bad mistake, because I had to turn my pocket inside out and wash it.

I showed it to my father and grandfather and then as soon as my father saw it, much to my dissatisfaction, it was promptly tossed into the chicken coop by my father and left there for several months until it was too big, and finally flew out over the top of the fence. Then it promptly took over the barn yard, from the loose chickens, ducks, and geese that were allowed to roam freely around the yard until they promptly ended their wanderings at the edge of my grandfather's hatchet, and ended up on the supper table. Fortunately, Benny (the turkey) did not. And not for the following Thanksgiving dinner either, which I was scared that he would.

He lived a happy bully life wondering around the farm for I think three or four years followed by three hen turkeys that somehow showed up during the next year. Where they came from, I still do not know. What I know is, Benny not only created about a hundred turkeys but he took no push or shove from man or beast. If you got to close to him or his hens, he would raise up his tail feathers, flap his wings and come straight at you until you moved away from his girl turkeys and him. Ducks and geese, roosters and cats, dogs and hens, my mother and sisters, all moved out of the way when he came too close to them.

My brothers and I had sort of trained him with a few good kicks to the tail so he didn't push us too far but the rest of the critters were on the lookout for him most of the time.

During the third year, Benny and his hens gave us no less than twenty turkeys. All of them except two more hens tasted very nice when stuffed with dressing and surrounded by fresh cranberry sauce, mashed potatoes, gravy, fresh vegetables, and hot biscuits. And so it went for the next three years. Benny strutted and gobbled, keeping his flock in tow and grandfather continued thinning the group at a rate of about one a month. We had stuffed turkey, turkey and noodles made from fresh eggs, and young smoked turkeys hung in the smokehouse along with the hams year round.

Also on our farm we had several cats and three dogs. The dogs never bothered Benny, his hens or any other of the fowl that wondered around. Once in a while, one of the dogs might chase the ducks just to watch them fly away and land in the pond behind the barn but I don't think any of them ever caught a duck for fear of being kicked into the pond themselves.

One of them caught a young chicken once, and was then kicked, pulled off by its ear, cussed and kicked again by my granddad as the other dogs watched from a few feet away and I think they thought catching a chicken was not worth the price they would pay for doing it, so they just let them do as they wished.

However one old tom cat named Snafuoo -- don't ask me how it got that name -- was a big, completely black tom cat, and he was also the leader of his own little clan of four female cats. He strolled around and laid around the barn, on warm rocks, on the fence rails, into and out of the house. He moved freely around and hunted around wherever and whenever he chose to for wild birds, mice, squirrels, baby chickens and one time, much to the disagreement of Benny, a baby turkey.

It so happened the day he chose to hunt the baby turkey, my two brothers, one uncle, father, and also grandfather happened to be unloading a wagon of hay into the barn and saw the whole thing. Benny, followed by the five hens, followed by fifteen or more tiny turkeys, came around the grain shed and began a slow pecking trip across the barnyard, picking up bits of gravel heading for the pond to drink.

Snafuoo came out of the barn and when he got to the corner, he saw the young turkeys. So he crouched down behind the footing and waited until the turkeys were within twenty or so feet of him. Benny, being just a little smarter than most turkeys, saw him and moved himself in between the cat and the babies, and went on slowly pecking his way across the barnyard, keeping a eye on the cat as he went.

Turkeys have very large, long, and sharp claws. They are not so quick to peck you as they are to fly up in the air and land on your face with all claws bared for a fight, and I might add, much faster than one would think.

So across the barnyard came the turkeys, and around the footing crept the cat until he thought the timing was right and he bounded out from his hiding place and made a run for one of the young turkeys. He thought he could run around behind Benny, catch one of the young ones and be gone as he had done so many times with young chickens. Except Benny moved out, then reached out with one clawed foot and caught Snafuoo by the side of his head, claws buried deep in the cat's fur.

The cat was taken completely by surprise and by the time it realized Benny had him, Benny also had a good grip on the cat's back side with his other foot and a beak, biting a chunk out of Snafuoo's right front leg. The cat weighed in at about five or six pounds, Benny at close to thirty. And the great turkey-cat fight was on as we all stood on the hay wagon watching in wonder as Benny first grabbed the cat and flew about fifty feet away from the young turkeys, dragging Snafuoo with him. He came down on top of the cat with both sets of claws buried in the cat's head and back then proceeded to turn the cat every which way but loose for about ten or fifteen seconds.

Snafuoo broke loose and was gone for a week somewhere. Benny shook his feathers and opened his great tail and then began to strut around the barnyard letting his hens and everyone else know he was still in charge. Unfortunately, Benny strutted and gobbled right under a twelve volt electric fence and as he stretched out his wings and raised up to Gobble. He touched the wire with the top of his head at the exact moment in time the voltage was passing through the wire. Benny screamed a loud gobble or two maybe, then flew several feet up off the ground backwards and when he came down, he was on his back with his feet sticking up in the air and not moving. We watched for a few minutes and finally my father said, "Killed him deader n' hell didn't it?"

My granddad replied, "Ain't that a damn shame!? After he just kicked the shit out of ol' Snafuoo too."

And my uncle answered, "I never thought a turkey would fight like that."

"I didn't either," someone answered, but I don't know who said that.

"Maybe he ain't dead, just knocked out," I chipped in, hoping for the best.

"He's dead," my father said.

"Yeah, he's dead," both my uncle and Granddad agreed after several minutes and after I went over and tried to get him to move.

"Turkeys can't take much electricity," my uncle said.

"Might as well go get some hot water," Father told my older brother.

"We ain't going to eat him?" I cried.

"I ain't going to let a twenty-five pound turkey go to ruin," Father answered.

My brother went to the house to get the water and we all finished unloading the hay wagon.

About a half hour had gone by I would guess as Benny laid there with his feet up in the air and the rest of the turkeys went on their way pecking their way down to the pond as though nothing had happened to their male counterpart. Benny. Poor Benny!

We finished unloading the hay and granddad went over and picked Benny up by his legs and carried him to the back porch of the house where my brother had dumped several gallons of hot water into a wash tub and turned on the hot plate under it. Grandfather laid Benny on the porch and he laid there while Grandfather went into the house and filled his pipe and came back, then sat on his stool and was ready, He sat there and smoked until the tub of water was hot enough and then as I watched in horror, he picked the bird up by his neck and lowered him into the tub of scalding hot water and left him there a couple minutes, pulled him out and laid him on the floor then began to pull his feathers out by the hands full. He started at Benny's underside and worked his way around the bird. He pulled and pulled and pulled until Benny was featherless, and Granddad was down to just the feathers in Benny's tail and the tip of his wings.

But as soon as his hand was wrapped firmly around the huge feathers in Benny's tail and he gave a yank on them, something happened, because Benny let out a loud "Gobble! Gobble!" and jerked himself out of Granddad's hands and took off across the barnyard, gobbling all the way and running sort of crooked and lopsided as he went.

Granddad sat there with his mouth open and so did the rest of us as Benny ran around as though he were looking for his clothes or something to cover his naked body with. It was a strange sight to see and everyone came out of the house and barn then watched as poor Benny gobbled and ran, then ran and gobbled. Then gobbled and ran some more and finally stopped. Then he simply looked for his family, saw them down at the pond and walked away after them, naked as a jay bird.

"I don't believe it!" Granddad said.

All us kids were laughing because of the funny-looking turkey walking around the yard with no feathers and finally my mother said, "You better go kill it, he'll die without feathers."

"No, he won't," answered Granddad, "They'll just grow back in a couple of months."

"Will they?" I asked.

"Why not, it's warm so he don't need them for a couple months."

It was warm, and sure enough, first there were little white pin feathers all over his body and then slowly, by the end of summer, Benny had returned to his own magnificent strutting self. His tail feathers were just as huge and the tips were just as white as they ever were. But he was the talk of the valley for several years at every Thanksgiving dinner we had.

Benny lived for almost twenty years. He fathered probably a hundred turkeys or more and was still the top guy in the barnyard when I left to join the Navy when I was eighteen.

Snafuoo? Well as far as I saw and can remember, he seemed to have lost his taste for, and developed a sort of fear of, turkeys for the rest of his life.

Christopher

He sat at the head of the long wooden table having breakfast with his wife and the twenty-six others lined up along both sides as the fire blazed in the huge fireplace warming the room. It was now the first day of February and time for his yearly trip to the trading post. Everyone had been on a one month vacation and now it was time to plan for the year's work ahead.

Most of them had gone back to Ireland, Scotland, or some other place out of the country. His wife and he had gone back to Norway as they did each year.

Now it was time to start work again. Everyone was well rested and excited about the New Year. They sat at the table laughing and telling tales of their vacations and their visits with families until he stood up, tapped on his crystal glass with a spoon, and got their attention. Everyone stopped talking and looked at the head of the table waiting for him to speak.

"It's time I went shopping. Does everyone have his list of supplies?"

Twenty-six sheets of paper were handed down the table from one person to the next until all twenty-six were handed to him. He read each one in turn and laid them at the side of his plate as he finished. On some he made corrections, on some he crossed something out and added something. Finally, he looked up and said, "Well done. Well done."

He got up from the table leaving the lists laying there. He had memorized each and every item on all twenty-six lists and had no need to carry them with him. "They get longer each year," he said softly speaking more to himself than anyone in the large room. "I hope they have all we need."

The chatter among the men returned as soon as he had left the room to change his clothes for the trip to the trading post.

He changed from the dark tweed suit he had been wearing while on vacation into some old leather pants and a shirt made from hides of caribou. He exchanged his shoes for some tall leather boots with fur around the tops and a wolf-skin parka with a hood on it. He was putting on the parka when his wife asked him, "Do you have enough gold to pay for all that stuff, Chris?"

He smiled and did a slight of hand trick, flicking his fingers, then showed her a gold coin. It was a old coin with no marking on it.

"I think I do, if I don't, I'll just have to get it on credit." He smiled, showing perfect white teeth.

"Oh! You always kid so much!" She laughed, then kissed him on the cheek and told him, "You be careful out here, Chris, there's a storm coming."

"Ha! I've made this trip so many times I could walk and carry it back if need be."

Two of the men had the sled hitched and ready as he came out of the building, two more we getting the animals up on their feet and freeing the sled from the ice. He walked from the front of the team to the sled, stopping to pet each animal as he passed them saying things to them, "Good fellow, How you doing? How you been? You get some rest?" And things like that, speaking in his soft voice until he took his place on the runner skids and kicked the tethers loose. Then his voice changed and he called, "Get up! Get Up! I know you're cold! Get up, pull! Tighten up! Pull!"

Six of the animals got up and began to pull, forcing the others to get up and they also began to pull, moving from side to side until the runners broke free and the sled began to move forward. He pushed on the sled and began to run behind it until it was moving freely across the snow, across the yard and out through the gate onto the open snow. He called out and encouraged the animals. "Pull! Pull! Let's go there now! Come on! Pull! Pull! That's it! Come on people, pull! Pull!" He ran behind the sled until it was moving too fast for him to keep up and he stepped onto the back runners and called out again, "That's it! Come on! Pull! Move out now! Run it out! Run it out!" meaning for them to run the stiffness out of their legs from lying on the cold snow.

The sled picked up speed slowly at first, then faster and faster until it was skimming over the snow and ice. The wind whipping his parka and turning his face white except for his huge beard and mustache and large eye brows, he stood on the runners feeling the cold on his face as he had a hundred times before and called to his team, "Gee! Gee! Pull! Run it out!!" meaning for them to turn left onto the flat frozen river.

The team turned down a small bank and then onto the frozen river running at a full gallop. He called over the wind, throwing his head back, "That's it! Run it out, guys and girls!!" and then he began to sing, *"Old Aunt Dina, went on to town,*

"Ridd'in on her billy goat and leading her hound

When the hound dog barked, the billy goat jumped, old Aunt Dina landed right on a stump

"A Figur're olie olie, a', A figur' re olie, olie a'

"She ain't a'gon'a make us biscuits today

"She jumped right up and rubbed her rear

"Then she grabbed that hound dog by its ear

"Picked it up and spun it around, the hound dog beat Aunt Dina to town

"Figur're olie, olie a, Figur're olie, ole a'

"She still might make us biscuits today".

The faster and louder he sang, the faster the team ran along the river. He hung on for dear life as the team raced along the frozen ice at a break-neck speed, the runners just touching the thin layer of snow over the five foot thick ice above the water. They ran all day and part of the night without stopping. Miles and miles they traveled down the river until he called to them during the early morning, "Whoa! Slow it down now! Easy now! Easy Now! Take it easy there! Slow it down a little! Now! Ha! Ha! Ha! Come on!" meaning for them to turn right and leave the riverbed. They came to a slow trot and turned right up a bank and onto a trail through small trees until they came to a well-traveled road and he called to them, "Now! Gee! Gee! Gee!" meaning for them to turn left onto the road. They followed the road at a slow trot for about a hour and he called, "Now Ha! Ha!" meaning for them to turn right again, then he called, "Whoa! Whoa! Lay! Lay!"

The sled was stopped in a grove of trees a short distance from the town and the animals laid down to rest. Steam was blowing out of their noses as they tried to catch up with their breathing from the hard run.

"Now you all just relax a bit while I go do my shopping," he said as he walked along them patting each one as he passed. "I'll be back before you can sing, 'Figur're olie, olie a' Figur're ,olie, olie a. She ain't gon'a make a biscuit today.'

He laughed and walked off through the trees and down the road to the town, puffing on his pipe and leaving a trail of smoke behind him as he walked out of sight from the team.

Everyone in the small town was awake and waiting for him to show up as he did every year at this time. Most years it was exactly right at the same minute of the same hour of the same day he would come walking into town, stop at the candy store and then on to the trading post.

This day was no exception. He walked down the center of the narrow street until he came to the candy store. He went inside and bought nine pieces of taffeta candy, put them in his pocket and continued on down the street until he climbed the three steps up to the door of the trading post and then went inside as most of the town people watched.

There in the center of the floor was a huge pile of things. Everything you could think of was there in a pile. Motors and cranks, shovels and rakes, wood, bolts, canvas and nails. There was paint, wire, tools, wax, and string, cloth and paper, rubber and glue, all in a huge pile taking nearly all the space in the trading post.

He greeted the storekeeper with a smile and a nod then said, "And a Happy New Year to you, Mr. Willows".

"Happy New Year's to you too, Mr. ...," because he could never remember his name. "What the heck is your name again? I'm so bad at remembering names."

"Christopher," he answered.

"Oh yes! Mr. Christopher."

"Not Mr. Just Christopher," he grinned showing his white teeth.

"Yeah. Christopher," the man repeated, then he smiled. "I knew that!" he said, "I just can't ever remember it. Well, I think I got all your things, I think. What in the world do you do with all this stuff every year?"

He looked at the old man smiling at him. It was the same every year since he had came here. He was as puzzled as everyone else in the town.

Each year in February, a small different man would come and bring a long list, then return in November and collect his things. Each February, this small man would come and order all the things he wanted from everywhere in the world and it would end up piled on the floor as it now was.

Once a year, this old man came to town and bought enough stuff to fill three huge trucks full, then disappeared. It was something no one outside the town believed and most of the people who watched him carry the stuff out of town, then disappear, didn't believe either.

"Might I borrow your wheelbarrow again, Mr. Willows?" he asked.

"It's right where you left it last year, Mr. .... uh. Christopher."

"I thank you, Mr. Willows," he answered and went out the back door returning pushing the wheelbarrow.

"And how much do I owe you this year, Mr. Willows?"

"It comes to eighty-three thousand dollars," was the answer.

"That seems fair. How much would it be in gold at today's prices, Mr. Willows?" Mr. Willows figured on his calculator and answered, "Exactly two-hundred seventy-three and a half ounces. You going to do that trick again?"

"If you wish," he said.

"No one believes me when I tell them you just make gold come out of thin air". He laughed, and then looked at the window and the doorway. He saw thirty or more people looking in through the windows at him as he pushed the sleeve of his parka up to his elbow so his forearm was bare, then began to flick his fingers. Each time he flicked his fingers, a gold coin appeared and he sat it on the counter until there were three rows of coins in several stacks, the coins all in a row.

"And one for good measure!" he smiled and flicked one more gold coin out of the air and sat it on the counter.

"Fair enough, Mr. Willows?" he asked.

"More than fair, Mr. .. uh, Christopher."

"And I thank you kindly, sir," he said, then began to load the wheelbarrow with things, stacking it so high it looked like no man could ever lift it and everything would come tumbling off it as soon as he tried to push it. But nothing ever fell, and he pushed it out the door and down the three steps, then up the street as people followed him trying to find out where he was going. Some would follow him, some would wait at the edge of town, and some along the road, but no one ever caught up to him. He would start pushing the wheelbarrow slow at first, then faster and faster, until he was running with it in front of him, and no man in the town could run as fast as him, even pushing the heavy wheelbarrow. He outran them all and disappeared into the trees. Then he would come back for another load and it began all over, him running and several people running after him trying to see where he went.

"It's like he just disappears into the thin air," several said. "He's got a hide-out in the trees somewhere," others decided. Some just stood looking and didn't even try to catch him.

"You all want a little head start on me this time?" He would laugh as he pushed the loaded wheelbarrow up the street.

At midnight, he was still pushing his last load up the street. People had offered to help him, but he refused all offers.

Then he was finished and returned the wheelbarrow to the back of the trading post and walked slowly up the street saying, "Happy New Year," to all the people who were all worn out from trying to catch him.

"His tracks just stop when he reaches the woods," one man told Mr. Willows as he sat on the front step of the trading post trying to catch his breath from running after the small man pushing the wheelbarrow as he watched the small old man walk away.

"It's strange," he said. "No man can run that fast and push so much weight at the same time."

"He seems to do it," Mr. Willows answered, and lit his pipe as he too watched the man walk away for another year.

"What does he do with all that stuff?"

"I think he has a secret gold mine in the mountains somewhere," Mr. Willows answered.

"He must."

"Yeah, he must, huh?"

"He must have some secret cave just outside of town he puts all that stuff in."

"Yeah, I think so," Mr. Willows agreed and went back into the trading post because >the show was over for another year and there was no sense thinking about something that had no answer to it. He had loaded wheelbarrow after wheelbarrow onto the sled until it was now stacked so high he had to use a ladder to climb to the top and load the remaining things on it. He tied everything on and then walked from one animal to the next taking the candy from his pocket and giving it to them saying "This is it. The last trip this year. Here you go, fellow, come on, get up now! Here you go!" And saying different things until all the animals were on their feet and ready to pull the sled.

"It's a heavy load we got this year! Pull! Pull!" He commanded, calling, "Gee! Gee! Gee! Pull!" meaning for them to turn the sled completely around and go back the way they had come.

The team strained under the heavy load until it was turned around and moving across the snow, then down the road and again along the narrow trail until they reached the river. He called, "Ha! Ha! Ha! Pull! Run it out now!" as they turned onto the frozen river and began to pick up speed.

It was after midnight and completely dark except for the moonlight as they pulled the sled faster and faster until he called. "It's dark now, and no one can see us," so then he raised his voice louder and called, "On Dancer! On Prancer! Up Comet!! Up! Up! Cupid! Fly! Fly! Fly, if you want to! Let's go home!! Fly! Fly!! Come on, Blitsen! Raise them up, boy! Let's go, time's a-wasting! Up! Up! Fly!! On Donner and Dancer and Prancer and Vinsen! Up! Up! Fly, fly!! On Prancer and Blitsen! Raise em' up, boy!"

And the sled lifted slowly up off the river ice and began to turn north as it picked up speed and rose higher and higher into the night sky.

"Ho. Ho. Ho. Old Aunt Dina went to town
A-riding on a billy goat and leading a hound.
When the hound dog barked
The billy goat jumped
And sent ol' Aunt Dina right straddle a stump". Ho. Ho. Ho

Several hundred miles to the north they flew until he saw the crystal dome and called out "We're almost home now! Down! Down!" And the sled settled to the ground just outside the gate. The team pulled it into the yard next to the big building and stopped as his wife and helpers came running out to unload the material off the sled.

He slid down from the top of the load laughing as the reindeer again laid down, blowing steam from their noses.

"HO, HO, HO, I love this job!! I truly do!" he laughed.

"Ho, Ho, Ho, Ho, Ho," he laughed as he walked with his wife, Mrs. Claus into the large building.

Slingshot

My Grandpa sat on the front porch of our old unpainted house in his old unpainted rocking chair with his feet up on the unpainted front rail with his pipe in his mouth but no smoke coming out of the bowl. It was, as usual, just hanging there from his teeth as he whittled. He was a first-class whittler but not too much of a painter. He said, "If God intended for things to be different colors he would have made different-colored wood." That was that. Nothing got painted around our old farm house.

He was whittling a dog inside a square on a ball as I stood waiting for him I to notice me. We, as kids, never spoke until we were spoken to first. We waited until the adult asked us what we wanted, or we caught "H.E. Double L."

So I stood for several seconds and watched him as he picked the tiny pieces of wood from inside the square with his pen knife until he stopped and looked at me.

"What's on your troubled mind, young fellow?" he asked as he lit his pipe, striking a match on the arm of his rocker. I looked at the arm and saw the groove where a thousand matches had been struck there before. He lit his pipe and tossed the match off the porch and said, "Well?

"Will you help me make a slingshot?" I asked.

He looked down at me and said, "Hummm.. Well.. That might be dangerous."

"I won't shoot anything. Just cans and stuff," I told him.

He added, "And my horses in the rump and a few windows and some birds and chickens and ... Nope!" He said, "You're too young. Ask me next year when you're nine."

"I'm nine now!" I answered.

"You are? When did you get to be nine? You were eight a few days back."

"It was my birthday two weeks ago, remember you bought me that hat?"

He had gotten me a Roy Rogers cowboy hat for my birthday present.

"Was that you?" He said without looking at me, "I thought it was that kid from down the road a ways."

"It was me, Grandpa."

"It was? Then where's that hat I spent my good money on? Why ain't you got it on your head?"

"I'm not wearing it right now."

"Why not? You're outside?"

"I sort of lost it," I answered.

"I know, it's out there in the barn where you took it off. You know when I'll make you a sling shot?"

"No," I answered.

"When you quit saying it got lost and start saying 'I lost it'. The goat ate your hat. Did you know that?"

"No, it didn't; goats don't eat hats," I laughed.

"It's upstairs in my room on the bed post".

"Then why did you say you lost it?"

"I just forgot for a minute."

"You been forgetting a lot lately. You forgot to do all your chores too?"

"No, I didn't," I answered and I was sure about that.

"You didn't clean off the front of your shirt," he said and put his finger on the front of my shirt, then when I looked down, he lifted his finger and banged my nose. It was one of his favorite things to do to me and he did it all the time, and I fell for it until I was about twelve years old.

"Don't learn too well, do you?" he grinned.

"Will you help me?" I asked.

"Help you what?"

"Make a sling shot?"

He leaned back and rocked a few times like he was thinking about it then he asked me, "You already ask me that, didn't you?"

"Yes."

"Well, what did I say?"

"You said when I was nine, and I'm nine."

"Did I say 'Tidily hi, tidily high, fiddly try today, I kissed my first girl friend on a bale of hay'?"

"No," I laughed.

"Can you say it?"

"No," I laughed again.

"Can't even remember it, can you?"

"No."

"That's because you're only eight and not nine."

"But I am nine now."

"You got anything that will prove you're nine?"

"I got school papers with my age on it."

"Are they As or Bs?"

"Mostly Cs," I answered.

"Better than I got, I got all Fs cause I didn't go to school, that's why I'm a dummy."

"No, you ain't, Grandpa," I laughed again.

"Are you sure you're nine and not eight and a half?"

"You know," I answered, then asked, "So will you?"

"What?"

"Make me a sling shot?"

"Oh, now you want me to make the whole thing by myself."

"No, I don't, I'll help you."

"Spell 'Geography'," he said.

"Grandpa E O George Rode A Pig Home Yesterday," I answered.

"Spell my name backwards."

I laughed, "It's the same both ways." His first name was Otto.

"Jump up and down and count to twenty five."

I jumped up and down and counted to twenty five.

"Pick your right foot up."

I lifted my right foot up.

"I didn't say lift it up, I said pick it up."

I reached down and picked my right foot up.

"Now the left one."

"I'll fall over."

"Alright, I guess you're smart enough."

Then he told me, "Go get me some matches, as many as you are old."

I went and got nine matches and counted them three times before I handed them to him.

He lit his pipe and then counted the matches.

"There's only eight here," he said.

"You used one."

"Oh ya, you are getting smarter. So how much is a cord of wood?"

"4x4x8," I said.

"What kind of wood?"

"Grandpa!" I exclaimed.

"You know your right from your left?"

"Yes."

Then go out there to the dump and get me the tongue out of a old pair of boots and get the right one, not the wrong one."

I started to ask which one is the right one but stopped myself after "which one is?"

"Alright, I guess you can live here another year. Go get the tongue," he said.

Like a lot of farms back then, there was a place out from the house where most of the trash was dumped, tin cans and other things. Ours happened to be up on the side of a hill and I tromped up there and spent I don't know how long digging through this and that until I found a old boot with a tongue still in it. (My older brothers had taken and used most of them.) But I found one and carried it back to my Grandpa the next day. He took it and said, "wrong one."

I looked at him hoping he was teasing me and after a few seconds he said "But it'll do." And he laid it up on one of the rafters above his head then said, "here," and he handed me a tin can (I think it had been full of beets) and one small round rock about the size of a small marble.

"Take this can down to the creek and fill it with round rocks no bigger than this one. Don't get flat ones or egg-shaped ones, round ones."

It took me over a week to fill the can with round rocks and I carried it back to the porch and to my Grandpa. He set it up on the rafter and told me, "Now go back to the dump and find me the laces out of two boots."

I searched and searched and looked at about fifteen boots and none of them had any laces in them. I got smart and took some of the leather lacings from the tack room (a small room where we kept horse harness and riding gear, saddles, and ropes) and brought it to him because I knew it was the same size and that was what everyone used for boot laces when one broke.

He looked at them and said, "I seen these before, where did you get them?"

"Out of the tack room," I answered.

"You're getting smarter every day," he said and put the leather thongs up on the rafter.

"Now comes the main part," he said, then said nothing else. I stood there for what seemed like an hour and he finally told me, "Oh, that's all today, come back tomorrow."

The next day was a Sunday and we didn't do much work on the farm so I had most of the day to do whatever I wanted to, but that came to a halt as soon as we had finished our morning chores.

"Someone in this family wanted me to make them a slingshot. Who was it?" he said.

"Me," I answered, then saw my dad looking at me with a look I didn't like to see.

"I don't remember you asking if you could have a slingshot?" he said.

I thought that was the end of it but Grandpa saved me by saying, "He asked and you said yes."

"When was that?" Dad answered.

"When you were feeding calves." Grandpa knew when my Dad was feeding calves you could talk until you were blue in the face and he would never answer you about anything.

"Oh," was all he answered and went outside.

Back then, men used to pour their coffee into the saucer and then drink it, don't ask me why, but that is what he did and then winked at me.

What he didn't know was I was getting wise to his tricks and a while later he told me to go find an inner tube, "Don't get one of those black ones, they don't work good, I want a red rubber one, the one we took out of the tractor tire a while back."

But I had seen him carrying one a few days ago and I watched him hide it under the grain shack. I went and got it and was back in a few minutes.

116

He looked at me, surprised, and said, "Got up early this morning, didn't you?"

"I saw you hide it," I answered.

He didn't answer me, just put it up on the rafter and went on his way to work in the field.

It took a week before he said anything about the slingshot and he told me the following Sunday, "Go get a ten foot ladder and take it down to that old oak tree by the creek."

Well, back then ladders were made from oak wood and they were heavy, almost too heavy for a nine-year old kid to carry, so I drug it three hundred yards down to the creek and under the tree but I couldn't set it up. He helped me that afternoon. Then he stood by it and said, "Come here, look up in the tree. You see that branch up there?"

"Which one?"

"The one with the big knot hole in it."

"Yes."

"See the one just above it?"

"Yes."

"See the one with the two branches hanging down?"

"Yes."

"See the fork in the one on the right?"

"Yes."

"Go up there and cut it down and don't fall off the ladder."

"It's pretty high," I said.

"And?" he answered.

"I can't climb that high."

"Can't died, Can took his place."

"I might fall and break my arm."

"Tough," he answered and walked away, leaving me there to overcome my fear of heights if I had one.

I guess I didn't at that time in my life but I do now. I can handle about ten feet but not much more.

It didn't bother me too much to climb the ten feet, but it bothered me a lot trying to stand on the top flat of the ladder and saw off the branch. I had to hang on with one hand and saw with the other one. And if you ever been nine years old and stood on the top flat of a ten-foot apple ladder and tried to saw a oak tree limb off with a three-foot limb saw you can understand what I went through for over three quarters of an hour. Then I had to carry the heavy ladder back to the barn. Uphill. I was about half way back when my Dad walked by and took it from me and carried it the rest of the way and put it away in the barn. I carried the branch back to the porch and left it there where it laid for another week before it was mentioned by my Mom who said to my Grandpa, "Are you trying to grow an oak tree on the porch?"

"Maybe," he answered.

"Then you sweep the porch," she said.

"The wind will blow the dirt away if you leave it there long enough," he answered.

"You're getting senile," my Mom told him.

"I already am. A little," he answered, then said, "What was we talking about?"

Everyone thought it was sort of funny except my mom who picked up his plate from in front of him and carried it out to the back porch and left it there.

"You sure make good vittles," he said, "wish I had some."

"When I get my porch back you can eat in the house."

He made one of his funny faces and said to me, "Why do you always get me into trouble?"

"I didn't," I laughed.

"Give it enough time and you will," then he looked at Mom and said, "Can I please have my plate back? I'll move it."

Mom went to get his plate and he looked at me and said, "You want to learn something?"

"What?" I answered.

"Don't say 'what?' Say 'yes'."

"Yes."

"You can't own something if you don't name it."

It didn't make much sense to me then, but it sure does now.

He got up after he finished eating and told my Mom, "Thanks for the vittles," and walked out the door to the front porch.

"What are vittles?" I asked.

"Another name for food."

"Who named it? Do they own it?" I was trying to make a joke.

"Don't get too smart," he answered then asked, "What are we doing?"

"Making a slingshot?"

"Oh ya, how much are you paying for this operation?"

"I don't have any money," I answered.

"Broke, huh?"

I didn't know what that meant so I answered, "No, I'm all here."

He laughed and answered, "Not that kind of broke, I was talking about no money, if you don't have any money you're broke."

"I guess I'm broke," I answered, not knowing why he even was asking me that.

He picked up the branch and made a mark on each of the forks and handed it to me, then told me, "We need to cut it off right here where I marked it."

"Ok," I answered.

"Well?"

"Well what?"

"Go cut it off and bring it back."

I took it out to the shed and sawed it off then brought it back. He peeled off the bark and cut a notch in each fork, then told me, "Go get your mom's scissors."

I stood there looking at him because no one was allowed to even touch my Mom's scissors.

"Well?"

"She won't let me touch them."

"Go tell her I want them." I went and asked my Mom if Grandpa could use her scissors and she said no.

"She said no."

"Go ask her again."

"She'll say no again."

"Go tell her to come out here and bring her scissors."

I went back in and told her what he said and she just looked at me and turned her back without answering me.

"She didn't say anything."

He got up and went into the house and came back with the scissors and Mom right behind him. She stood there as he trimmed the leather and cut the two strips of rubber and then she took her scissors back into the house.

He sat there and tied the rubbers to the forks, then made holes in the leather and tied it to the rubber strips and the slingshot was done. He pulled the rubbers a few times and let them snap back then told me, "Go out there and close the gate for me."

I got about fifteen feet and he shot me in the butt and it hurt. I almost started crying but I stopped myself and turned and looked at him.

"Hurt didn't it?" he said.

"Yes."

"So now you know how it feels. So don't be shooting my horses in the rump with it."

"I won't."

"You better not," then he stood up and put the slingshot in his back pocket and told me, "Let's go."

I followed him out to the grain shed and he picked out a small piece of broken window pane and carried it with him while he went to the storage shed and picked out a gallon jug. Then he carried them to the grain shed and took his .410 shot gun down off the rack and put a shell in it.

"Come on," he told me again and I followed him out behind the barn.

He sat the jug on a fence post and the glass on the fence rail then handed me the slingshot.

"Think you can hit that glass?"

"I think so."

"Well then. When you get the notion you want to shoot out a window, you come here and shoot that glass, you got it?"

"Yes."

Then he raised the shot gun up and shot the jug, blowing it into a thousand pieces. He looked down at me.

He handed me the slingshot and told me, "Here! And when you get the idea to shoot me in the butt to get even, remember, if you do, I'm going to shoot you in the butt with this shot gun. Got it?"

"Yes."

He walked away.

I never did shoot that piece of glass or a window, or a horse in the rump. Or my Grandpa in the butt to get even with him.

The Last Ride of Jim Spencer

Jim Spencer lived in a sort of remote part of Arizona. He was a cowboy and a bull rider after he got out of school and the Marines. Before that, when he was in high school, he was one of the best track and field runners in the state but he was from a small farm and never had the time to be in all the meets so he never really made good in track, but until the day he died he could stand flat footed on the floor and jump up and kick an eight foot ceiling. He could jump over a four-rail fence or run and jump over a horse's back and walk on his hands for about half a mile. He could run backwards as fast as most men ran forward and he made a lot of money betting he could do it. And the thing about him was, he was only five foot two inches tall. Just a person who had that special muscle ability. He was just a very strong man for his size and a very likeable person full of fun and always making jokes and telling tall tales. The funniest man when he was drunk you could ever meet in your life

But his favorite thing was betting. He would bet on anything and he lost most of the time. Silly bets he knew he couldn't win and still he would bet and just hope for a happening so he might win but he hardly ever did. Two days after payday he was broke and borrowing money from anyone who would loan it to him. He would set around in the tavern or restaurant bumming beers in the bar or drinking coffee in the cafe and sitting in the bunk house on his bunk trying to think of something to bet on or a way to make a lot of money.

He wanted to win the U. S. Championship Bull Riding, but he never made the finals. He made money at it but hardly enough to pay for his expenses. He always came home broke or nearly broke and after buying beer for everyone he was broke and back to trying to bet he could outrun someone or kick out a light on the ceiling or walk on his hands from here to there and back but he had done it all so many times everyone knew he could do it and never bet with him.

Then he happened to meet a man who had twin horses. Not just twins, but identical twins. No one could tell them apart and he got to thinking about a couple things and one of them was the story about a guy who rode his horse from one small town to another thirty-one miles away in two hours. He knew for a fact no horse in the world could do it because it was almost all up hill around a mountain. But, using his ability to run and jump he knew he could run up over the mountain in two hours but no one ever would bet with him because he had done it before.

He left for Colorado in January and met with the man who owned the two mares and told him his idea.

"You bring the two horses down to Arizona and put one in hiding somewhere and bring the other one to this tavern on a Sunday and talk about how much endurance it had and it could run fifty miles or so. I'll mention the story about the guy who rode around the mountain in two hours and you say your horse could do it. He smiled and said, "And the betting will start hot and heavy. But I'll ride the horses and get off and run up over the mountain and get on the twin when I'm on the other side and ride it down to town. I know I can do it in less than two hours, maybe an hour and forty five minutes. After a couple days of talking they agreed to do it in May when the weather got better.

Jim went back and did what he always did as he waited for the horse to arrive and it did on the second Sunday in May. The fellow rode the horse up to the tavern and tied it up then said he had ridden it all the way up the hill from Phoenix since eight in the morning, a distance of almost fifty-five miles in six hours. No one believed him.

So the argument started and started growing with Jim Spencer right in the center of it.

It took a while but he slowly turned the conversation to the story about the guy and his ride around the mountain.

"Hell, my horse could do that easy, she wouldn't even break a good sweat doing it," the man bragged. And the betting started and the betting got heavier and heavier and finally it was decided a week from today they would bring the horse and ride it around the mountain in less than two hours.

They took the second horse over the mountain on Saturday night and one man stayed there with it until Sunday morning, then left it tied under a tree where Jimmy Spencer could meet up with it as he came over the mountain.

There were several thousand dollars bet but by the time the weekend came there were over two hundred people waiting, some at one town and some at the other and the betting was getting completely out of hand.

The next thing that happened was the fellow said his man who was going to ride the horse never showed up. So they waited and after two hours, Jim Spencer said, "Hell, I'll ride the damn horse, I think she can do it, and I got a hundred twenty dollars that says she can."

The bet was made and Jim got on the horse and someone called the other town and said exactly what time it was and Jimmy dug his heels into the horse and it took off down the road and turned up the trail over the mountain for a little over a mile, then Jim jumped off the horse and took off on foot up over the mountain on a path he had ran more than twenty times. He was ahead of his time by almost ten minutes when he climbed over a few rocks and just as he reached the other side he got bit by two rattlers, one got him on the arm and the other one got him in his lower leg. He knew he was in big trouble and he still had over five miles to go even if he wanted to get himself help. He tied off his arm and his leg with his belt and bandana and kept going. He reached the second horse with over ten minutes to go but he was so weak he could hardly climb into the saddle and spur the horse forward. He managed it by tying himself on with the reins around his waist and he rode on.

There was a hundred-fifty people standing at the road watching across the clearing for him to come running out, but what they saw was his horse sort of wandering around a half mile from the road and then slowly walking to them with Jim slumped forward in the saddle. They ran to get him and by the time they pulled him off the horse, Jim Spencer was dead from the snake bites.

The whole story came out then and everyone was mad at first then felt so sorry for poor Jimmy that they all just called off the bets and said it was a pretty good plan and too bad it didn't work out for him.

The man took his two horses back to Colorado and they buried Jimmy Spencer and decided May 16th would be Jimmy Spencer Day in the two taverns each year.

Two of the women went and bought two pine trees and one was planted at the tavern and one was planted at his grave. Neither of them was ever watered and both trees died within a few months. Jimmy Spencer Day came and went without anyone mentioning it for several years but the small sign hung on the wall of the tavern and then one day someone did mention it and was told, "Hell, that's just another one of those cowboy tales you hear around here. I don't think the man ever lived here in the first place."

Junk Yard Alice and the Round Man

Where the round man came from, no one really knew.

It was a very hot day in the desert just on the outskirts of Phoenix, Arizona. The three men who worked at the junk yard were all taking a afternoon break from the 110-degree heat, drinking beer and sitting on three old wooden chairs under the roof of the shed where most of the work was done, when it happened.

Across the field from the southeast there came a huge twisting spiral of dirt, dust, and debris, along with paper and other things. The twister had picked up from the ground as it travelled from who knows where, straight at the junk yard.

The three men sat and watched it until they saw it was going to pass directly through the junk yard, and then they ran for cover as it crossed the back fence and came at the shed. They locked themselves inside the shop and waited for it to pass. It did after rattling the roof nearly off of the shop and taking most of the tin roof with it.

They waited for a few moments, making sure it had passed and opened the door, then came out of the shed to see most of the roof had been carried away along with their chairs and the case of beer they had been drinking from, plus some trash and other things. In fact, the shop was cleaner than it had been in years.

"What the hell?" remarked one of them.

"It blew the roof off," another said.

"Hell, it took our beer with it!" the third answered.

"And our chairs," said one of them.

Then the first one said, "Yeah, but look what it left!'

126

All three looked down at the small fat boy standing in front of them, completely naked. He seemed to be maybe three years old and he was as big around as he was tall. The round man had come home. From where? It was never found out.

Searches were made and questions asked. No one knew where the boy had come from. They traced the path of the twister back across fifty miles of desert but no one claimed him.

"Well! I guess we just keep him until someone comes looking for him," the owner of the junk yard told his men and that was how it came to be.

A month passed then a year and another year and another. The little round man was contented to run around naked or half naked if he happened to find some old clothes in a car in the junk yard and play. Or work. Or sleep wherever he got tired. In, or under cars. In the shop or on the roof of the shop, it didn't matter to him. The whole yard was his home and he seemed to be completely happy.

He began school, but did not fit in at all because of his ill manners and greasy clothes and body. His found clothes were ill-fitting and his greasy round belly always stuck out from his shirt. After five years of school, he never returned and did his studies in a bread truck in the junk yard as he slowly converted it to his private room.

It was sold for scrap iron one day and he was again out of school and a place to sleep. "Round boy!" (He was called back then).

The owner told him, "You might as well clean out that old house up by the gate and live in it."

So with the help of the hired men, he cleaned out the house and moved in. Slowly he accumulated things and furnished it half way, using truck parts and car parts and things found in abandoned cars and trucks.

His house, after a few years, looked like a museum, with old things hanging on the walls and the trunk of a 1956 Ford filled with pillows for a couch, a car seat for a chair, bucket seats for table chairs, fenders hanging on the walls, a bed from a truck for his bed and mismatched utensils found in and under the seats of cars. And so on it went on until the round boy was seventeen, and more of a round man than a round boy.

It was on a day in November. It was raining hard and he had just finished cleaning out a car that had been towed into the junk yard. In the trunk, he had found a pair of hair clippers and decided to cut off his ten-year growth of hair as he was tired of trying to keep the grease and oil out of it. So he intended to shave his head like the other men.

He stood in the shop and plugged in the clippers. They worked, and he began to cut off the several pounds of greasy black hair. He had the top of his head shaved and was working on the sides when it happened.

A huge bolt of lightning hit the shed, flashing across the metal roof causing it to shake and shudder and forcing the rain water to run back up the slope of the roof and down through a small hole directly above the round man's head. At exactly the moment the water landed on the round man's head, the electricity caused a tremendous overload in the electrical wiring and that surge came down through the hair clippers and into the round man's wet head, down through his body, and out through his toes.

His eyes turned red and his hair, what was left of it, stood straight out from his head, his knees buckled and his toes curled up inside his found boots and he was lifted up off the floor a few inches then landed eight feet away from where he had been standing. Right on his feet!

"Wow! Oh Man!! Oh Man!!" one of the hired men cried.

"Am 1 dead?" asked the round man.

"You're standing," one answered.

"I am?"

"Yeah, you are. Did it hurt you?"

"I'm still smoking, ain't I?" he answered and walked away, forgetting about cutting his hair for the time being.

But something had happened to his brain when the electricity passed through it. He now remembered every single part in the huge wrecking yard and where it was, when it came in and where it had came from. Plus he remembered most of every book he had read and a lot of other things he had never thought about before.

But he was also electrified. His fingers could shoot a current of electricity five feet, and he excelled in shooting these bolts of current right into the butt of his fellow workers and whoever else happened to bend over at the wrong time, plus he could walk around with fluorescent light bulbs and light up anything. And in a matter of a few days all the hair on his head fell out and never grew again. He sold his clippers for a dollar and bought a burrito, then walked away eating the burrito, happy as he ever had been, with little sparks flying off the nails in the heels of the boots on his feet as he walked back into the junk yard.

Slowly the electric charge diminished and he became the round man again, except he could still remember almost everything asked of him.

He was now five feet six inches tall and five feet one inch around with a bald head and a greasy face and body. But he went on with his life such as it was. He sat on his stool under the shed, read car books and racing magazines, sold parts from the junk yard, told people where everything was and where it came from and did the best he could do with what he had to work with. He had a few big fat girls who came around and gave him burritos and he was happy to get them. They gave him t-shirts and he was happy to get them all greasy as soon as he touched them. And so was the life of the round man in the junk yard on the outskirts of Phoenix, Arizona.

He slept in the huge dent in the center of his bed.

He sat on the metal stool in the center of the shed where it was always shady, ate burritos, drank beer and talked to people about nothing, mostly.

But mostly he asked them if they knew what his name was.

"Yeah, I do. You're the round man."

"Not that name. My real name."

"No idea," was always the answer.

He wished he had a name of some kind even if it was a dumb name. "Ronny the round man," sounded nice.

"Jake the round man," was OK.

"How about 'Tony the round man'?" He asked lots of people.

"Call yourself anything you want! What the hell does it matter to me? Nothing, I suppose," he thought, but he wished he had a name like everyone else he knew.

He sold parts and remembered things and wished his life was different. Mostly.

Then one day the owner walked up to him and said, "Well, Mr. Round man. I'm leaving. It's all yours. You're on your own now. Have fun, and maybe I'll see you some time".

Then he never came back. So the round man was even lonelier than he had been before, because the nearest thing to a family he ever had just walked out the gate and didn't even wave goodbye to him as he sat on the stool under the shed and ate his burrito.

Alice was different. She knew where she came from and she knew who her mother and father were.

Her father was in Texas somewhere and her mother was walking away from the 1962 green Tudor Buick Road Master she was sitting in watching her mother walk away up the driveway of the junk yard where she had wanted to sell the car for enough money to buy a bus ticket to somewhere. But didn't want to wait and didn't want to take the girl with her. So she told her, "Alice, you stay here, I'll be back if I can."

She watched her mother walk away and knew she was never coming back, so she got out of the car and tried to get into the junk yard by hammering on the lock of the gate the car was parked in front of.

Ralph Conklin drove to work from the restaurant he had just left and parked his Ford wrecker truck behind the Buick and walked around it, then stopped dead in his tracks as he saw the six or seven year old girl hammering on his lock with a hunk of iron she had found.

"Hey! You? What the hell you think you're doing to my gate there?" he yelled at the tiny girl.

"I'm trying to get this gate open so I can find something to eat, my big guts are eating my little ones," and she returned to hammering on the lock with the hunk of iron.

"Hey! That's my lock you're knockin' all to hell and back! Stop!! I got a key!!" Ralph yelled and grabbed the iron from her hand and moved her out of the way.

"Where's your mom?"

"Gone."

"Where's your Dad?"

"Gone."

"Where do you live?"

"Here! In that Buick Road-Master."

"Where's your mom?"

131

"Gone. I'm hungry, you got anything to eat? I could eat a dead mouse if you catch one for me, look at my ribs sticking out here," and she raised her dress and showed him her ribs, she also showed other things because she had no panties on.

"Whoa!! Put it down! You showed me enough!! I believe you!" he cried and turned his head.

"Well? You got any food in there?" she asked.

"Yeah! I got some lunch meat and stuff." He answered as he opened the gate.

"Any milk?"

"Chocolate is all I got," he answered.

"I like chocolate," she answered and followed him into his office house.

"You live here?" She asked. "Yeah, I do, why?"

"It's a God damn pig pen!" she said and went to the refrigerator and opened it.

"Whose car is that blocking my driveway?"

"Mine now!" she answered, loading her bread with lunch meat and pickles. He watched her spread mustard, then mayonnaise, and then catsup on the sandwich. She put three pieces of meat then five pieces of cheese on it and took a big bite as she carried the quart of chocolate milk to the table.

"You ever clean anything?" She mumbled with her mouth full.

"Where's your Mom?"

"Gone."

"Where's your Dad?"

"Gone. You got a clean glass?"

"No. Who the hell are you anyway, kid?"

"Alice. I'm Alice. This table is a God damn mess! Don't you ever clean anything?"

"Quit cussing."

132

"Well it is."

"So what? Whose car is that?"

"Mine now."

"You ain't old enough to own a car."

"So buy it from me."

"I ain't buying nothing from you! What the hell you doing here anyway?"

"I'm deserted. Pull it in if you want."

"Pull what in if I want?"

"The Road Master. I got my things in it."

"What things?"

My panties for one thing," she answered and drank from the carton of milk.

"You stay right here! Don't move! Just eat and stay here."

He went out and pulled the Buick inside the yard and came back into his office house. She was making a second sandwich, stacking two kinds of meat on it, then cheese and mustard and mayo then catsup, and a few pickles for good measure.

"Will you bring me my panties? My butt's got goose bumps on it. Don't you got no stove in here?"

"No, I ain't got no stove and I ain't responsible if your butt's got goose bumps on it, who the hell .. who brought you here?"

"My mom, then she left me. I'm deserted now. Look!"

She turned and raised the back of her dress and showed him her goose bumps.

"Good God! Girl! Put it down!! I'll get your panties for you."

"Get the blue ones with legs on them."

He brought in her plastic bag half full of old clothes and asked, "This all you got?"

"That's it, Chester!" she answered.

"What the hell is going on here?" he looked at her as she took another big bite of the sandwich and a drink of milk.

133

"I'm getting pretty full now," she smiled at him.

"So am I," he answered. "What the hell you doing here?"

"Well, I got to live somewhere, don't I?"

"Here? You're moving in here? Oh no, you're not!"

"I got to live somewhere, don't I?"

"Not here!"

"Then where?" she asked and got up, then walked through the house looking at the piles of car parts and junk laying around. She came back and asked, "You got a gun?"

"Yeah! Why? You see a rat?"

"No! A hog pen. Just shoot it, then burn it, and we'll build a new house," then she asked, "So where do I sleep at in here?"

"You don't sleep in here, I sleep in here."

"I'm too little to sleep on the street," she answered.

"Well, you can sleep here until I find out where your mom is."

"You won't. She's gone. I'm deserted. You got anything to clean with?"

"Clean what?"

"This God damn pig pen!"

"Stop saying that! You're too young to cuss."

"You going to help me?"

"Help you what?"

"Clean this mess up!"

"No! If you want it clean, clean it. I got work to do." He went outside and she went to work cleaning the house as best she could. Every time he came in she was busy dragging things around and cleaning, sweeping, and wiping down things. By midday he came in and found her asleep on his bed, covered up with an old blanket. But the house was halfway clean and all the dishes were on the counter draining in a rack she had found somewhere.

"Oh Christ!" He muttered "What do I do now?" And what he did was he took her to supper at a restaurant he went to every day and brought her back with him.

She sat at the table and looked at him until he got so nervous he told her to stop looking at him. "You need a shower," she said, "You're all greasy."

"So what?" he answered.

"So it's not good for you, you could die from grease poison in your ears."

"You can't die from grease poison. Who the hell told you that?"

"Where do I sleep? Not in your greasy bed?"

"Sleep on the couch."

"There's mice in it! I saw two of them."

"Sleep wherever you want to," he answered, then took a shower and went to bed.

He woke up with her sleeping next to him curled up in a bath towel. She woke up and looked at him.

"Well, you took half of a shower anyway," she said.

He looked in the mirror and saw one side of his neck was still black from the grease and several other places. He took another shower and made sure he was clean this time. He spent half the day fixing her a room in the back, next to his. And so it went for a year until she told him, "You got to get some kind of paper that says I'm your kid so I can go to school next month."

"How do I do that?"

"How do I know, I'm six. You're forty-three," she answered.

"Wise ass," he muttered, and left.

"Well! I got to go to school don't I?" she called after him.

"I didn't," he answered.

"I can tell," she answered back.

He talked to a friend and found a way to get a birth certificate with his name as her father and Alice started school.

Every day for six years, she skipped off to school, did perfect work, and skipped happily home again carrying her lunch box and books. Then she cleaned his house and tried to cook. It was decided after several years of burnt food that she was much better at working on cars than she was cooking food.

Alice entered junior high and excelled in school and got straight As on every paper she finished.

Alice was very good at school and working on car motors and every other part of a car or motorcycles. By the time she was seventeen, she had two cars, a pickup, and three motorcycles.

It was on the first Saturday in June after she finished high school the accident happened. A car fell off a stack of cars and landed on Ralph. It was the very same car she had arrived in thirteen years before, the 1962 Buick Road Master.

She ran to where he was laying under the car and cried as he told her, "Alice, I want you to go behind the house, under the tree on the west side, and dig up the can of money I have buried there. Then sell this place and go to college, that's my last wish, and thank you for living with me all this time." Then he died in her arms.

Alice buried Ralph and dug up the can of money he had buried, then sold the wrecking yard and went off to college driving her 1967 Mustang and pulling a small trailer with her two favorite motorcycles on it. She went off to a college called Cal. Tech. somewhere in California. Four years later, she graduated as an engineer of some kind and was ready to begin her life, except she didn't know what she wanted to do with her life. All she liked was wrecking yards, hot rods, and motorcycles, so ...

She stood beside her car and drank a bottle of beer, then laid the bottle on the ground and gave it a spin. Whatever direction the neck pointed to was the way she would go. Lucky for her, it pointed east. Had it pointed west, she could have only went two miles before she ran into the ocean. But it didn't and she headed east pulling her trailer behind her '67 Mustang.

She went from coast to coast and back again looking and trying to find a place where she felt at home and finally she came to Phoenix and drove along a road where there were wrecking yards lining both sides of the pavement. She drove slowly along, looking, but saw none that looked good to her. She turned onto another road and then onto a different road and finally stopped in front of a small wrecking yard on a side street with a big gate with a funny looking man made of tin fastened to the gate and a sign that said "Route 66 starts right here."

She got out of her car and walked in through the gate and down the drive.

"What ya need?" Asked a fat man sitting on a stool.

"A home!" she answered and walked right past him.

"Hey! Where you going?"

"I'll be back, don't worry," she answered and walked around the junk yard then back past the fat man and into the house by the gate.

"Hey! What the hell you doing in my house?"

"This is a God damn pig pen!" she said, then asked "You married?"

"No!"

"What's your name?"

"They call me the round man."

"That's it? Ain't you got no name?"

"Yeah, that's it," he answered.

"So how about I call you Ronny? 'Ronny the round man?'"

"Sure!" he answered, taking a bite of his burrito.

"You gonna help me clean this place up, Ronny?" she asked.

"You moving in?" he asked, puzzled.

"Sure, why the hell not?" she answered.

"Yeah! Why the hell not?" Ronny the round man answered. He tossed his burrito away to the birds and began to carry car parts out of the house.

Jake's Mail Order Bride

Elsie May Walker was twenty eight years old and not the prettiest girl in the small town she lived in: Jerome, Ohio. She was a sort of sandy-haired stout-hefty girl nearly six feet tall and slightly over 150 pounds, unmarried and had no prospects of ever getting married, so it seemed to her and her family. Not that they wanted to get rid of her but she complained a lot about her situation and maybe tried too hard and drove away the few men who were available in the town of 1200. It was 1968 and a lot of men in Alaska were without wives. Need I say more?

So the story begins.

Elsie lived on a small farm just outside of Jerome, Ohio, with her mother, father and five brothers. She was a real corn-fed Ohio farm girl who could milk a cow and toss a bale of hay as far as any of her brothers toss her brothers over a cow and further than any two of them, and there were a few times when one of them made her mad and she had tossed her brother. She could plow a field and fix a flat tractor tire if there was no one else around to do it for her.

Just a few days after her twenty-ninth birthday she saw an ad in a weekly paper that read:

Fishermen, Gold miners, Ranchers, Timber men and other Hardy Men in Alaska need wives. There are seven men to one woman in Alaska. Are you Lonely? Alone? Not happy?

If you want to get married, send $5.00 and a short letter telling us about yourself to: And it gave an address; maybe,

806 zippatie do dah lane somewhere; U. S. Of A

Elsie May wrote:

Dear Sir;

I am twenty-nine years old and come from a farming family, one girl and five boys. I am not a sissy girl. I am not the best-looking woman, but I'm not ugly either, average is what I would call me. I am a good cook and keep a clean, neat house. I would like to meet a man who is at least six foot tall and not over fifty years old because I would like to have maybe three children.

Elsie May Walker

She enclosed a picture, not of herself, but that of a woman she got out of a picture frame at the drug store then put it in a small paper frame and that woman was damn good looking. She mailed off the letter with five dollars and gave them her address.

Two weeks later she got a letter back thanking her and it said she would hear from a man in Alaska soon and of course she told no one in her family what she had done.

Jake, who everyone called Blacky, because of his long black hair and black beard and black hair on his arms and everywhere else including two very large bushy eyebrows, was not a gold miner, or a rancher or a fisherman, he was in short, a bootlegger. But not really that either.

He went to Alaska when he was twenty years old with the intentions of fishing or mining but ended up running a tractor building roads for the county and that was how he happened to find the spot by the lake he wanted to live on. So he filled out the papers and filed on a small (ten acres) piece of land on the bank of a lake called "Two and a Half Moose Lake." (Don't ask me how it got its name because I do not know.)

Anyway, he worked here and there for the county and on his days off, he cut logs and built a cabin on the lake which just happened to be chock-a-block full of fish, nice big fighting fish.

And over the first few years a lot of men who he met and some he hadn't met came there to fish and of course the first thing a man will ask when he comes to your cabin to fish is "You got any beer? Or what have you got to drink?"

After getting tired of buying beer and having other men drink it, Jake began to sell it and he kept selling it and earned a almost good living at it even though he never bothered to buy a license or file taxes on what he earned selling the beer. Then he built six wooden flat bottom boats, got a deal on several small motors and rented them to men who came to fish. Then, over the next few years he built five small log cabins 12' by 12' with bunks, a stove, a table and not much more in them, but each of them had a name above the door and a couple sets of horns nailed up on the front of them and the whole place looked pretty good with a nice little dock and a rock lined trail to and from each cabin. A big fish smoker right in the center of it all so men could smoke their fish when they were still nice and fresh and a few pork ribs were also cooked in the big iron pipe it was made out of (stolen from the pipe line?) Then Jake's place just sort of became known as "Blacky's Lodge on Two and a Half Moose Lake". This all took a few years, 13 to be exact, and then it went on like that for a few more years and kept getting more and more people coming to stay and fish for a few days.

But, the one thing Jake, or Blacky, whatever you want to call him, didn't have was a good cook. And he was not one himself, in fact, if he had to depend on his cooking to make a living he would have been dead by now. Pancakes and ham and fried potatoes. He could almost cook, if the stove, which was made out of a fifty-five gallon drum with a smaller drum inside it and a piece of the same pipe he used for the smoker (stolen from the pipe line?) barbecue inside the smaller drum to hold the wood, then he placed a nice thick piece of flat steel on top, and it worked pretty well, if you didn't expect too much from it, but it kept the cabin warm and when it was working just right and if he had not drunk too much of whatever he was drinking that day. He did make a good pot of red beans, onions and ham hocks with a little red chili powder in them. He dished them out for $1.50 in a nice big bowl with a couple hunks of sourdough bread and he sold a few fishing things, hooks and line and sinkers and lures and stuff like that he bought at the sporting goods store and doubled the price on. He didn't sell a lot, but he sold some. And he had a sign that said "If You Take It- Pay For It" tacked on the counter above a can for them to put money in, and the good part of that was, most of them didn't have the exact amount to put in the can so they just put the next larger amount they could make.

Mostly people just did for themselves, they cooked their own food on one of the three campfire places he had built out of rocks and they made their own beds or slept in sleeping bags or in a tent out in the yard if they didn't want to pay ten dollars for a cabin and weren't afraid of bears. And most of them were so well mannered they kept the yard nice and clean and often spoke about the place as if they had a part in it which a lot of them did, not a big part but enough of a part so they came back time and time again and brought friends with them, maybe a license plate they tacked on a wall or a old bucket they found and set out in the yard for decoration. And there was quite an assortment of old things sitting around, like broken boat motors and worn out tools.

He didn't pay too much attention to them that way and more or less let them do as they wished.

"Well now, don't that look good there?" he'd say even if he thought it was just another piece of junk he had to walk around or trip over. But he kept a keen eye on the beer and whiskey sales and boat rental so he ended up making a pretty good living during the summer and didn't have to work out anymore.

But he learned how to let everyone know how broke he was all the time and made pretty good tips as the bartender, and he told a good story too, that helped. So one weekend, I don't know which one it was, but some customer, or friend, said about the same time Elsie May wrote her letter, or maybe a little sooner I'm not sure,

"Jake, you know what you need around here?"

And Jake answered "Yeah! A good cook."

And the person answered, "Here you go right here, it says they got two hundred to chose from," and he handed Jake a newspaper he had brought to wrap his fish in.

Jake looked and read an ad that said:

"We have over two hundred lonely women looking for a husband in Alaska. All ages and all sizes. Send five dollars and a short letter telling us about yourself"

At first he said no, but after the drinking started and the other men talked to him he decided it couldn't hurt to spend five dollars and see what came out of it, so with the help of his friends he wrote:

Hello;

My name's Jake Uklikson and I own a small fishing lodge up here in Alaska and I wouldn't mind having a wife if she was a good cook and didn't mind roughing it a little. I figured it can't hurt none to write a letter or two if you want to write me, but it takes a month for me to get a letter from down there so don't get in no hurry about it. And I ain't rich or nothing like that so don't get your hopes up on that part.

Thanks a lot" Jake; or Blacky (whatever you want to call me) and he sent five dollars.

Six weeks later he got two letters on the same day, one from Elsie May Walker (the one she wrote to the company) and one from the company. It read:

Dear Mr. Jake Uklikson; AKA Blacky,

After reading your letter and carefully going through our female clients, (Elsie was the only one they had), we thought you might be interested in Miss Elsie. If not, please write us again and don't forget you must send another five dollars to cover the cost of research.

Jake read the letter and looked at the letters AKA and asked, "What does that mean?"

"Also known As," his friend answered.

"Damn! That's pretty smart, ain't it? Who thought of that?"

"Probably some smart guy," was the answer.

"Well let's see what she has to say," Jake said and opened the other letter which was just a copy of the original, but it didn't matter because he couldn't tell the difference anyway.

He read it then handed it to his friend and his friend said, "I think she's the one for you, buddy. She says she's a good cook and if she had five brothers, she's got to be tough, she says right here she ain't no sissy girl."

"She sure don't look very tough," Jake answered.

"Yeah, but that's only her face, if she came from a farm I bet there's a lot more to her than shows in that picture."

"How much more?" Jack asked, thinking maybe she had a huge big butt or was fat as a hog.

"Ask her for a full length picture before you commit yourself."

"Hell! She can't look no worse than I do," he sort of laughed, then said, "Maybe I better shave."

"Christ, you haven't even met her yet! Slow down!"

So I guess he slowed down and then wrote her a letter.

Hello; It's from me; Jake AKA Blacky (he liked that aka thing),

I'm writing to you because the match-making people gave me your letter and you sound pretty good to me and a friend of mine too. I don't know what to say. I'm better at answering than I am at asking, so if you write me and ask some questions I'll be glad to answer them for you if I can.

You got a full length picture of you I could look at? I ain't thinking nothing bad about you, just it would be nice to see all of you. If we don't get together, I'll send it right back to you.

Jake, AKA Blacky

Then six weeks later, he got a letter and a picture from Elsie May.

Dear Blacky; I like Blacky better.

That was not a picture of me. I cut it out of a frame that was in the drawer here in the bedroom, I didn't think I looked good enough to send a real one of me, but after I thought about it, it was a stupid thing to do. This is what I look like now (picture) -- (reader, use your imagination, and don't put a wart on her nose or something like that). A lodge sounds real nice to me and on a lake too. I like fishing a lot, "Trout, we have Trout here and catfish".

You told me to so here are some questions you can answer
Do you have any children? yes no
Have you been married before? yes no
Do you have electricity? yes no
Does it snow a lot more there than here? yes no
Do I look alright to you? yes no
Do you have a lot of dogs? yes no I like dogs
How old are you? Over thirty under fifty
Do you have indoor plumbing? yes no
Could I have a full length picture of you? yes no

145

I don't know what else to ask you, write me back if you're still interested after seeing what I really look like.

Elsie

He looked at the picture and said, "She ain't too bad looking, kinda pretty. She's got a nice face and nice smile on her and I like her hair".

His friend said "She looks to me like she could cut a cord of firewood with a hunting knife. She ain't no girlie girl. Looks to me like she'd fit right in here if you could get along with her."

So Jake, AKA Blacky, wrote back:

Dear Elsie no, no, no, no, yes. No, over thirty, forty one, no, yes.

He wrote her the letter and said, *"I'm expecting to get plumbing in this spring and I have a generator for electricity but we burn wood for heat up here, maybe you do too if you're on a farm.*

I got six boats I rent and four cabins I rent too, but mostly we just do a lot of fishing and not much else but a lot of talking. What we need is a cook, so if you don't want to get married maybe you could just come on up and cook for us during the summer.

Three or four kids might be good if they were mine."

Then he wrote on the back of the picture,

"Don't look at it too hard, it might make you sick! hee haw"

Jake

But I have to stop for a few lines and tell you, Jake had another girlfriend already, named Millie, yes, Millie the moocher. AKA a six hundred seventy-five pound, five foot ten inches tall at the shoulders, big-eyed, long-faced, fat-lipped, drink-stealing, beer-can-Sucking, whiskey-drinking, foul-smelling, pushy, four-legged drunk if there ever was one. Yes, Millie was a moose. Jake had rescued her from a mud bog when she was only a couple days old and then he raised her. Millie loved Jake and followed him all around. She would nuzzle up against him and lay her head on his shoulder except when she was too drunk to walk, then she just leaned against her tree in back of the cabin and went to sleep for a day or so. Sometimes he and she would just set in the yard, him on a tree stump and her standing right close to him and they would drink a case or a case and a half of beer and a pint of whiskey. But then I still don't know if she was following him, or the can of beer he carried in his back pocket for her to steal. And that's all you need to know about Millie except if you happened to be sitting at the bar in the cabin and had a beer in front of you, or a drink, if Millie came in you best just get up and stand back and let her do what she wanted, and that was go along the bar and drink every can of beer and every drink sitting there, and if you didn't move, she would simply use her head and knock you off your stool then drink whatever it was sitting on the bar in front of you.

So the letters came and went for about a year and Jake went to town and called Elsie and talked to her for about an hour on a Sunday.

Elsie said she would pay her own way up to Alaska because if it didn't work out she didn't want him to be obligated to her or her to him. And on April Fools' Day 1969, Elsie May got into an airplane and flew to Alaska and Jake went to Anchorage to meet her with his friend.

They stayed in a motel in town (separate rooms) for three days, talking and discussing things and they got married, and then went back to the lodge.

Elsie May walked around all over and said "It could use a little fixing but I like it, Blacky. I'm real proud of you. Where is the bathroom?"

And Black said "Oh, Oh", kinda like, "I forgot that part. It's out there!"

Well, that's when the trouble started.

Elsie May had never had sex and she was pretty shy about doing it in case the marriage didn't work out. But she was more worried about doing it without taking a shower and him not taking a shower. So they went back to the motel and stayed three more days, then she gave it a try and found it to be a pretty darn good thing. Jake thought it was a good thing too and decided to stay in the motel another week while he had his friend start building an indoor bathroom with a tub and shower in it.

Then Elsie told him he had to shave off the beard because it made her face sore.

She told him he had a week to get the indoor plumbing finished so she could have hot water without having to heat it on the stove.

He had the same week to get a different stove if he wanted her to cook. She didn't mind a wood stove because she was used to one. In fact, she said, "If I had my druthers just keep the wood one, but not this wood one."

He had to take a bath or shower before sex and he had to take one everyday hereafter.

He had to stop drinking fifteen or twenty beers every day and only a couple shots of whiskey, not a half a bottle every day.

He had to stop burping out loud and stop peeing out the back or front door, whichever one was closer to where he was at the time. No spitting on the floor and using the f. word three or four times in every sentence he spoke. And that was before he even opened the door after they came back from the short honeymoon.

Jake was about ready to call the whole thing off then and there if she was just going to be bossy all the time, but he liked the food and he liked the sex and he kinda liked Elsie too and he knew she was more then likely right about it all and she knew how to make sausage from scratch every morning. And it felt pretty good to be sleeping with a handful of breast. Nice to feel in your sleep he thought.

She told him, "We need a cow and some chickens, and a place to grow a nice little garden."

She told him where she wanted it and how big she wanted it and he told her, "You can't have a garden because the moose will just eat it."

She told him, "Build a fence around it."

Then she told him, "We need to start a real business here and keep books so we know where we're at in the fall and don't go broke in October." And you need to get a license so you don't get arrested.

"They don't arrest people up here," he said, "They just shoot them," but then he did admit he sort of went broke every year but he resented her telling him what to do and how to do it all the time even though it had only been about fifteen hours.

And he was about to tell her to pack her things and go back to the farm but he liked the sex, and he liked her cooking and he kinda liked her too, and she was more or less right about it all when she told him, "If you want to act like an animal go out there and live in the woods."

It was the third Saturday and there was about a dozen people there fishing and drinking and eating and having a really good time meeting Jake's new bride.

It was in the late afternoon and there was eight men sitting along the bar drinking beer and drinks with Jake behind the bar talking and joking with them, when guess who walked in through the front door?

"Where the hell you been?" Jake asked the moose who paid no attention to him at all and started her trip along the bar, pushing men out of the way and off their stools and then picking up the can that was in front of them, clamping a good lip-lock on it and raising her head, then sucking the beer out of the can and sucking the can flat. By the time she got to the last can of beer. Well, wait a minute.

Now you know, everyone in Alaska has guns, and Jake had about seven of them around, hanging up and leaning against the wall here and there but he also had a Ruger Black Hawk .44 Magnum in a scabbard hanging at the end of the bar on a wooden peg he had made just for that purpose about three feet from the stove where Elsie May happened to be trying to cook.

Everyone said, Millie the mooching moose had a look of pure terror in her eyes for about three seconds as she dropped the last beer can on the floor, then looked for another one but saw Elsie May in front of her six feet away. The moose looked at Elsie May, and then she was dead. Because Elsie May watched the moose suck down seven of the eight beers and that was enough for her. She reached over, took the four-pound handgun out of its scabbard, looked to see if there was bullets in it, then cocked the hammer and fired one shot, right exactly between the eyes of Millie the mooching moose. She dropped like a rock to the floor and laid there on her knees with her eyes wide open, still looking at Elsie May.

"Son of a Bitch," said someone real slow and soft.

"Oh My God!" said another kinda fast and loud.

"She killed your moose," another one added, looking at Jake, AKA Blacky.

"You killed Millie," Jake AKA Blacky said, looking bewildered at his wife.

"Who?" Elsie asked.

"My God! You killed her!" Jake said again.

"What were you going to do, let her drink everybody's drinks?"

"She's been doing it for nine years," he answered.

Elsie looked at Jake then down at the dead moose and said, "Well, too bad for her, ain't it?" She twirled the handgun about six times forward then about five times backwards and six or seven times forward again, then put it back in the scabbard. Then she said, "Some of you guys help me get it outside and hung up so I can dress it out."

"What?" cried Jake.

"Dress it out," Elsie answered, "take the guts out of it and skin it before it goes bad."

"What?" He cried again.

"What's wrong with you?" Elsie looked at him like he was nuts or something.

"I've had that moose for ten years, she was a pet," he cried.

"Well, now she's food," Elsie said, then walked around and took one hind leg and started to pull the moose out through the back door. Three men helped her. About an hour later, Millie the moocher was a skinned moose carcass hanging from her back legs on the limb of the tree she had leaned against for the past eight years.

Jake had stood in the doorway and watched as his new bride expertly gutted and dressed then skinned the moose, letting all the innards fall into a wash tub she had brought from the cabin.

By then, everyone except Jake's best friend had left for somewhere.

"What are you going to do?" he asked Jake.

"She ain't no girlish girl, you were right about that," Jake answered.

"She sure as hell ain't," his friend answered, trying as hard as he could to not laugh.

I wasn't there when it happened, but I was there before Elsie came, and I came back sixteen years after and heard about it from one of their four daughters. Their two sons were out fishing.

When I was there the last time they had twenty boats and sixteen cabins, a restaurant and bar, a sporting goods store, and a small garage.

The road had been made wider and graveled and they even had a nice big neon sign down at the highway saying:

"Blacky's Lodge and Restaurant. 3 miles ->
Motel rooms, Cabins, Boats for rent
Day Week, or Month. Great fishing!

But I guess Jake, AKA Blacky never took another bite of moose meat for the rest of his life.

Glances

It was not a big bar but an old bar; in fact, it was the oldest bar in the town with a huge Brunswick back bar that had lions' heads on the top of it with lanterns hanging out of their mouths. In the time back before electricity the lanterns were filled with oil and lit at night and the mirrors reflected the light out into the rest of the room. Mostly the same people came there day after day and the crowd didn't change too much. The bartender had a big handlebar mustache, wore striped shirts and a bow tie like they did fifty years ago, and carried with him a halfway-bald head, but he had been there for thirty years and never been in love, so he said, but he was a good tenor in the old days when they had quartets.

The salesman came from somewhere back east and had never been in the bar before but he finished his day's work a few doors down the street and just happened to stop in for a drink or maybe two and as it ended up, several more than three.

She was turning twenty-one that day and her friend happened to take her to have her first drink to celebrate her turning twenty-one at last. After all, it took her twenty-one years to do it and it was quite an accomplishment at that.

So the two of them went into the old bar and sat in a booth and ordered a drink of what I do not know and would not care to guess. The drinks arrived and each of them had a straw in them so the girls did not have to lift the glasses and be unlady-like. They sat politely in the booth sipping their drinks and the first girl who was older noticed the salesman looking at her friend and not just looking but sort of glancing at her, then looking in the mirror at her in long stares, so she said to her friend.

"That guy is staring at you."

"Which guy?"

"The old guy at the bar."

She turned and looked and he looked away but as soon as she stopped looking, he again looked at her, first in the mirror, then he turned and looked at her.

"He's doing it again," her friend said.

"Well, what can I do about it?" she asked.

"Go tell him to stop."

"I can't do that. I'd be too embarrassed."

"But he's just staring at you."

"You go tell him to stop."

"He's not staring at me," she answered.

"It doesn't bother me that much," she answered.

"It's really rude," her friend returned.

"Don't look at him."

"I can't help it, he's doing it again look!"

She turned and he turned away.

She got up out of her seat and walked to the bar and stood by him then said, "You're staring at me."

"I know I am," he smiled at her.

"Well, I don't like it," she said.

"Oh, well, I'm sorry," he said.

"So stop, will you?"

He smiled again and asked her, "Would you please step here beside me for a second?"

"Why?"

"Just, I want to show you something."

She stepped forward and stood beside him and he said, "Look in the mirror, look down the bar at the people."

She looked and saw three old men and four old women all sitting at the bar and all of them mostly drunk and talking loud about nothing at all.

"If you were me," he said softly. "Who would you look at? Them, or you girls?"

She went back to her seat and told her friend, "He's not hurting anything, let's just go."

John's Legs

This is one of those stories I don't know if I should even tell. Some might think it offensive and some might think I'm sick for writing it but I think it is worth telling because it is just a part of real life and it's a true story. In a way it was funny to me and to John (not his real name) and if he reads this I know he won't mind me writing it, so I'm going on ahead with it.

It was about eighteen years ago when I used to drive a taxi on the weekend for a friend of mine. He drove all week and I drove on the weekend for extra money. Normally I drove from around ten in the morning until about three in the morning Saturday and Sunday, but if I got too tired to drive I would just park it at his house and go home. Then I went to my normal job at seven on Monday morning.

I remember it was on Saturday night and it was really raining hard when I was called to a local tavern in the suburbs. I didn't park the car but stopped in the street and as soon as I stopped a man who had no legs came out of the Tavern walking on his hands carrying his torso. I was amazed to watch him as he opened the passenger's door then reached up, then took a grip on the rain rail above the door and with one hand lifted himself up and swung his body into the car and onto the seat. He gave me a address across town and as I started to drive he said, "I'm going to get my legs back."

"You're what?" I asked, not believing what he had just said.

"I'm going to get my legs back. I sold them to a guy and he's never paid me for them so I'm taking them back."

What could anyone say to that? I didn't answer him. He seemed just a little bit too drunk and I was sort of, well, not scared but leery? Is that a good word? He talked almost all the

156

way there and mostly about his friend who had not paid him. The amount I don't think was ever mentioned.

It took maybe a half hour to drive to where he had directed me and when we stopped in front of a older two-story house that had been painted several different colors. I kind of knew why he had not been paid and was wondering if it was actually legal to sell your legs to another person, but I didn't mention that either.

So we stopped and I parked the car at the curb and he got out then walked on his hands up the sidewalk and then up maybe five stairs onto the porch, and knocked on the door.

Oh Yes! Another fellow without his legs answered the door and they started at first talking and then it got louder and as I watched, they got into a wrestling match, and then a fist fight on the porch.

Without you being there it is pretty hard to describe, two men without legs fighting and wrestling, punching and rolling around on the porch for several minutes, I would say at least five. Then it was over and both men went into the house and the door closed.

A few minutes later, this man walked out of the house, down the stairs and got back into the taxi. His eye had a nasty cut on it and his mouth was bleeding a little and he didn't look too very happy.

He looked at me and smiled then said, "Got um! Let's go back to the tavern."

We went back.

He got out and walked away back into the tavern on his repossessed legs.

Me? I got a story and a seven dollar tip out of it.

Alligators

It seems to me that people are, Stop. Let me re-phrase it. Nothing on this planet concerning life is more important than the habits your parents teach you. Now notice, I didn't say lessons, I said habits. They can teach you to drink or cuss or be a thief or a million different bad things and you can learn the same things from the people around you, but habits take a long time if they're good habits, like picking up after yourself, working steady, being honest about money or being considerate of others, but not going too far, there is a very thin line between loyalty and stupidity.

No one in this story is stupid, maybe a little ignorant, but being ignorant isn't a bad thing, it sounds bad but it's just not knowing something. As soon as you learn about it you're no longer ignorant, but you are no smarter than you were before. You're smarter if you want to learn it and find out how to learn about it then learn about, that process is smartness, not intelligence, but it is a part of being intelligent.

Lucky is the child who knows what and where he or she wants to go in life at very early age so they have a direction and spend their time going in a straight direction.

Some people spend their whole life going in a round-about circle, looking for that direction and not really getting anywhere. So if you read this and have small children, remember: it's up to you to make or break them.

He was twenty. He had just finished his second year at agriculture college and then came home for the summer. He hadn't planned on coming home, but the death of his father made it necessary. Not that he wouldn't have came home anyway but he disliked very much the circumstances that brought him home.

The death of his father was bad enough after losing his mother less than a year ago, but now he had to not only face the truth to himself but he had to explain it to his older brother, who had not gone to college so his younger brother could. The plan was to make the three-hundred fifty acres of farm land pay off, not just earn a living from it, and he was the one going to school to learn how to do it. But the truth was he had no interest in farming, and after two years of taking classes he was not interested in, he had made his mind up to leave the farm and travel for a year at least around the country and take part in the correction of the government which seemed to him to be going to hell in a hurry. His intentions were to travel, meet people and then go into politics and try to do something right.

It would be very hard to try and write how he felt as he got off the bus and walked through the depot to meet his brother. But I would think he was very hesitant, sad and reluctant to go right into explaining his intentions to his brother, but he was positive he didn't want to stay on the farm not any longer than he was forced to. He had been injured quite badly when he was fourteen by getting his right foot caught in a mowing machine and he lost all of his toes and a quarter of his foot. He had a slight limp but he walked alright on solid ground or pavement, not on soft ground, because he had to have a hard leather plate in the bottom of his right shoe. That was the main reason he didn't want to be a farmer but not the most important reason.

He tried to not talk about college and kept the talk about other things during the four days before the funeral. He had decided to wait a week after then try to explain what his plans were and he was hoping his brother would be a little bit understanding and not just explode in anger. To his surprise it was his brother who started the conversation by saying to him, "You know Jimmy, that college thing was never really my idea,

159

it was Dad's. I know you were never really a farmer at heart, so if you want to change your classes to something you really want to study, I'll still support you as well as I can."

"I don't want to change my classes. I want to quit altogether and travel for a year if you think you can get by here without me helping you," he answered.

"So what about your half of the land?"

"You can have it, as far as I'm concerned," he told him.

"It's a lot to just give away."

"If I ever need any of it I'll have you send me a acre or two," he sort of laughed.

"I'll keep the land and you take the insurance money."

"I didn't know there was any."

"Not a lot, but a few thousand dollars, maybe twenty," his brother told him.

"I don't need that much," he returned. "I want to buy a motorcycle and just travel and work here and there and talk to people, maybe write about them."

"So let's just put it in a bank account and if you get into trouble you can draw on it."

"And if you need it you can draw on it," he answered.

And that was more or less the end of the conversation about him leaving. He took six thousand and bought a road bike and a backpack and left the farm with six hundred dollars in his pocket and five checks in case he got into trouble. He left Wisconsin a week later and traveled east to the Atlantic Ocean, then turned south. When he got to New York City, he went straight through, not wanting to take a chance on leaving his bike anywhere it could get stolen and he had no wish to talk to any city people. He headed for the Deep South. He wanted to see the real people and talk to them, ask what they wanted, and what they liked and expected of a Congressman or representative. He rode down into

Kentucky and stayed there for a month, working in a small saw mill, and living in a motel close by. He found it not as easy as he had thought to get people to talk to him about what they wanted. Most seemed pretty contented just as they were.

What amazed him the most was nearly all of them said exactly the same thing the people in his home town said word for word. They had jobs and houses and food on the table and seemed to be getting along just fine without changing too much.

He went north up into Tennessee and spent a month there working as a painter's helper. The people were about the same and they spoke about the same things, their jobs and families and what kind of beer they liked best and what kind of cigarettes they liked to smoke. All in all he was pretty disillusioned about the whole thing.

It was September and starting to have a chill in the air and rain in his face as he rode south into Louisiana, He was looking for some kind of job, but not looking really hard, he was thinking about Arizona for the winter. He had never been there, but he had seen lots of pictures of the Grand Canyon and he wanted to see that for sure, maybe spend the whole winter in Arizona and then go on to California and see L.A., Hollywood, then go on north to the redwoods and maybe up to Canada next summer. But he was in no hurry as long as he stayed out of the heavy rain. He rode down into Shreveport and took a road west along the swamps and looked at the huge clumps of moss hanging from the trees, and looking for a safe place to park the bike and roll out his sleeping bag somewhere.

The two lane road turned and wound around small houses and over a lot of small bridges and finally he came to a sort of park with a drive-through hamburger place and a sign that said *Camping sites. Three dollars a night.* He went in, ordered a hamburger and fries, and was sitting under a huge tree on a red and white bench when she came walking down the road. At first he didn't really pay that much attention to her but as she came closer he couldn't take his eyes away.

She looked to be maybe sixteen or seventeen. She had no shoes on but was carrying them in her right hand. She had on a plain cotton dress with a sort of blue pattern of flowers on it and as she walked the wind sort of blew the dress in between her legs and outlined them, but it was her hair that he looked at. It was so black he it looked blue and it hung down to her waist, the wind was blowing it away from her face and then sort of lifting it like it was being sucked up away from her head, she smiled and her teeth were just as white as her hair was black, she was fifteen feet away and smiling as she walked past, then she stopped and turned and walked over to him.

"That be your'n bike there?" she smiled.

He had his mouth full of the hamburger and had to chew and swallow before he could answer her. He nodded his head and sort of mumbled, "Uh huh."

"Shore is a purddy thing ain't it," she said with some kind of accent. She looked at the name on the fuel tank and touched each letter as she sounded out the name "Mo toe Gus ee."

"Mo to gu sie?" she said.

"Motogusie," she repeated.

"Yes, you did it," he answered.

"That's it? That's how you say it?"

"Yes," he told her.

"Shore is purddy, ain't it?"

"I like it," he said.

"Bet it would go a hundred miles an hour, won't it?"

"Faster than that," he answered.

"How far can you go in one day?" she asked.

162

"I don't know, maybe eight or nine hundred miles if I didn't get too tired. I rode four hundred yesterday coming down here."

She looked at the license plate and said, "That's way up north, ain't it?"

"Yeah, way up north," he said.

"You going back up there?"

"Not this year, I'm going to Arizona first, then over to California."

"How far away is that?"

"About eighteen hundred miles, I think. I'm not sure."

She stood there looking at the bike and he watched her face as she was thinking.

She turned and flashed a perfect smile at him. "You got a name?" she asked.

"Jimmy."

"Sara Lee, Sara Lee Bruie'at."

"Cajun?" he asked.

"Ka, jhon," she answered and laughed, "You're in Ka, jhon country now. Creole, dis is da bayou down here."

She reached and rubbed the seat of the bike, then turned her face to him again and smiled, "I bet dis bike here could go all the way to Arizona in one night I bet," she smiled again.

"If I didn't get so tired I'd fall off," he laughed.

She smiled a long knowing smile and said, "Bet you could give me a ride home?"

"Where do you live?"

"Just down dis here road a piece, bit more'n a holler, not too far."

"You want me to give you a ride home?"

"Shore do," she smiled again.

"So how far is a holler?' he asked.

"As far as you'll can holler, I reckon, I don't know for sure."

163

"You like alligators, Jimmy?"

"Never seen one up close but I don't think so," he answered.

"We got lots of them in the river by our house, I can show you one if you want to see for yourself."

"I can probably live without seeing one," he answered.

"You like corn bread and grits?"

"Never had grits, but I like corn bread and beans," he answered.

"Know what I like?" she asked.

"What?"

"Malted milk shakes, strawberry ones, but I never get one cause I don't have any money."

"You want me to buy you one?"

"That's what I'm asking," she laughed and showed her teeth again.

"You got the blackest hair and whitest teeth I ever seen," he said.

"Creole," she answered. "That's how we are down here in the bayou, black hair, white teeth, and no sense," she laughed again then said, "I got eight brothers and sisters."

"That's a lot of kids," he answered then said, "You want a malted shake?"

"Sure do," she laughed again and rubbed the seat of the bike.

"Shore is a purddy thing, ain't it?"

He walked to the window of the drive-in and ordered a strawberry malted milk shake and the woman inside whispered to him, "You best watch yourself young man, or she'll be on the back of that thing when you leave here. Lord knows she ain't got nothing to stay around here for," she handed him the paper cup and said, "$1.25." He gave her two dollars and said "Keep the change, thanks."

164

"Lordy me," she said and walked away. He heard her tell someone in the back, "That Bru'at girl is about to snag herself a husband I'm thinking."

He turned and looked at the girl and she was sitting on the seat of the bike holding onto the handlebars and smiling. Her dress was pushed up almost to her thighs and he looked at her bare legs. He thought she was the prettiest girl he had ever seen in his life.

"Here's your malt," he said and handed it to her.

He watched her suck on the straw as she held the cup in one hand and hung onto the handlebar with her other one. Her eyes were looking straight at him. They were almost as black as her hair.

He sat back down on the bench and watched her until the cup was empty and she got off the bike and tossed it into a trash can.

"First time I ever ate sitting on a Motogusie," she laughed.

"You ready to go home?"

"Not yet, I still got bout a hour before I got to get there," she answered then walked around and sat on the other side of the bench facing him.

"You be about twenty I reckon."

"I'm twenty exactly," he said.

She sort of turned her face a little and said, "I'm being seventeen. I'm the oldest."

"Prettiest too, I bet," he returned.

"Maybe," she smiled at him.

"You're sure thinking hard, ain't you?" he said.

"Shore am," she said and smiled at him, then asked "What they got there in Arizona?:

"Cactus I hear, lots of cactus."

"Them sticky things?"

165

"I think so."

"And rattlesnakes."

"And rattlesnakes," he repeated.

"We got cottonmouths down here. Mean ones."

"I've heard."

"Ain't none in our river. Let I never seen one yet."

"Let?" he repeated.

"Let. You know when you look for something and don't see it."

"Never heard that one before," he chuckled.

"Well I don't know, that's what they say down here. I told you we ain't got no sense."

"You want me to give you a ride home?"

"I'm still a thinking bout it. I might get in trouble if'n my paw's home."

"What kind of trouble?"

"Ow I don't give a good hoot if'n he is home," she said and smiled at him again then asked, "You won't wreck us or nothing will you?"

"I'll try not to," he answered, then told her where to put her feet on the pegs and told her, "you better tuck your dress in under your legs or it will be blowing all over the place."

She sat on the back of the bike and got ready, and then he got on and started it.

"You OK?" he asked.

She put her arms around him and he felt her breasts pressing against his back and almost wrecked it before they got started. He rode only twenty-five miles an hour for the couple miles to her house then she directed him into a small dirt driveway that went for a hundred yards and they were in the front yard of the house. Before he got the bike turned off there was seven kids around it, all of them asking questions to Sera Lee.

166

"Who's that?" "What's he doing here?" "Why are you riding on that thing?" "Is that a Harley?" And about fifty more until she told them all to shut up. They all ran off a few feet away and stood there looking at them except one girl who looked to be about ten or eleven with long black stringy hair that looked like it hadn't been washed in a few weeks, her dress was tattered, torn at the hem and dirty.

"You fixing to run off, Sera lee? And get married?" she asked.

"Shut up, Mary Ann!" Sera almost screamed at the girl. Then she ran off yelling at the top of her voice.

"Momma! Sera's fixing to run off with some guy on a motorcycle out here". Then she ran into the house and out of sight. But he could still hear her telling her mother her sister was fixin' to run off and get married.

The house sat up on several poles about eight or nine feet off the ground with the back of it hanging out over the river; there were two boats tied to one of the posts. It was a small, maybe three-room, house, all clapboard with no paint on it anywhere. He could see three small windows all covered with clear plastic. It looked just like some of the houses he had seen in magazines - - hillbillies lived in back in the hills of Kentucky or somewhere, and it looked like it was just about to fall over backwards into the river.

"You fixin' to run off and get married, Sera Lee?" he asked.

"Maybe," she smiled at him, her eyes sparkling like two black diamonds. "You want to meet my Momma?"

"Sure," he answered, then seen a man sitting on the back porch, he was sitting there looking at them for a few seconds and then he stood up and sort of screamed.

"What the hell you doing, girl? What the hell you bringing that thing here for? You get in the house and you, fella, you get the hell out of here!"

"Don't leave," she said, "He won't do nothing, he's drunk."

"That your dad?" he asked.

"If you want to call him that," she answered, then called back, "You shut up Paw! He gave me a ride home and he want to meet momma."

"I don't want that damn thing in my yard," he yelled back.

"Just drink your 'shine, paw, and leave us be."

He sat back down and didn't say another word, just sat there rocking and sipping from a quart jar, then drinking water from another jar.

"He don't do nothing. He don't work or nut'in," she said then said 'come on and meet Momma".

He followed her into the house and stood in the doorway not believing anything so pretty as this girl could have ever come from a place like this. The floor was covered with dirt and the only furniture he could see was a old table and three chairs. There was a wood stove against the wall and a woman was standing in front of it doing something.

"What ya making, Momma?" she asked.

"Same thing I make every day you bring any one home, Sera Lee."

"Three dollars, what they paid me for cleaning their house," she said and handed the money to her Mom.

"Don't let Paw see it," she said as the woman stuffed the three bills into her pocket.

"He don't need to know nothing bout it," her mother answered, and then looked at Jimmy.

"This is Jimmy. He gave me a ride home from the drive-through, he bought me a Strawberry Malt too after I sort of coaxed him a little."

"What kind of coaxing?"

"I just smiled real pretty, didn't I, Jimmy?"

He didn't answer. He was still looking at the inside of what was supposed to be a house.

"Where do all of you sleep?" he asked.

"Around," she answered, mostly outside if'n it ain't raining and the river ain't too high."

He tried to look into the other room but couldn't see very well but he saw there were no clothes anywhere in the house. What the kids had on was all they had, he guessed. All of them were barefooted and ragged and standing out on the porch looking in at them.

One of the boys asked him, "You one of those biker men?"

He laughed and told him, "No, I'm a Agriculturist."

"What?" the boy returned, looking funny at him.

"Farmer," he said, "but I'm traveling around to see the country."

"Ain't much to see round here," the boy answered, then said, "Sept kids."

"Momma, if Sera Lee runs off and don't come back, can I sleep in her room?" the girl asked.

"You can hush your mouth, Mary," her mother said, then wiped her hand on her dress front which looked to be dirtier than her hand was and said, "I'm pleased to meet you, young man. We ain't got much to offer you less you want a plate of greens and grits."

"No, thank you," he said.

"We just poor folk round here," the woman said, and turned back to her cooking. She looked tired to him and he felt sorry for her.

"Sara Lee! Bring me another jug o' water," her Paw called from the back porch.

"Get it yourself," she answered, then took his hand and pulled him back out through the door and down around the house where the two boats were tied.

"Where we going?" He was not wanting to leave his bike in the yard.

"Billy Bee, go stand by his motorcycle and don't let no one touch it and don't you touch it either," she told the oldest of the five boys standing there. She untied the smallest of the two boats and got in it then said, "Well come on".

"Where we going?"

"Across the river."

"Why?"

"Why do you think?" she laughed then said, "Not that!"

"Then why?"

"So we can talk without all those brats hanging around us."

She untied the long narrow boat and stood in it then told him to get in, "Is it safe?" he asked.

"I reckon, it ain't sunk so far, but you best sit so 's it don't tip over with us." He sat in the end of it and she stood up and pushed with a long pole. The boat slid across the river and landed on the other bank. She got out and tied it to a tree limb.

They walked a few feet up the bank and she sat on a log that had fallen over. He sat next to her and she turned to him and said, "Can I go with you?"

"You don't even know me," he answered.

"I know you're a good man," she said, then told him, "I don't expect nothing from you, I just want to go somewhere so's I can have a life."

"You haven't much of one here, have you?"

"I'm just afraid I'll end up like my Mom in there with nine kids and nothing else."

"It looks to me like any man around here would want to take you away."

"There ain't no men around here, they're all like my Paw, worthless as a dead skunk."

"What are you going to tell your mom?"

"I'll tell her I'm leaving."

"She won't care?"

"She'll be happy for me if I don't end up with a bunch of kids somewhere and no man to take care of them. I can get work cleaning houses somewhere. I know I can."

"Did you finish high school?"

"I went to the ninth grade and then Paw made me quit, I didn't want to but he made me".

"You could finish high school," he said.

"Where?"

"Anywhere."

"You gonna take me with you?"

"I guess so," he said.

"Tonight?"

"Now if you want to leave."

"Paw would call the cops if he knew I left. We have to wait till he goes to bed about nine o' clock. Then he wont know I'm gone for two days because Maw will tell him I'm cleaning houses in town."

"We could be in Arizona in two days," he answered.

"They won't come after me there, will they?"

"How they going to know where you're at? Your paw don't know nothing about me, not even my name, so how would they ever find you, but after you leave with me I'm keeping you."

"I was thinking you would when I seen you watching me walk down that road, I put on a good show didn't I?"

"I don't know about that, but you sure made me look," he said.

"You gonna take me for sure? You promise?"

"I promise," he said.

"If you go back to the drive-through and wait, I'll come there after nine. I got to talk to Momma and make sure she wants me to go, I know she does but I got to ask her anyway."

They talked for a while and went back across the river. He left to wait for her and she went into the house and told her mom she was going of to Arizona with him.

"What you want me to tell you Paw?"

"Don't tell him nothing for two days so he can't call the police and have them bring me back."

"I told you she was fixin' on running off with him, didn't I?" the girl interrupted.

"Shut up, Mary! Don't you say a word about this."

"Okay, Momma. Can I sleep in your room Sara?"

"I won't be sleeping there no more," she said.

"So can I sleep in her room, Momma?"

"Yes. Now go outside, Mary."

"You gonna get yourself a bunch of kids like us, Sara?"

"God No!" she answered and then told her, "Go outside, Mary, and don't say nothing to the rest of them. We don't want Paw to know. The girl went outside and Sara helped with the supper then did the dishes. As soon as her Paw went to bed, she left and walked the two miles to the drive-through.

"You got any Levi's?" he asked.

"I ain't allowed to wear them."

"You got to have pants on and a coat, you ain't even got a coat do you?"

"Don't need one down here it don't ever get cold."

He took a pair of Levi's out of his pack along with his coat and told her to put them on over her dress. She did and they left Arizona. The next morning Mary stood behind her Mom and said, "I told you, didn't I?"

"Yes, you told me, Mary, go outside."

"You think she'll have a bunch of kids like we got here, Momma?"

"I hope not, now go outside."

"I bet she took her dress off when they went across the river."

"Now why would you say that?"

"You think she did?"

"What if she did? What difference does it make?"

"I'm just thinking ahead Momma, you know, in case?"

She ran outside and her mother stood at the stave crying, partly from happiness for her oldest daughter and partly from sadness about the others.

The Bear

He heard it, but it was a long ways off. The sound of a drum, maybe. He tried not to hear it and tried to go back to sleep and finish his dream. He loved this dream so much. They were together and he was driving his truck and she was sitting beside him and smiling at him saying, "I love you, you're my hero." Then they were in the river in Mexico swimming naked, and then on the grass and he was making love to her. She was so small and her skin so smooth and her hair long and black and he loved her so much, but then the dream changes as it always did and he hated it, and tried to move it away, out of the other dream he wanted to go on forever. But it was there, just like it always came. They were on the grass and then he was in the jungle. It came to him like a colored movie.

He was back in the jungle of Vietnam and it was raining hard, he was soaking wet and his feet hurt from being so wet for such a long time, his lower legs hurt from his wet pants legs rubbing against them, then he saw him. Just like he always saw him in this dream.

Corporal John Morrison standing a few yards away from him and the young woman kneeling down in front of him with him holding her by her hair and pointing the .45 at her forehead.

"Don't kill me please, Joe," she cried, "Me no north, me South girl, me no soldier, Joe, please no kill me, okay? Okay? Joe?" she begged.

He stood there and watched his platoon leader as he unzipped the front of his pants and took himself out then told the girl, "You suckie, suckie I no kill you."

"Ok, Joe," she said, "I suck good, ok? I be your suckie girl, ok? No kill me, ok?"

174

He watched the girl lean her face forward and suck on his platoon leader for several seconds then pull her face back and swallow several times trying not to throw up.

"You ok now, Joe?" She smiled up at him. Morrison pulled the girl up onto her feet by her hair and pushed her out to a arm's length away from him then turned her loose and squeezed the trigger. The girl's head exploded as she was hurled back several feet then turned upside down and over a dead log, landing on her back with her legs still up on the log.

"You crazy?" he had yelled at his corporal.

"You keep your mouth shut," Morrison had yelled back at him, then smiled and said, "What do you think she was thinking just before I blew her brains out?" He watched Morrison put his .45 back into the holster and then raised his rifle and aimed it at his head.

"What the fuck are you doing?" Morrison said, and he squeezed the trigger. Morrison didn't move, just slumped straight down to the ground, dead.

"Now you know, don't you?" he said and went on his way, trying to find the rest of his platoon.

Now she was back in his dream and he tried to keep her face in his mind, she was at the stove cooking, making him food as he went up behind her and put his arms around her waist and kissed her. Then, they were on the bed making love again, he tried as hard as he could but something was interrupting his dream. A tap, tap, tap, tap, every second or so, he closed his eyes tighter but he couldn't make it stop, he pulled the heavy blanket over his head but he was awake and the dream was gone.

He laid there for several minutes listening and trying to figure out what the sound was then realized it was a drip outside the bedroom window.

It had turned warm during the night and the snow on the roof was melting, causing the water to run off. It had melted a small hole in the snow on top of an oil drum sitting beside the house and the water was dripping down on it, through the hole and hitting the metal lid. Tap. Tap. Tap.

He laid there listening to the hollow sound a few more minutes and then threw the covers off himself and turned over then sat up on the side of the bed.

He rubbed his face and felt the winter's growth of hair covering his cheeks and chin and most of his neck. The hair on his head was matted from not being washed for days and he stood up and looked at the empty rum bottles on the floor. He counted eight empty fifths laying in different places where he had dropped them and they had rolled to a stopping place and laid there waiting for him to pick them up.

He looked to see if any of them had anything left in them and saw nothing.

He walked down the short hallway in the trailer and kicked three more bottles out of his way as he stepped over them and went into the bathroom and peed. He stood there listening to the urine hitting the water in the stool and looked at himself in the small mirror. He finished, then searched in the drawer below the sink and found a pair of hair clippers. He stood there in front of the mirror and cut the hair from his face and head until there was only a tiny stubble left and a large amount of reddish brown hair on the floor. He turned on the hot water, then got his face wet with hot water to soften the stubble, took a bar of soap and lathered his hands then rubbed it on his face. It took three latherings to shave off the rest of the hair on his upper lip, chin, face and neck. He turned on the hot water in the shower and stepped in.

"God damn!" he said, then said it again and began to wash his body with lava soap and half of a cotton towel. Fifteen minutes later, he stepped out and stood naked in a large pile of reddish brown hair lying on the floor. He didn't bother to sweep it up, he just walked over it and went out to the kitchen area and put water in the coffee pot and then fresh grounds and sat it on the counter and turned it on. He went back into his bedroom and got dressed.

It was still dark outside as he poured a cup of coffee even though the maker was not done making it. Some of the coffee fell to the hot burner as he held his cup in under the stream and again when he sat the pot back on it. He stood there and watched it sizzle for several seconds before it evaporated.

He moved across the room sipping the black coffee realizing he had put way too much coffee in the filter. It was strong. He stood looking out of the front window for nearly a hour and watched the sun slowly turn the dark sky to pale light gray color, as light as it was going to get for another month. It was raining harder now and the snow was melting faster.

"Break up," he thought, "It must be April." But he didn't really know what month it was or even what year it was. All he knew was it was break up and he was awake and it was time to stay sober. Soon the snow would be starting to go and the bear would leave its den and head for the river as it did each year but this year he was going to kill it or it would kill him.

He got another cup of coffee and sat down at the table watching it get lighter and lighter for three hours before he tried to make something to eat. He was on his second pot of coffee and standing at the stove when he heard the ice breaking up on the river seven miles away. It sounded like a distant thunder claps and then another and another rang in his ears, then it stopped for a while and he ate his eggs, potatoes and bacon.

It took him three pots of coffee and into the early afternoon before he got up and took a cardboard box with him into the back bedroom and started a trip through the house picking up empty rum bottles and beer cans. He picked up eighteen rum bottles and about forty beer cans, then sat them outside the front door. He then went back and picked up all the paperback books he had read during the four months he had been alone in the trailer. He picked up clothes and bits of food, dried-out sandwiches with a couple bites out of them and bowls still half full of soup or whatever he had started to eat then didn't finish. He picked up spoons and forks from all over the house and food wrappers. It was getting dark again by the time he had finished sweeping and throwing out things. The house looked halfway like it had been lived in by a human being and not an animal of some sorts.

He walked out to the back of the house and looked at his propane tank, he still had about fifty gallons left and the generator wasn't running so they must have fixed the down power lined the snow had brought down a month before.

"Hell, I'm good to go," he said and went back into the house. He turned on his radio and sat back in a chair and read a book for three hours then went back to bed.

He tried to dream but the tap, tap, tap, on the drum kept him from dreaming and he laid in bed and read until he finally fell asleep early in the morning. and the dream came back just for an instant.

He was with her again on their trip north when he was bringing her home. Walking down the street in Seattle, then in a hotel room on the bed kissing her face. Then others came into his dream and he woke up and laid there listening to the water dripping down on the drum for a few seconds and then drifted off again.

He lay on his back and sort of slept, but sort of remembered the sight of her laying along the creek where she liked to walk. He had followed the blood trail until he had seen only one foot because the bear had tried to bury her and come back later for a second helping of the meat.

He woke up and sat upright in the bed, his face covered with sweat, his legs and feet tangled in the covers. He got up and made more coffee. He wanted a drink but there was none in the house. Again he sat at the table, drank two pots of coffee and waited for it to get light.

It was sometime in April, he knew that now, and he knew it was a Thursday, he had heard that on the radio but he didn't know what the date was until he heard it. April 16th, 1995. He was going to be thirty-eight years old in six days.

It was light now but the area was completely fogged in, He couldn't see the road sixty feet from the front of the house but he could hear the water running down the ditch. Teckla and Joe would be here tomorrow or the next day to check on him. He could count on that one for sure.

It was in the afternoon and the fog had lifted, he was standing in front of the window looking at the mountain for signs of the bear when he saw the beat up old four-wheel-drive pickup drive up the hill and turn into his place, then stop.

He watched the huge Indian woman and her small Eskimo husband get out, her on the driver's side, him on the passenger's side. He knew Joe had had a drink or two before coming up.

Tekla told Joe, "Don't you just go there! Get those things I need to clean up his house".

"You work too much cleaning," Joe answered.

"You spend too much time not working, lazy," she answered.

"Well, I work when we need things," he said.

"You work when you need whiskey, you drink too much of that stuff all the time," she answered and carried the cardboard box up the steps and into the house pushing past him without saying hello.

"You dead yet, Jimmy?" she asked as she sat the box on the kitchen counter, and then said, "Oh, I guess not, you're sitting up at your table. We brought you some food to eat, I made moose stew with potatoes and carrots. Joe is out there bringing in some things I need to clean your house. You live like a pig now."

"Hello to you too, Tekla," he said.

"Well, you do, don't you?"

"I guess so, if you say so."

Joe came in and said, "Hello, Jimmy; she thought you were dead this year so we came early so if the house was stinking too bad we could just burn it down with you in it."

"That was nice of you," he answered.

"You got whiskey here, Jimmy?"

"No, I'm all out."

"She wouldn't let me bring some, so I did anyway." He took out a pint of Four Roses and sat it on the table and Tekla came and took it and put it in her coat pocket.

"Work first," she said.

"What work?" he asked.

"You don't work, that's the thing with you," she said.

"Look, Jimmy, I lost three more teeth." Joe pried up his top lip and he could only see four teeth in his upper mouth and none in his lower jaw. "I'm getting new ones as soon as four more come out. I tried to get new ones but they said I still had enough to eat with, so they didn't give me any this year."

"You can still drink whiskey, can't you?" Tekla answered, then said, "Go get the other things out of the truck. I got to clean this house good today."

"She makes me work all the time, Jimmy," Joe said and went out the front door.

"He should work, then we don't have to eat moose meat and fish all the time. He drinks too much whiskey for me. It makes it hard on me all the time, Jimmy."

"Joe works in the summer," he said.

"Just when you tell him to work, not when I tell him to work, it makes it hard on me, Jimmy."

"I know it does, Tekla," he said.

Joe came back in and sat the box on the counter and Tekla told him, "I'm cleaning this now. Go put it over there. You don't think too much either." Then she turned to Jimmy and said, "He makes it hard on me all the time."

"We going to clean the road tomorrow, Jimmy?" he asked.

"Not for about three weeks," he answered.

"You going to go try and kill that bear again?"

"Don't talk about that to him," Tekla turned and looked at her husband.

"Why you talk about that for, I said don't talk about it".

"As soon as it thaws out enough and I see him come off the mountain."

"He's going to kill you too," Tekla told him, then walked to the table and stood looking down at him. "It ain't the bears fault he's a bear, he didn't know she was your wife or nothing, he was just being a bear and he got hungry, so he killed her."

"And I'm going to kill him."

"He's going to kill you. I know he is, I dreamed that he killed you by the river."

"I dreamed I killed him by the river, so that makes us even."

"You never dreamed nothing about that. My dreams come true. Remember when I dreamed Joe was in the river and I went and pulled him out by his foot?"

"She pulled off my shoe and threw it in the river," Joe answered.

"It just came off when I was pulling you out, I should have kept the shoe and let you drown."

"It was a good shoe, too, only a month after I got it."

Tekla came back and set the bottle of whiskey on the table and said, "Here! It's better to hear you drink than hear you talk."

"She's afraid of me," Joe said. "That's why she gave me back the whiskey." He took a drink of it and handed it to Jimmy; he took a small drink and handed it back.

"Tastes good, huh?" Joe said.

"Tastes good, huh?" Tekla echoed, looking over her shoulder with a disgusted look on her face.

"See, she's afraid of me," Joe said.

"Remember when you got drunk that time and I hit you with a pan on your head?"

"Maybe she's not afraid of me," Joe laughed, made a scared-looking face, and then asked, "Want me to clean the road when you let that bear kill you? If you don't come back, I'll have to do it myself this year."

"Drink your whiskey and shut up," Tekla told him.

"See, she's afraid of me, alright, I scare her all the time with things I say. She's afraid I'm going out to the lower states and marry a young woman after I get my new teeth."

"And then I'll take them away and give them to you after you get done working," Tekla laughed then said, "You live like a pig in a pen, Jimmy, don't you ever wash your dishes when you eat out of them?"

"Sometimes I do," he said.

"Sometimes you don't, too," she returned and told them, "You men go sit on the chair over there so I can clean the table".

Tekla cleaned the house part way, then washed his dishes and set the table with the moose stew and different things she had brought with her and then told him, "Maybe you might not go this year after that bear. It don't make no sense to me to just kill it when it don't know what it did."

"I know what it did."

"I don't know how to talk sense into you, Jimmy."

"Yeah? Well you're just wasting your time trying, Tekla. I'm going after it as soon as it comes down from the mountain."

"Let's eat," Joe said.

"You eat, but you don't work," Tekla answered and served Joe a plate, then smashed the meat so he could eat it without chewing it. They ate and Tekla and Joe got ready to leave. She said they would be back in the morning if it wasn't snowing or if it wasn't too foggy.

"You want me to get some groceries for you, Tommy?" Tekla asked.

"Yes, if you would please, and get me some trail supplies."

"You go to get them yourself, I won't help the bear to kill you," she answered and then they left.

It was dark now and he sat in his chair and tried to read, but he felt hungry again and ate more stew, then some of the cake Tekla had brought him. He slept better and didn't dream at all.

He got up early and made coffee then went into the back room and got his guns down and began to clean them. He was just finished and standing, looking up at the mountain with his spotting scope, when Joe and Tekla came back.

Tekla set to work cleaning the rest of his house and Joe set right to work drinking more whiskey and getting in Tekla's way until she told him, "Go outside, bring in those things before you drink whiskey."

"See, Jimmy, I have to work all the time," he said and went out to carry in the groceries Tekla had brought up to the cabin. "I'm going down to the lower 48 and get me a young woman who has a lot of money and don't make me work too hard every time," Joe kidded, smiling at Tommy.

"It's raining hard, and it's cold out there, Jimmy!" he said as he sat the first box on the floor. "If it turns to snow we're all in trouble this time up here," then he drank the last little bit of the whiskey he had brought the day before. "Maybe the rain might wash out the culvert."

"No, it won't, Jimmy," he answered and set his spotting scope back up in front of the window Tekla had just finished cleaning.

"Is it up there yet? You see it, Jimmy?" Joe asked.

""Go get the rest," Tekla told him and waved a large spoon at him."I'll hit you with this," she said.

Joe brought in the last box and told Jimmy, "I think I better go down there and look at the culvert and see if it is washing out."

"It's in the hall closet," Jimmy answered.

Joe said nothing, just looked at Tekla as he went to the hall closet and took out the half gallon of Four Roses Whiskey he had hid in the culvert last fall.

He sat it on the table and Tekla walked over and took it, then sat it on the counter by the stove so he couldn't get it.

"Work first," Tekla told him.

"What work?" he asked.

"Don't you have to work on the tractors?"

"Not in a rain as hard as this one is out there," Joe answered.

They made their living by maintaining the thirty-nine miles of gravel road. Joe drove the road grader twice a week from one end then back the other way and kept the drainage ditches open.

184

Jimmy owned the tractors and worked part time but he mostly let Joe work so he could earn money, except the two or three months it was so packed with snow and ice no one drove on it except him and maybe Joe if he came up to the cabin.

"I just have to put the batteries in them so the motor will start is all."

"Go do it and then drink whiskey."

"It's too early, it might freeze again and ruin them," Jimmy told her.

"It won't freeze again this year, too much rain. When it rains it don't freeze, when it's foggy it don't rain." Remember 'when the sun is out it don't snow,' I taught you that," Tekla told him then told him again, "Work first."

"She's afraid I'm going to go to the lower states and get me a young wife, that's why she keeps me tired out working all the time." He put on his coat and went out the door.

Tekla took the half gallon and poured some of it into the pint and sat it on the table, then took the jug with her. She put it under the sink in front of where she was standing.

"He makes it hard on me all the time, Jimmy," she said and went to the back room, his bedroom.

"It smells like a rotten foot in here," she called, then said as she came back out of the room, "It stinks in there like feet. You need to stop thinking about the bear and think about keeping yourself clean or you're going to get sick and die."

"I don't care if I do, Tekla," he answered.

Tekla picked up a large wooden spoon she used to stir the stew pot and hit him on his head, a nice hard thump.

"Ouch!"

"Stop being crazy!" she said and walked back into his bedroom and called out, "You live like a pig in here".

"Quit reminding me," he called back.

The mountain was completely fogged in but he stood looking at it anyway.

"Any good-looking women up there?" Joe asked as he took off his coat, hung it on the hook and sat down at the table. He took a drink of whiskey and said, "Tastes good, I was supposed to tell you something but I think I forgot what it is."

"What did I forget to tell him?" he called.

"He's got a lot of mail at the store," Tekla called back.

"Oh yeah. Jimmy, you got a lot of mail at the store, I remember now."

Tekla finished cleaning the house and cooking several dishes for him and they left after she shook her wooden spoon at him and told him, "Don't live like a pig so much and don't think crazy anymore till we come back here."

"I won't," he smiled and said, "thank you." He handed her some money and they drove off down the hill.

It was dark now and getting warmer. He could hear the water running off the roof now in a steady stream. The road was running and the snow was falling off the branches of the fir trees up behind the house making a soft crashing sound as they fell and the creek behind the house was running again. Spring was close and he knew as soon as water seeped into the bear's den it would come back awake and start down the mountain. He sat in his chair and read for a while, then took a shower and went to bed. Again, he didn't dream and slept for eleven hours without waking up once.

It was light when he woke up. A clear day, the sky was patchy with puffy white clouds but it wasn't raining and it wasn't foggy. He could see to the top of the mountain and it was still covered with snow, no bare patches of ground. He made coffee and looked through his spotting scope. He had to go to town today and get his new traps and trail gear he had ordered before the bear got away without him seeing it.

He drank his coffee and ate some of the food Tekla had made, and then went out to put the battery back in his truck and start it. Joe had already put it in. He thought *"Joe is really a good worker but he and Tekla don't see things the same way. She thinks he should have a steady job and work five days a week but Joe wasn't made that way"*.

He started the truck and moved it to the front of the house by the door, then went back inside to let it warm up and dry out a little before he drove it. He left an hour later and drove down the road; it was full of chuckholes and ruts from the rain washing across it at every curve. He would tell Joe to come and grade it tomorrow before the water overran the ditch and cut across the road so deep no one could drive over it, and then it would be hard to repair.

He went first to the hardware store and picked up five new steel traps and then to the grocery store, where the post office was also located in the back corner of the main room, and picked up a small box of mail he had gotten during the past six months. He looked first for the checks from the state for his work on the road. He found them and took them to the bank and got some cash for Joe and Tekla, then drove to their house.

They lived in a small two-room sort of log-board house with the bathroom added onto the back of the kitchen. Built by the state for natives a long time ago, it set several yards up from the river's edge. They had the right to have a new house built at no cost to them but they never had it done even though he told them to several times.

"I'm used to old things and the old ways." Joe had told him a few years back.

"In the new houses you can't have some things I have. You can't have a fish trap or pelts inside like I got, and ivory. And I have those things in here from my relatives before me when it was a place with no name. I think some of the things I have offend you white people, like the bones of my great-grandfather's hand. He was a good hunter and his hand guides mine when I hunt the whales in the summertime. If we move to a new house, then I have to bury those things and I don't want to, I want to keep them. If I'm dead, then the white man can bury them, but not me, so I'll stay here in this house until I die."

He stopped in front of the house and went inside. It was warm from the wood cook stove and Tekla was sewing a large patch quilt blanket by hand. Joe was working on a fishing pole.

"You bring me some whiskey, Jimmy?" he asked.

Tekla looked at him, then at Joe. "Think of something else," she said.

"Fixing my fishing pole is work; it's the old kind of work."

"You're the old kind of lazy," she said, then smiled and said, "Hello, Jimmy, you want something to eat?"

"No, thank you," he answered, then said, "Joe, you need to come and clean out the grader ditch in the morning, the runoff is about to cut across the road."

"Want me to come today and start?" he asked.

"You can if you want to, but I don't think you will have enough time to do much before dark."

"We'll come in the morning, early," Tekla answered.

"She won't let me drive, she thinks I'll go down to the lower states and find me a young wife down there."

"When you drive, you break my truck and you drive so slow, you never get nowhere," she said then shook her head, "He drives over rocks and breaks tires."

Joe had a tendency to just drive anywhere, if there was a road there or not it didn't matter to him. There were four beat-up old trucks in their backyard that Joe had destroyed by driving them through the brush.

He handed Tekla four hundred dollars from the checks he cashed and left.

He went back up the hill. The road was almost washed out at several turns and he had to use four-wheel drive to get across them, but he knew Joe was a good operator and he would put the road back in good shape in a few days if they could get up the hill. If not, he knew Joe would just walk in and take the grader back down and pull his truck up, so he wasn't worried about that. If Joe didn't show up, he would drive the grader down and meet them at the bottom of the road at the highway, then follow the grader back up the hill.

He carried the traps into the shed and placed them with the four he already had hanging on big hooks on the wall and went into the house. He sat at the table and looked through his mail, throwing most of it away as soon as he looked at it. He read three letters and put them in a drawer. He read the fourth one four times, and then put it in his wallet for safekeeping. He stood at the window, searching the top of the mountain until dark, then read part of a pocket book and went to bed.

It was raining again in the morning and he was woken up by Tekla calling to him from the front room, "You ain't drunk, are you Jimmy?" she called, then came into the bedroom and stood looking at him.

"No, I'm not drunk," he said and sat up in the bed. "Where's Joe?" he asked.

"He's gone down the road with the grader. We had a hard time coming up here."

"Yeah, I know, I did too. Damn! I must have been really been asleep, I didn't even hear him," he answered, then said, "Mind if I get dressed?"

"Thought you were drunk cause you got some money yesterday."

"I ain't drunk, I'm naked," he said.

"Sounded like you had a saw in here cutting wood, but it was just your snoring."

She left the bedroom and went out to the kitchen and made coffee and something for him to eat, then started doing his laundry.

"How do you get so dirty when I'm not here?" she asked.

"I practice," he answered, then put on his coat and went outside and began cutting fir boughs. He intended to boil them and put all his things in the water to completely hide his body smell from the traps. Last year the bear had sprung every trap and took the bait and put it all in one pile, letting him know he knew he was trying to catch him. This year would be different. He would get to the river first and have the traps set, then lead the bear around to where they were. He spent all day cutting boughs and stacking them in the shed so the smell would saturate the area. He put his hunting gear, boots, coat and guns in among the boughs and covered them over with more boughs, then went back into the house. It was getting dark and he was worried about Joe. He started to drive down the road and look for him but Joe drove the grader back into the yard and came into the house.

"You got some whiskey for me?" he asked Tekla.

"You eat!" She said and carried a plate of food to the table for him then gave him some milk.

"I don't like milk," he said.

"Put some whiskey in it," she said.

"The road open?" he asked.

190

"A little, not all of it, but I cleaned out the curves so the water don't go across the road. Tomorrow I'll have most of it, but it's going to take a week to make it safe again".

He turned and looked at the mountain through his spotting scope. It was too dark to see anything.

"You going home tonight or staying here?" he asked.

"We're going home," Tekla answered.

"That road is bad down there, it got worm too fast this time," Joe said and reached for the pint of whiskey Tekla had sat on the table for him. He took a drink and said, "Tastes good." He handed the bottle to Jimmy and he took a small drink. "Want more?" Joe asked.

"No," he told him.

"Want to play cards?"

"No."

"Want to play checkers?"

"No."

"Tic-tac-toe?"

"No."

"You in a bad mood thinking about that bear?"

"No."

"Want me to tell you about when we went to hunt whales last year?"

"No."

"You just thinking about something?"

"Joe! For Christ's sake! Drink your whiskey," he sort of laughed.

"He's just worried about you," Tekla said.

"I know he is," he answered, then said "I'm fine, Joe, just drink your whiskey, alright?"

"I don't like to drink it by myself," Joe answered and put the lid on the bottle, got up, then put his coat on and went outside.

"He thinks that bear is going to kill you," Tekla said, "And I do too."

"Maybe it will," he answered.

"I think you want it to."

"No, I don't."

"I think so, then you won't have to think about her anymore."

"Tekla!" he said and looked at her.

"Alright. I guess we'll go home now. I'll see you in the morning."

"Thanks, Tekla," he said and watched her put on her coat and leave.

It was clear in the morning and he could see small patches of open ground on the mountain, but no signs of the bear. He was looking at the mountain when Tekla and Joe drove in. Joe started the grader and went down the road and Tekla came into the house and started doing things.

He went out to the shed and got out the oil drum and set it on the iron rack he had built, and then gathered some wood for a fire. He was going to wash all his clothes he intended to wear in the water after he boiled the fir boughs in it to hide his human smell. He started a fire and filled the drum with water. He took his hunting knife and peeled several fir boughs, letting the needles and small branches fall into the water. It took four hours before the water was hot enough to put his hunting clothes in. He let them soak in the water until the fire went out a few hours later. He took them out and laid them in the boughs to let them dry and absorb the scent of the boughs. He dumped the seven traps into the water and left them there.

Joe made two complete trips up and down the road and he drove the grader into the yard and climbed down. "You finished?" he asked Joe.

"No, I only got the mud and slush off of it, there is a lot of water running down there, it got warm too fast this time," then he looked up at the mountain and said, "When that snow up there melts it's going to come down here and fill the creek up, then the road is going to be running a lot harder than last year. It got warm too damn fast if you ask me this time."

He didn't answer and Joe said, "Looks like you're getting ready."

"I am ready," he said and walked back to the house with Joe following him.

Tekla set the table for them to eat and no one said much. Joe didn't even ask for whiskey. Then as they were leaving, Tekla stood in the doorway and said, "It's God damn crazy, you thinking about killing that damn bear like you do." Then she closed the door and he watched them drive away. Joe looked like he was tired; he had been on the road over ten hours grading it.

It was clear again in the morning and the snow was melting at a faster rate than he had seen it in the eight years he had been up here. Water was running across the yard in front of his house and down the road, covering almost half of the drivable area. He stood at the window and watched the mountain through his spotting scope for signs of the bear, and the water washing gravel down the road making new ditches for Joe to fix. He saw no bear signs, but the bare patches of ground were getting further up the mountain and he knew within a few more days, the bear would come out and start its trip down the mountain and down to the river. It would be hard to follow him, but if it was raining, it would be easy for him to stay close to it without the bear smelling him.

Joe arrived and Tekla came in the house to fix food while Joe started the grader and went down the road without talking to him first. He was glad; he didn't want to talk about it anymore.

He stood looking out of the window and Tekla never said hello to him, just started doing something with the food.

He spent most of the day watching for the bear and even after Joe and Tekla went back home at dark he stood at the window watching the mountain.

It was dry the next day. No rain, but some fog, and he was half mad about it. Then it cleared in the afternoon and he searched back and forth and up and down across the mountain to see if he had missed the bear coming out. He saw no signs of it and was contented it was still asleep in a den somewhere up there.

Two days later he saw it. He watched it as it came out of a hole in some boulders and stood there getting used to the daylight then went back into its den. It was not fully awake today but tomorrow it would be and he had to get ready and be gone by daylight or he might miss it. He spent the better part of the night getting ready and he walked across the road before it was light the next morning, carrying the eight heavy traps and his camping gear along with both guns, and headed along the creek down to the river about twenty miles south.

He crossed the creek and found a good place, then set his spotting scope up on a rock and sat there waiting until shortly after daybreak. He watched the bear come out and start down the mountain, stopping every few seconds to dig in the ground and eat something. He watched it until it was halfway down the mountain and then it turned south and started its journey to the river to wait for the salmon to start running. He picked up his gear and followed it, staying about a half mile behind. He climbed until he found where the bear had turned south, then it was easy to follow. All he had to do was follow the dig marks the bear left in the ground as it foraged for roots and other things to eat. He followed the bear three miles the first day and made

194

his camp in a hollowed-out place in the rocks. He set his string of tin cans and small bells around in a circle several feet away in case the bear smelled him and turned around. A hungry grizzly bear will eat anything it can catch, him included, and he didn't want that to happen.

He followed the bear several miles along the side of the mountain and then down into the valley. Then the bear did what he had thought it would do but it did it sooner then he had figured. It crossed the river. He would have to go another two miles before he could cross in the small rubber raft he had left in a tree during the summer. He saw the bear twice as it moved slowly along the river bank on the other side and he followed it, keeping in the brush so it couldn't see him moving or smell him. He came to the tree where his raft was but it was too late to cross the river. He waited until morning and crossed in the raft.

The bear had crossed back during the night and was now where he had been, he seen it and knew it had gotten his smell even though he had done everything he could have done to prevent it. Now the bear was after him as much as he was after the bear.

He spent the whole day sitting at the edge of the water with his rifle hoping the bear might come to the river close enough so he could kill it from his side. He saw it but it was too far away and it was standing up trying to get his scent. He watched it stand up several times, testing the air, trying to smell him.

"Come over here," he coaxed under his breath as he watched it through the scope on his rifle but the bear moved on down the river.

Joe and Tekla had came to his house at about nine in the morning and saw he had left. Joe climbed up on the roof of the trailer and looked at the side of the mountain. He saw Jimmy a mile away, climbing up to where the bear had turned and came back down. "He's up there already," he said.

"Crazy, crazy to go chase a bear like that!" she said then told Joe, "We better go get some help and go up the river and find him or bring back his body if the bear eats him."

"He's too tough to eat," Joe answered, but didn't believe what he said.

"You drink too much whiskey," she said in not a very nice tone.

"It's going to be tough to go up the river with the ice coming down," he said.

"We'll go get Roger to help us. His boat can go up in the ice."

"Maybe," Joe said, then said, "Maybe not," then added, "It's going to take four days on the river to get to the falls."

"He won't be at the falls, he'll be above them. The bear wont come to the falls until June, it will stay up and eat mice and scrubs on the ridge until it's warm."

"You know about bears, I know about whales," Joe said, then sat quiet until they were at Roger's house.

Tekla told Roger that Jimmy had gone after the bear. He called another friend and they agreed to meet on the river in the morning at daylight then drove back home to pack things. Joe took his rifle and other things from his shed and loaded them into the back of his truck without Tekla having to tell him to do it.

He slept, but not to soundly, surrounded by the string of tin cans and bells tied together with twine, so if the bear came in contact with the string he would hear it and be ready when it entered his campsite. It never came and he was up at light and moving slowly down the river looking for signs of where it had been. It was still on the other side of the river and he would have to cross over again to find its trail.

196

He loaded the small raft and crossed again. He deflated it and put it up in a tree, then headed on down the river. He picked up the bear's trail after four hours. It was a long ways in front of him. He had found many holes the bear had dug and all of them were full of water. He figured it was at least six hours in front of him. He had lost most of a full day going back and forth across the river.

He made camp and strung out his makeshift alarm system then went to sleep in the tent. He was back on the trail at daylight and almost to where he knew the bear would spend the next three months before the salmon run started down at the falls. By the afternoon, he saw fresh signs of the bear and it was no longer moving in a straight line south. It was where it was going to stay for a while. He stood and looked at a huge area where the bear had torn the ground up digging for mice. He made camp and set out his cans. He ate and then cut branches to make a fish trap for catching bait. Fresh fish was the thing bears liked and he was going to catch a lot of them for his traps.

Tekla, Roger, Ben, and Joe were seventy miles down the river and just starting up when he made his camp. Ben was helping Tekla as she used a long pole to push the hunks of ice away from the boat. It was about all the twelve-horsepower outboard motor could do to move the heavy wooden boat forward against the fast-moving current. They were making about one or two miles an hour up the river.

He woke up when he felt the tent move. At first he thought the bear had come in the night, and then he realized his tent was really moving. It had started raining again and the river had come up almost three feet and was washing his tent away with it. He had to move up to higher ground or get washed away by the river.

He moved the tent a hundred fifty yards up the bank to a high place under the trees and tied it down again. If it got too flooded he could always climb a tree for a couple days if he had to and wait for it to go back down.

At daylight, he stood looking at where his tent had been. It was covered with three feet of fast-moving water. His fish trap was gone and he was too far away from the main stream to catch fish. He had to move down the river a half mile to below the falls to where he knew there was a high bank and put in another fish trap. It took him all day to finish.

The next morning, he took five of his bear traps and the fish from the trap and carried them a mile up above the falls and into the trees. He secured two of them up into the trees six feet above the ground, tying them to huge limbs with the chain attached to the trap, and placed three on the ground around the trees then stuffed them with the fish he had caught and went back to his camp and waited for morning to set the other three traps.

He got up and it had stopped raining. The river had dropped a few inches but not enough to make much of a difference. He emptied his fish trap and put the fish in a sack and carried the other traps back up into the trees.

All the fish from the day before were gone. Foxes and ravens had picked them clean. He had to do something else and that was catch more fish but the more he put there the more foxes and ravens would come to eat them. He was in a dilemma of sorts.

He decided he would put the traps on the ground in a circle and put the fish in the center of the ring and cover them over with tree limbs. If the foxes tried to get them, they would be caught in the traps and then get eaten by the other foxes and he figured the ruckus would keep the birds away and maybe bring the bear to the fish. He tied all the traps together by hooking the chains to another trap and arranged them in a large circle around a good-sized tree, then cut several tree branches and tossed them on top of the fish he had caught. All he wanted was for the bear to get caught long enough so he could shoot it and kill it. He left for his camp and set in the tent waiting until it was dark. He wanted to hear the bear bellowing because it was caught but he heard nothing from the trees. He went to sleep and got up in the morning, emptied his fish trap and carried the fish back up to the trees. It was raining again, hard.

There were foxes all over the place, four of them were in the traps, and about thirty were eating them. They ran when he came close and he threw the fish onto the limbs and started to walk away.

The bear was twenty feet away and looking at him, then it started forward at a slow hunting walk looking at his face as it came to him.

His rifle was ten feet away, leaning against a tree, and he tried to get his handgun out from underneath his slicker as the bear came at him.

He raised his slicker and fumbled with the tie down on the holster and finally got the gun out in his hand, but the bear was fifteen feet away and moving faster.

He fired at it and missed its head, but hit it in the right lower shoulder. The bear flinched, then charged him.

His second shot hit the bear in the left shoulder and it went down for a second, then got up and came forward then raised up to strike him.

He fired again and hit the bear in the chest but it didn't stop. His next shot was at point-blank range three feet from the bear. He aimed and fired into the bear's open mouth and killed it. But he tripped on the chains of the traps and fell backwards as the momentum of the bear kept it coming forward and it fell forward and as he fell backward, the bear fell directly on top of him. He tried to move to the side but he was too slow. The six-hundred pound bear fell on top of him and pinned him under it.

He was pinned under a six-hundred pound grizzly bear and could not get free. His legs were crossed and pinned and his left arm was on his chest with the bear on top of him, its head laying beside his. He tried to slide out from under it but he was tangled and his coat was trapped in one of the traps he had set, holding it in a iron grip. He would have to get out of the coat to get free if he could get out from under the bear's weight and there was no way he could get out unless the foxes ate enough of the bear so he could move it. That was going to take a week and he was positive they would eat him first, or as much of him as they could get to.

He wanted to cuss but there were no cuss words he could think of to describe the mess he was in. He tried to move his left arm. He tried to reach it with his right hand and help to pull it free, but he couldn't reach it. He laid there under the bear for an hour, trying everything he could try to get free but he was pinned and he was trapped and that was it. He couldn't reach anything to help pull himself free and he couldn't push the bear off of him. It took another half hour and he thought if he could get to his hunting knife, maybe, maybe, he could cut the bear open and then hack off enough of it so he could get free.

"You're dreaming," he said it out loud, then felt a movement a few feet away, behind his head. He looked back and saw two foxes sitting looking at him and the bear, trying to decide if they should come forward and maybe have a snack.

He raised the handgun and fired at them but missed. They turned and ran. He knew they would be back sooner or later. He had one shell left in the gun and if need be he was saving it for himself. He was not going to be eaten alive by foxes.

"What the hell do I do now?" he said out loud and tried again to move even his left arm or slide sideways. He was trapped and there was no way out he could think of at the moment. He was tangled in the fir boughs and his coat was clamped in the bear trap and his legs were crossed so he couldn't double them up for leverage.

He tried to slide his right hand in under his left arm and managed to move it a little by letting out his breath and then shoving his hand forward but all the clothes he had on were not a help. The material was hanging on and wadding up, keeping his hand from sliding in under the bear's wet fur. He tried pushing his left arm out from under the bear but it was stuck and partly wrapped in the slicker and the trap was holding his right hand a few inches short of reaching his left arm.

"Son of a bitch!" He cussed and grunted, then started to get mad. It took him almost an hour and he finally reached across his body and found the handle of his hunting knife, then tried to pull it back across his body an inch at a time as he let all the air out of his lungs and then pulled as hard as he could pull. But he couldn't maneuver the knife into a position where he could cut the slicker enough to free his left arm.

"You're pissing me off, bear!" He grunted and finally jerked his right hand free with the knife still in it. He had been under the bear over three hours and his body was going numb. He couldn't feel his lower legs and he couldn't feel his left arm. The pressure was cutting off his blood and he knew if he didn't get free soon he was going to lose his lower legs and his left arm even if he did manage to get free. He tried to think and feel each part of his body but from the shoulders down he was getting numb and more numb and he knew if he didn't get free he was going to be dead in a few hours. He was wet from the ground water soaking up into his clothes and he could feel his heart

201

overworking itself to try and pump blood through his compressed body. Then he saw them. Now there were five foxes sitting, waiting.

"Get! Get away!" He screamed at them and they ran off a few feet but then turned and set there watching and waiting. He pointed the handgun at one of them and fired before thinking. Now the gun was empty.

He killed the fox and two others grabbed it, then ran off to eat. It took all of his maneuverability to get the cartridges one at a time from his belt and reload the gun. He had been under the bear over four hours now. He laid there and waited, then when the foxes came back he shot one, and laid back to wait again. He took the hunting knife and tried to cut the bear open. He cut and cut and finally he had a small opening in the bear's belly. He cut off pieces of the bear's guts and tossed them to the foxes. Now it was getting dark and more foxes were coming and sitting and waiting. He wiggled and tried to move by breathing in and out as hard as he could, making a little room for his blood to get through his veins, he wiggled his toes and his fingers on his left hand and cut and sliced with his right hand. If he could get the belly of the bear open, the guts would slide out and make the bear lighter. At least he would have the heat from the bear's body to keep him worm during the night. He might make it until daylight if he was damn lucky.

It was dark now and he was getting weaker and weaker. He thought the smart thing to do would be to just shoot himself in the head and be dead and have it over with but he said out loud, "You ain't going to kill me like you did her, you bastard!" and he tried again to move. He pulled and pulled at the bear's intestines, pulling them out of the bear and cutting them off, tossing them away as far as he could toss them. He could see the foxes as they scrambled to grab the fresh meat and run off with it.

Then he passed out for a while and came back to consciousness and started again. He passed out and came back and passed out and came back and passed out.

Then he was dreaming he was floating in the air and his body was tingling. He could move his legs again and his arm was free and he heard bells and heard voices and he knew he was dead. He wanted to see her and he tried to look for her. If he was in the afterlife, she had to be there waiting for him. He wanted to see her. He opened his eyes and looked at the smiling face of Tekla looking down at him.

"You crazy?" she said. "You don't lie under the bear when you skin it! You skin it, and then you lay under it."

The Bartender

He always said a bartender had to be a friend, a father, a union sympathizer, a mental health counselor, and a psychiatrist. Plus being smarter than his customers and more patient than a saint.

He was most of them; at least he tried to be most of the time. He never really wanted to be a bartender but he needed a job and it was offered to him. Then he just never wanted to go to the trouble of looking for a different one. He had been here twenty-six years going on twenty-seven.

He was twenty-two and a week out of the Army when he walked into this bar restaurant to take a rest and have something to drink. He had been looking for a job and just happened to say that to the waitress, who told it to someone and someone told Leo the owner, and he came from the back room and looked down at him, then said "stand up."

He stood up and Leo said, "He's hired. Show him what to do," and he walked away back to his office.

Then the waitress took him behind the bar and taught him how to be a bartender by handing him a book and telling him, "If you don't know, ask. Most people know how to make their drinks."

He knew everyone on the street and all the surrounding streets for seven or eight blocks. All of them that drank in his bar anyway. He had watched most of the kids grow up eating in the restaurant with their parents, then come in for their first legal drink. He never bought a single one of them a free drink because he didn't like a single one of them. Now they were his customers. Leo's customers.

He had heard it all, every story, every divorce case, every arrested son and every pregnant daughter. Every cheating wife, girlfriend, husband, boyfriend, cousin, uncle and a couple of aunts. Everything and anything anyone ever thought of in the world, he had heard it, seen it, tasted it, refused to taste it. Smelled it, felt it, looked at it, and it was starting to get to him. He wanted a change but just didn't want to go to the trouble of looking for one, nor did he know how to accomplish it. So he came to work at five every night, six nights a week and poured drinks, polished the glasses and wiped the bar until it shined as he listened to the same stories and tired old jokes, mostly from the guy who wrote this.

Everyone at one time or another said he looked out of place behind the bar because he was such a big man. Not fat, just big, six foot three and two hundred eighty-eight pounds in his birthday suit. His hands made the drink glasses look smaller than they really were. He had changed his appearance more times than he could remember, long hair, short hair, beard, bald head, shaved hair cut, glasses, contacts. suits, sweaters, mustache, handlebar mustache, side burns, pork chops on his jaws, neckties, bow ties, string ties and gold chains of every variety he could find, he had three hundred of them.

Twenty-six years of walking four blocks to work and walking back home to the same five-small-room apartment. He doubted if his phone had rung a hundred times in the last twenty years, no one ever called him and he never called anyone, they just waited until whoever saw whoever in the bar at night. He had cars and never drove them, three pickup trucks and never hauled anything in them, two motorcycles and never rode them, a bicycle that had been hanging on his storage room wall for fourteen years and never taken down, money and change all over the apartment, money in coffee cans and in cocoa cans and quarters in Alka-Seltzer bottles from when they used to come in tall green bottles the exact size of a quarter. He had change and money in jars, milk jars and two-gallon water jars, peanut butter jars, jam jars, and gallon pickle jars, cookie jars and candy jars he had carried home to put change in. He had three bank accounts and no longer kept track of how much was in each one. There was loose money in drawers and wadded up ones and twos and fives on his dresser, and in its drawers and in the bathroom drawer. He carried about a hundred home with him every night and never spent much, only $275 a month for his rent and $18 for the phone, $2 for his coffee in the morning when he liked to sit and read the paper, and maybe five for breakfast when he ate it. Everything else he ate at the restaurant for free. His pay was $385 a week, so he took home about a thousand a week and had for the past seventeen or eighteen years and he had nothing to do with it. He hadn't cashed a pay check for longer than he could remember. Now Leo, the owner, deposited them in his account for him.

He didn't know which account, or how much he had in there and didn't really care either.

He bought clothes, but he no longer liked the way they were made overseas and he quit buying them about ten years ago. He had enough anyway, his closet was too full, the hall closet was too full and three storage room hangers were full. Clothes in plastic bags and clothes in plastic storage boxes on the floor. Winter and summer and spring and fall clothes. Suits and casual, shorts and sweaters. Running clothes and working clothes. Walking clothes and over clothes. Cowboy boots and English shoes, tennis shoes, brown shoes and black shoes, black and white shoes. White suede shoes and loafers, zip-up boots and slip-on shoes, golf shoes he never wore. Too many to wear.

Pictures of people he no longer even remembered who they were, and he didn't care if he ever found out. But he never tossed them out. They just sat there all over the apartment on everything a picture could sit on. If there was a vacant spot, there was one there, and the walls were full. Pictures of kids that mothers had given him because they were so proud of their little boy. Then when he turned out to be a gangster, they changed their tunes. He didn't care. The place was filled with pictures of women, families, dogs, cats, and cars, houses and Christmas tree lights, hamsters in cages running, parrots on perches talking, Easter Day hats and parades, candy bunnies still in the boxes and stuffed bunnies, Santa Clauses and Easter bunnies, candy Easter eggs, chocolate reindeer with red noses, plastic ones, some of them lit up at night until the batteries went dead, teddy bears and stuffed animals, wrapped-up gifts he never opened. Birthday presents and Christmas presents and presents from women who were interested in him when he wasn't interested back, but not anymore. Small gifts from Leo, watches he bought from his brother for five dollars. They all lay on the floor behind the stuffed chair. He didn't care enough to even move them.

The carpet had a defining trail worn in it from the front door to the hall closet, to the right end of the couch, to the bathroom, to the bedroom and back to the couch around the other end of it, then back to the front door. The rest of the carpet looked almost new.

The refrigerator was empty, clean and unplugged, and the cupboards were empty except for things he had stored in them, a few dishes and some things people gave him from the bar, he had quit buying food that just spoiled a long time ago. The stove sat unused with a skillet and coffee pot still on it sitting beside three coffee cans of change and a package someone had gave to him some time back, he didn't remember who, wrapped in pretty paper with a white paper flower on it and unopened, it just sat there. He never went into the kitchen. He had gotten fat then quit eating and got too skinny so he joined a health spa and never went. Bought an exercise machine and never used it, bought a jogging suit and never went jogging. Became a vegetarian and ate meat anyway and finally just quit trying to change. So he walked the four blocks to his apartment every night, six nights a week at 2:34 am ... opened the door at 2:58 am and then hung his coat up on the hook on the inside of the door, walked to the couch and turned on the TV set, turned off the TV set after flipping through about eighty channels. He saw enough TV at the bar. "Victor, turn it to Channel??" "Victor, turn it up a little will you?" "No" was the answer. "Victor, can we watch the ball game? Football game? Hockey game? Soccer matches? Boxing? Wrestling? Motorcycle races? Stock car races? Tennis match? Game shows? Indy car races? Soap operas? Soap box derby or the news?"

He had seen too much TV. Then he would turn off the TV and go to bed. Get up at one in the afternoon and shower, shave, dress, walk across the street, and eat breakfast at Crocker's, then walk down the street three blocks and drink coffee at Pickit's news stand and coffee shop and read the paper. Then it was four in the afternoon. So then he walked back along the street six blocks to work where he walked through the restaurant saying hello to a few customers. "How are you? Enjoying your dinner? Nice to see you." Then through the kitchen to say hello to the cook. "How are you Toni?"

"Fine, Victor, you want something to eat?"

"Maybe a turkey sandwich and a small salad, OK?"

"Sure, want me to bring it in to you?"

"Thanks, Toni."

"No problem, Victor."

Then he would take a clean apron off the shelf and carry it with him into Leo's office and pick up his till.

"How are you today, Leo?"

"Same as always."

Then he would go behind the bar and change his shoes, taking off his street shoes and slipping into his soft soled work shoes, then putting on his white apron and tying it in front, making sure the laces were exactly even and the bows were the same size, then rinsing out and folding his seven new bar towels in half then into thirds and setting them on the bar where he wanted them. Then arranging the bottles like he wanted, turning down the volume on the TV and then standing there behind the bar waiting for a customer to come in or eating whatever Toni had brought him that day. Or cleaning bottles or glasses or lining them up in neat rows. It never got busy until after seven and not really busy then. It wasn't a hot spot, just a neighborhood place. And he was part of it, a small unimportant part, but a part. At least people said, "Hi, Victor," as they walked past him in the coffee shop or on the street but not one of them over twenty-seven years knew his last name.

So he stood there behind the bar looking out into the restaurant area at the three waitresses, three of maybe seventy-five who had worked during his employment and he wondered why he had never been interested in sex. Any kind of sex. Everyone talked about it, told jokes about it, complained about it, bragged about it, fought over it and lied over it, made movies about it and wrote books about it. It had to be important and he listened to them talk about it, but he knew nothing about it and was not interested in it, had never experienced it, and had no desire to ever experience it. Every person looked exactly the same to him except some were men and the others were women, some tall, some short, some fat and some thin, some loud and some quiet but all the same when you looked at them through his eyes. Things walking on two feet, eating, talking, laughing, crying and drinking then leaving and coming back.

Then Leo walked through the bar, "Have a good night, Victor, I'm going home."

"Yeah, see you tomorrow, Leo."

"Hope so."

So again he stood there behind the bar and looked out into the restaurant and one of the waitress came into the bar and stood there a second then said, "You're such a quiet man, Victor, are you bored?"

He looked at her, one of the better-looking people who came to sit or stand in front of him. Her skin was smooth and her hair neat, her teeth white and her breath smelled good, not old like some of the men.

"No, I'm just here, same as always. I'm not bored, I'm not excited, not sad or happy."

"That's kind of a strange thing to say," She looked funny at him then asked, "But why not?"

"Because I'm not a real person."

"You're not?"

"No."

"No, then what are you?"

"I'm a caricature in a short story."

"You are?"

"Aren't you?"

"Maybe, I don't know, I never thought about it," she answered then said, "Gee! I hope not."

That's the difference in me and you. You're looking at it from the inside and I'm looking at it from the outside. I know what and where I am. I'm just a thing some nut cake sat down and created because he had nothing better to do on a Sunday

210

afternoon with his time. And he wanted to entertain his friend who is a real bartender so he made up this place and my place, me and you and everything else on the last six pages.

"So he makes me look like some freak with a house full of stuff I don't use and he uses you to find a way to end the story. So if you don't like it, maybe someone else will write you into a different story and make it the way you want it."

The Bicycle

Twenty-five years ago I was driving on a street in Seattle. I don't remember the street but I remember it was in the summer because I had a convertible car and I had the top down. I was at a stop light when across the street in front of me rode this man on a bicycle, not just an ordinary bicycle but one of those old bicycles, a Schwinn maybe. One made in the late forties or early fifties with the big fenders and whitewall tires, a head light and taillight. What was so different about it was the man had painted it black and white so it looked like a police motorcycle. On each side of the compartment on the frame where the light batteries are kept, he had placed two Seattle police decals.

Mounted on the handlebars were two small red lights with a blue light in the center and on the back fender he had placed a bar and there he had mounted the same, two red lights and one blue one. It also had two white saddle bags mounted on it and where he got it I do not know, but a nickel-plated siren was mounted on the frame just in front of his right knee.

But it only started there. He was completely dressed in black leather, from his boots to his black leather coat, and he had a white helmet with riding goggles on his head, a duty belt with nightstick and handcuffs. He had a radio of some kind hooked onto his coat with a mike attached to his shoulder. He did look exactly like a police man mounted on an old bicycle, with one exception. He had silver tips and spurs on his boots. Then of course he was not one. Maybe in his mind he thought he was but he wasn't

Some would call him a name of some sort but what he was does not matter today, because after being gone eighteen years I returned to Seattle and what was one of the first things I saw

212

pedaling along a street? You guessed right. The same man, who was now at least seventy-five years old, but he looked the same.

What's the point? If there is one, I don't know what it is, but maybe it's a sort of success? Anyway, I have been thinking about him and I wondered if anyone ever acknowledged him in writing, so I went to the library and looked for something in the past newspapers. I found nothing. I wanted to take a picture of him so I went looking but I never found him. No one seems to know where he lives.

I just thought it was interesting.

The Biggest Lie I Ever Told My Dad

And never got beat for

The year was 1953 and I was eleven years old. Which was then much different then than it is now.

People weren't too much worried about their children getting hurt as they are now and I think they were more adult then than they are now. Those who lived in the country anyway, not the boys who lived as I did in the country on a farm at the foothills of the Cascade Mountain range in Oregon. Is it right or wrong? I do not know, but back then it was right, and now, I guess it's wrong. Personally I think children are too protected and much too idle. Spare the rod and spoil the child? Idle hands are the devil's workshop? In my case back then, the rod was a bamboo fishing rod.

My day began at 4:15 in the morning with a rap on the door by my Dad and then he would go outside and do his morning relieving off of the back porch. That was also a common thing back then out in the country when the outhouse was fifty yards away and it was 24 degrees outside, and maybe 35 degrees in the house before the fire was built. It was not uncommon to wake up and find icicles hanging from the rafters inside our (my two brothers and my) bedroom on certain colder mornings.

Our first chore was to milk the thirty-five head of cows we kept and this was done by hand after feeding them and washing them. Then the milk was cooled and put into 15-gallon milk cans that now have become a antique collector's item along with the head stations used to hold the cows in place while they were being milked, and many other things we used on a daily basis back then.

How things change as time passes. A cut finger was usually cured by cussing a couple times (if we were out of earshot of the grownups) and then spitting on it, and if one was available, wrapping a piece of cloth around the cut, but most often it was just left to heal by itself. But if it was sort of a bad cut and if you were to show it to my Dad, he would look at it and then tell you, "It's two feet away from your heart, don't worry about it. If it turns green, we'll just cut your finger off."

Or the next real cure was teat balm. That cured everything from cut fingers to blisters on your hind end after you did the wrong thing.

Now when I look back on it, I would like to say, "It's funny now to think about it." Well, frankly, it wasn't funny then and it's not funny now. It was a hard life for an eleven-year old kid. We worked from 4:15 am until 7:30 am then went to school and came home, then worked from 4:15 pm until 7:30 pm, then went to bed and got up and did it again except on the weekend. Then we had off from 7:30 in the morning until four in the afternoon.

Me? I liked to go fishing, so when I got the chance I would get on my horse, Judy, and with my dog, Bob, off I would go to the creek or sometimes to a lake seven miles up in the hills, called Ann Lake. It was in April, sort of the last of April or the first part of May I don't really remember that well, but it had turned sort of warm and the snow was all gone as was the ice along the banks of the creek and it was a Saturday. The sun was out and as soon as we finished the chores, I asked if I could go fishing.

"Where you going?"

"Up to the creek," I answered but my intentions were to go to the lake and catch a couple big browns.

215

"If you're going to the lake, take your brother with you. I don't want you going there by yourself, there's bears coming out now," my Dad told me.

Taking my younger brother with me was not my favorite thing back then, but later it still wasn't my favorite thing either. But I had no choice, so we both got our horses and headed up the through the pasture and up the trail to the lake, me in front and my brother following on his horse named Pea 0 ho, a small paint who was smarter than my brother and I both put together.

We had gone about a mile from the house when I happened to see something I admired ever so much, a fir bough, exactly the right height and still covered with about two pounds of snow. Then, me being the kind and loving protector of my younger brother, I had no choice whatsoever but to catch the branch as my horse walked past it, and of course I held on to it until it was bent about as far as I could bend it and making sure my brother was in exactly the right place at the wrong time, I just had to let it go. The bough shot back and you can guess the results, my loving little brother was hit flush in the face with a wet fir bough and a huge wad of wet snow, nearly knocking him off of Pea 0 ho and causing the horse to buck and toss him off onto the ground.

Now you might not think a nine and a half year old boy could yell out twenty-six cuss words without repeating one of them twice, but he did. Then he threw about ten rocks at me and let go another fifteen or twenty more cuss words directed at me ending with "I'm going back and tell Dad you spooked my horse and it bucked me off."

Had he left out the "spooked my horse" part, I would not have been too worried about it, but spooking a horse was one of the unforgiving things you didn't do around my Dad, so I knew I was in trouble as he jumped back on the horse and went back to the barn. I went onto the lake and went fishing, hoping I could catch at least twenty fish to bring home and then use them as a bargaining tool to keep myself from getting a good licking.

A year before, my older brother and two of his friends had built a raft to go out onto the lake on and it was a good safe raft but I was not supposed to use it when I was by myself but I always did anyway. It was tied up at the edge of the water down a steep bank by a very good fishing place near where the creek ran into the lake. There were always a lot of nice big fish in that place and in the springtime they were fat and firm from the snow melt so I tied up the horse and took my fishing pole down the bank and out onto the lake I went.

Boy did I catch some fish. I think I caught at least thirty fish in about three hours. I threw about half of them back into the lake because they were too small but I kept fourteen. I remember that very well. Fourteen of the nicest fish I had ever caught or have ever caught to this day, every one of them at least two pounds. So I had a good big string of fish slung over my shoulder as I climbed back up the bank and walked right between a sow black bear and her two cubs who were up in a tree on the other side of the trail.

Man o' man, here she came at me, snorting and bawling and she had no intentions of stopping. So I did the only thing I could think of. I threw the string of fish at her and hit her on the face with them. I guess she decided the fish would taste better then a young boy who had just messed his pants. So she stopped and I took off like a rocket up the hill using both hands and both feet at the same time. The bear I think ate a couple of the fish and got more energy from them because here she came again, right up the hill at me and my trusty horse jumped up in the air and bucked then showed me her bravery by breaking loose and taking off for the barn at a full gallop with Bob the wonder dog right in between her front legs leading the way.

Me? I think I would have passed both of them except I went the other way into the woods and up a tree after stopping to pick up several good rocks. I sat on the branch and waited for her to come after me but I guess she was thinking I had gone back to get the fish because she turned around and never got to the tree.

But I didn't know that for sure and so there I sat all afternoon and into the evening. Then as I was about to get down, guess who walked by under the tree? Ol' black momma bear and her two cubs. So there I sat almost all night on a tree limb fifteen feet above the ground.

I was sure my Dad and brother would come looking for me right after they finished doing the chores but they didn't and it got darker and darker and colder and I was shaking so bad I almost fell out of the tree several times. Then you talk about being scared? I looked down and there it was. A huge black thing covered with fur looking up into the tree right at me. I knew it was a big old grizzly bear and I was going to be eaten. I could see its eyes looking at me. Big ol' brown eyes and a row of white teeth shining in the moonlight. I had to pee really bad and I did. Believe this or not, but I peed and it ran down the leg of my jeans and I moved my foot, letting it run out of the pants leg hoping it would run down on the bear and scare it away. It didn't work.

Then it went away and I sat there in a pair of wet pants, cold and scared and hungry, and I hated fishing and I made up my mind I was never going to catch another fish as long as I lived or ride a horse again or have a dog. Why? Because I knew I was going to be killed and eaten by a bear before morning as soon as I fell out of the tree. But if I didn't and I lived, Bob the dog was in for a cussing. The coward.

218

Then the worst thing that could have happened, happened. It came back and there were two of them right below me. I still had the rocks with me but my hands were too cold to even grip them, let alone throw them and do any damage to two grizzlies, so I just sat there looking down at four eyes looking back up at me for what seemed like at least three months. Then, the big one started to climb the tree. I started climbing higher but I was too cold and couldn't hang onto the branches and the bear was bending the tree over. Slowly the tree bent and I was getting closer and closer to the ground. Then it had me.

I felt this paw or, now I know it was a big hand, gripping my right leg and pulling me down out of the tree. I wanted to scream and yell for help but I was too scared to even whisper, so I just closed my eyes and said good-bye to my mother, my older brother, my horse, my dog, my dad, my younger brother, and my teacher. In that order.

Then I was on the ground on my back and it still had a hold of my right leg. I waited for the bite to come that would kill me and put me out of my misery, but it never came. I laid there with it holding my leg for a long time, and then I opened my eyes and good grief! What did I see? Two huge hairy-looking things standing there looking down at me. I thought they were men wearing some kind of fur coats at first, then the big one turned loose of my leg and took a hold of my arm and lifted me up to my feet, then it put both of its arms around me and pulled me up against it. I thought it was going to eat me then for sure, but it didn't. Then the smaller one came and stood against my back and they both just stood there for a long time squeezing me in between them and I started getting warm again. The big one kinda rubbed my back and patted me on the head like I was its kid or something. It kept making a kind of moaning noise like it was saying "you're OK, kid." And it patted my head real soft like and rubbed its hand in my hair like Aunt Alice always did. It seemed like a hour, maybe, that they just stood there against me letting me get warm and I was thinking they didn't want to eat a cold kid so they were warming me up so I would be easy to chew or something.

Then the big one moved away and took me by my left arm and started to pull me along through the brush with the smaller one following along behind me. I knew they were taking me to their house so they could eat me but they just kept walking and dragging me along through the brush until we got to the gate in the upper pasture of our farm. Then the big one put his or her hands under my arms and lifted me up so I was looking right into its big ol' brown eyes. Then it kissed me right on the face, then sat me over on the other side of the fence and kinda smiled at me. They had big ol' teeth just like yours and mine except they were a lot bigger and their eyes were shining in the moonlight like they were real happy about what they had done for me. Then they just turned and walked away back into the brush and were gone. 1 took off running like all get out back to the house and right up the stairs into the bedroom and jumped into bed with my clothes still on. Well, I was immediately kicked back out by my older brother who said 1 smelled like 1 had peed my pants and I said, "I did! I did! I was up a tree and these big old bears pulled me down and brought me home!" Well, you know what my Brother answered?

"DAD! He's home!" and the bedroom door came open and there was my Dad with his belt folded in half ready to do his job on my butt. I started talking like crazy, telling him what had happened and he stood there looking down at me, then after I finished, he said, "That's the damnedest lie I ever heard a kid tell anyone." Then he just turned around and went back to bed.

No one believed me, even after I took both brothers up to the gate and showed them these big footprints in the ground. No one ever believed me and I never believed it myself or told anyone about it for a long time until one day I saw on the TV these people saying there really was a Bigfoot up in the mountains. I never said there was and I never said there wasn't, but I can tell you this, there used to be back when I was a boy in 1953.

And you know what else? When I went back to the lake a week later, someone or something had been using my fishing pole and left it on the raft for me. And I know I dropped it up on the trail where the bear came after me. And you know what else I did? I left them two toothbrushes and some toothpaste because I'm telling you "Bigfoots have got some bad awful breath".

The Doorman

What a happy man he was for nineteen years while he stood at the front door of the hotel on Charles Ave. under the canopy with the red fringe hanging down and the white and blue sign across the front of it (The Charles). He swept the red carpet several times a day and never failed to help anyone with their things, be it whatever, he took pride in helping them inside, carrying their bags or clothes or packages.

If he had ever, and he had many times, seen a picture of a doorman in a magazine, he was him or he tried to look and act better than any doorman he could imagine. Standing rigid with his hands behind his back, white gloves clasped, hat straight, shoes shined to a high glow, pants cuffs exactly one half inch from the ground and exactly even with the top of his shoe heels, the crease straight and sharp down the front, brass buttons polished, tie straight and coat tails pressed and hanging straight to the bottom of his trouser pockets. He stood looking straight ahead, smiling and greeting passers-by.

His name? Oh, let's just call him James.

James arrived every morning at 6:06 carrying a small brown leather suitcase and walked into the hotel, through the lobby and back into the laundry room where he changed his clothes and removed his newly-shined shoes from the suitcase and put them on over fresh socks. He would stand and brush his coat and trousers of any lint that happened to be on them and walk out through the lobby and take his place on the small rubber pad two feet to the right of the front door.

First to arrive every weekday and Saturday morning was the owner of the Hotel, Charles M. Rockingham, a short man, slightly overweight and one might call him a little overbearing and sharp of tongue. He carried no concern for his employees in his vocabulary and it was not uncommon for him to call one or more of his sixteen employees stupid, moron, or a few other selected names, when it suited him. In nineteen years, he had spoken to James twice. Once he said, "That coat button is coming loose. Tighten it up".

The other time he said, "Get a new pad. That one is looking shabby."

Both times James had answered, "Yes, Sir," and that was all they had ever spoken to each other except for James saying, "Good morning, Mr. Rockingham," as he held the door open for him at 7:08 six mornings a week for nineteen years.

Many was the time he had seen a reliable employee walk out of the hotel after being fired for some small infraction of the rules or a slight negligence of some sort. Many times, they would stop and try to complain to James about what had happened to them and each time all James would answer is, "He's tough to work for, I'm sorry," but he stood at the front door for nineteen years and waited for it to happen to him.

It was on a snowy Saturday morning in December a week before Christmas when it happened. The sidewalk was covered with a thin coat of ice and very slippery. James had asked the maintenance man three times to please come and spread some salt on the sidewalk in front of the red carpet but there was no rock salt in the hotel, so the maintenance man had gone to buy some at the store and hadn't gotten back.

At 8:30 in the morning, a limo had arrived and stopped in front of the canopy and James had stepped forward and opened the back door. A lady started to get out of the car and James extended his hand to her and said, "Let me help you. The sidewalk is very slippery this morning."

"Take your hand off of me," she answered and stepped out onto the sidewalk and as she stood up, both feet slid out from under her and she landed on her fanny on the sidewalk. "Oh my God!" she cried, "I think I broke something!"

"I tried to tell you the sidewalk was slippery," James explained.

"You let me fall," she cried.

"I'm so terribly sorry. Are you hurt?" James answered and tried to help her to her feet.

Her driver ran around the car and lifted her to her feet and helped her into the hotel, telling James, "It's alright, just get the luggage, will you please?"

"It is not alright!" the lady cried as she was helped through the door held open by James.

James then took the three pieces of luggage out of the trunk of the car and carried them into the lobby and handed them over to the head bellhop and retook his place at the front door.

It was only a matter of a few minutes until Charles M. Rockingham stuck his head out through the door and said four words to James: "You're fired, you moron!" and he went back into the hotel followed by James who followed him into his office and stood in front of his desk and tried to explain what had happened. "I'm not listening to you. Get out!" was the reply.

"But I would like to explain if I can".

"You can't! Get out!" And with that James simply smiled and said, "Please call in my time so I can get paid."

Charles Rockingham picked up his phone and instructed the bookkeeper to pay James what was owed him then looked up and said, "Now get out!"

James smiled and said, "Thank you you old son of a bitch!" and he turned and walked out. He stopped to get his money then went into the laundry room, picked up his two other suits and his suitcase with his street shoes in it and left the hotel.

Then he walked directly across the street, talked to the manager of the hotel there and then took his place at the front door. He looked exactly the same except for one small thing. He had a gold chain attached to the top button of his coat that stretched across his chest and into his left top coat pocket and on the end of the chain in the pocket was a silver whistle.

James stood smiling in front of the door as he had done for the past nineteen years but now when he saw a car with a driver that he recognized, he stepped out onto the curb and blew his whistle, letting the driver know he was now at a new location. Eight out of every ten drivers turned and said to their passenger, "Do you have any preference to where you stay?"

Eight out of ten passengers said, "No," and the limo would make a U-turn at the corner and stop in front of James, who then happily stepped out and opened the door for them and said, "Thank you for staying with us. I hope you enjoy it as much as we will," as Mr. Charles M. Rockingham looked out through his front door and cussed softly under his breath as he watched another of his former guests walk into the Georgian Hotel.

Where does the attorney come in?

Well, let's go back to the lady who slipped and fell on the sidewalk. Sometimes a good hard fall will change a person's attitude. It might be a financial fall, an emotional fall, or just a good hard fall on your butt, but a fall is a fall and it is almost always followed by embarrassment, then anger, then vindictiveness, then by, if given enough time, apathy, and then remorse for the anger and bad thoughts, then with some people who have a sense of morals, forgiveness.

So after two days of rubbing her butt and her husband and driver telling her it was her own fault and James had tried to

225

protect her from falling on the slick ice, she gave in and agreed it was in fact her own fault and wrote a small note to the doorman saying she was sorry, then handed it to the bellhop who told her the doorman had been fired and was now working across the street. And he seemed to be just as happy there as he was here.

"Well I'm not satisfied with that," she said to the bellhop and told him she wanted to see Mr. Charles Rockingham at once. The bellhop told the purser and the purser told the bookkeeper and the bookkeeper told Mr. Rockingham and he went up to see the lady. She told him politely the fall was her fault and to re-hire the doorman but he refused. She demanded he re-hire the doorman and he again refused.

The lady then packed up and moved across the street where James had also moved too and told him she wanted her attorney to get him his job back.

"Thank you, but I really don't want it back." he answered. I have been expecting it to happen for a lot of years".

"Well, nevertheless, you should be compensated for what he did to you," she said.

"Really, I'm fine where I am," he answered, giving her his best smile.

"Well, I'm not," she said, and went into the hotel.

James stood his post and forgot about the whole thing. He was in fact quite contented and having a good time coaxing the guests away from old sourpuss Rockingham. Each time he saw him looking out the front door, he would smile and wave politely to him. He was in truth making a lot more money in tips from the guests. His conclusion was cheap managers have cheap guests and old Rockingham was a cheapskate to say the very least about him.

A few days passed by and James stood rigid and shining in front of the Georgian looking like a US Marine in full dress at a parade, greeting patrons and opening doors and carrying luggage and receiving good tips for doing it.

Finally old Rockingham, after losing several of his best guests, made up his mind that he had better swallow his pride and do something about it before he lost all of them. So he sat at his desk and wrote out a check then walked across the street and stopped in front of the smiling James.

"James, I'm sorry. I want you come back. Here," and he handed James the check.

James never looked at the check, just folded it in half with the amount inside and handed it back to him. He smiled and said, "There is a very thin line between being stubborn and being stupid and on the other side of the coin, there is also a very thin line between being loyal and being stupid. Have a good day, Mr. Rockingham."

So Mr. Rockingham returned across the street and as days passed, he stood at his front door and watched James do as he had done for so many years, standing proudly in front of a different hotel, looking so sharp and clean, as his business slowly moved away across the street.

My Visit with a Flying Saucer

So right off the start you're not going to believe this any more than you believe my visit with God, but it's as true as anything you ever heard from me, or a preacher or a politician.

The year was 1954 when we lived in a old house on a sort of abandoned two-lane road. We walked about a half mile to catch the school bus each morning and then of course we also walked back in the evening. This really has nothing to do with what I'm about to write but I was thinking about that road and how the pavement had all melted and the tar was coming up through the gravel, or the gravel was settling down through the tar and when it got hot the tar melted and tiny bubbles came up. When you stepped on them they popped like bubble wrap. It was fun except it kinda made a mess on the bottom of your shoe. And if you rode your bike over it, the tires would sort of stick to the road making it hard to pedal. Then when you got off your bike if you left it in gravel or dirt, the tar would get hard again and stuff would be stuck to your tires and you had to scrape it all off before you could ride your bike again. The same with your shoes, or you could just walk into the house with tar on your shoes and get the tar beat out of your hind end by your mother.

I took a short cut across Nevada in 1993 when I was driving from Arizona to Seattle. I had driven for almost a full day and night and was ready to find a place to get a few hours' sleep. I was out in the center of the desert between Reno and Las Vegas a hundred miles from nowhere so to speak. I parked off the road out in a sort of cleared field where there was a dirt road maybe leading up to an old mine, a farm house or something else. I had just stopped to sleep for a while and had laid out my sleeping bag in the back of my pickup, ready to rest, and was sitting on the tailgate of my truck having a smoke, when I saw it. At first I thought it was a large helicopter but it didn't make any noise. It moved slowly across the sky maybe four hundred feet up and maybe twenty miles an hour. As I watched, it first went north to south, then back to the north, then it turned and came west, right at me then stopped maybe a thousand yards away. Then I saw it was not a helicopter but something else. What it looked like was a big round aquarium.

It had windows all around it divided by posts of some kind like ordinary windows. I would say it looked like the top of the Space Needle in Seattle. Needless to say, I was not going to stick around and find out what it was. I got into my truck and tried to drive away but the truck would not start. I sat there looking in my side mirror at this thing for several minutes and then it moved closer, maybe a hundred feet behind me and the lights inside it came on and I could see the people in there looking out through the glass windows. But they didn't look like people; they looked like the pictures of aliens from outer space, large hairless heads with huge eyes and small mouths. Just holes where the nose should have been like I had seen in books and on TV. Some of them weren't as space-looking as the others. A few of them looked to be maybe halfway from what we look like today to what they looked like in the books. They were taller than the others and bigger. Their eyes weren't as large and they had some kind of a cover on their heads. All the others were wearing a silver sort of shiny suit but these few had on a green suit.

Some of them had big eyes and large heads with tiny small ears and small mouths. Their bodies were thin and their arms and legs were long and thin as though they hardly ever used them. I sat there for a long time waiting and wishing it would go away.

I had heard about people being taken into these things and being operated on. I was scared as all get out to say the very least. Not that I thought it would do any good but I locked both doors and rolled up the windows, but then I noticed this sort of I guess you could call it a stinger come out of the bottom of it and go down into the ground like it was drilling a hole. Then it sort of made a sound like it was pumping something out of the ground and I kinda figured it was taking on water. All the beings inside were happy and sort of moving around and then drinking from these sack-looking things.

So I thought they took on water and every one inside had a drink.

This lasted for almost a hour as I sat in my truck and watched.

Then, this is the part no one is going to believe. I still don't know if it was a dream or if it was real.

It just vanished. One second it was there and the next second it was gone. I heard this bang like thunder as though it just popped out of the air and the air closed back where it had been. Bang! And it was gone. I tried to start my truck and it almost started but then, then it was back and only about a hundred feet from my truck. It sat there about fifty feet or maybe less off of the ground and the lights came back on. I saw there were more people in it now. Maybe a hundred, or the ones that were in it had moved to stand in front of the windows, but I think there were about a hundred of them looking out at me. Maybe there was more in the back that I couldn't see.

Here's the thing. Two of them looked like a normal human being. They were in front of the others and standing side by side in the center of the front window looking down at me and talking. They had on those green suits and a cover over their heads. It looked to me like they had on big sunglasses. I couldn't hear what they were saying but they looked right at me then the light went out inside and a different light came on from the

230

bottom of it and these two were lowered down onto the ground. I could see them coming down but I couldn't see what was lowering them, it looked like they were just floating down on a air stream or something, I thought they were coming to get me but they walked off away out into the desert and I never saw them again. I don't know what happened to them and I don't know if they were men or women or one of each. But they looked to be perfect humans just like you or me look today. And the reason I say today is what I saw during the next few hours, or minutes, or maybe seconds, I don't know, it's not what people are going to look like in 3007.

I tried to start my truck several times and drive away but the battery was dead and I was just sitting there in the seat scared out of my wits and ready to get out and run as if that would do any good. But it was the only thought I had.

Now only the greatest science fiction writer in the world could make this story up and I'm not that person. But here's what happened and if I wasn't as old as I am and didn't have the heart problems like I have I would never tell this story because I already see it coming to pass. It was like I was at the drive-in movies, I saw this tiny light coming from one of the windows and then a picture came onto my windshield and started playing like a movie as I sat there watching it.

It was a sort of history from 1940 or about that time to the year 3270 and I guess that is the year they were from. It showed a hundred or more things I do not really remember because it all went by my eyes so fast, and I was so astonished by it.

It kinda showed a camera going along through a city somewhere along the streets. The first thing I saw was the American flag which had a police badge in the center of the stars and they were hanging all over every building. Everyone had some sort of blinking-eye thing on their forehead just above their left eye. I saw people starving to death all over the streets in cities I didn't recognize. They were lying on the sidewalks and sitting on the pavement begging passers-by for food.

The year flashed 2023 and letters came across my windshield saying the bees were all dead, and the fish in the seas were mostly gone. Then it showed huge long rows of glass buildings that looked like greenhouses with hundreds of people standing on the outside of them behind fences made of rod iron looking in. They were all very thin and their eyes were sunken in like you see pictures of starving people. I believe this was somewhere in the center of the USA, maybe Iowa or Kansas, I don't know. Maybe even Texas. But there were armed guards all around the fence with guns of some sort and every so often one of them would shoot one or two of the people touching the fence. It looked to me like they were all waiting to be fed.

Next I saw wars all over the world and people being killed all over the world. Robot-flying planes were flying around shooting out rockets at buildings until they got shot down. People were being lined up in rows of three wide and shot down by laser guns or some kind of a weapon that did not shoot out bullets but a stream of energy, maybe electricity. It seemed to be maybe a thousand at a time were being killed, mostly older people, then scooped up by men in tractors and dumped into large trucks and hauled away. It looked to me like this was in the far east somewhere.

The year flashed by, reading 2048, then the picture sort of traveled around the planet showing huge areas of water. I saw the ice on both poles had almost completely disappeared and the water table had risen up and most of the coastline was gone. Most of the South Sea Islands were gone. Florida and almost all of the south was gone underwater. All of lower Mexico was gone under water. Millions of people were walking to the higher ground and dying like flies as they walked then being picked up by these men in machines and loaded into huge trucks that seemed to have a gas furnace in them and the bodies were burned as they were put into the trucks. There were tents and makeshift small houses all over with people just sitting and waiting for something to happen to them.

Then the year 2066 flashed onto the windshield and there was a definite change in the structure of the human race. There were no fat people. They were all smaller and much younger as though all the older people had died or been killed. I would guess the average age was twenty-five. The air was filled with a sort of dense smog from so much water covering the earth creating a high amount of humidity. It was raining almost everywhere it showed dry land. People had not much hair and it seemed to me their heads were larger and their eyes were larger, and their bodies smaller. At least thinner, maybe one hundred pounds. There were not so many people then and most of them seem to be just sitting or lying in camps all over the dry parts of the planet. Buildings were underwater all along the coastlines. I saw New York City, and all of it was halfway underwater. The tops of thousands of buildings were sticking up out of the water and thousands of boats were going every which way. Most of them had sails or paddlewheels on the back of them. Every building had gardens growing on top of them in glass buildings.

Then it started again and the year showed 2131.

Almost all the earth was covered with snow and ice. Huge building were being built all aver the planet, high narrow buildings that all looked alike, maybe fifty stories high with huge green rooms on the top five or six floors where food was being grown. There were glass-covered walkways going from one building to another and all of them were hooked together. I could see people who looked like the people on the aquarium-looking thing going back and forth through the passageways riding on what looked like some kind of a belt. Most of them had no hair and most of them were dressed alike in a shiny light tan suit of some sort; it looked to me like they were plastic.

2141. The humidity was so unbelievably bad the entire earth was covered with fog. The sun had come back and the earth was warming and the water was all evaporating. The polar caps were returning and the oceans were thawing out, but the humidity was so bad visibility was only a few yards and people's eyes were a lot larger or they had on some kind of protective glasses so they could see through the fog. Everyone was wearing some kind of a silver suit I thought because of so much moisture in the air that they were some kind of plastic waterproof clothing.

Buildings near the coasts were beginning to show and they were all covered with green slime but men, or people, were in machines with long legs on them that went down into the water and they were cleaning the buildings with huge water jets washing the slime off of them and trying to make them workable or livable again. There were huge monster-looking helicopters flying around with huge hoses sucking up the slime from the streets and then dumping it along the shoreline, rebuilding the coast, I guess. I couldn't tell; the picture only lasted a few seconds.

Then it showed 2173 or 2207; I didn't see it well enough to remember. But the picture went around the planet and I saw there were almost no animals left, but the ones that were left were all very small, even cows and horses were about half size, and there were robots all over the place, all kinds of them doing everything.

Everything was automatic. I saw no cars or trucks but a lot of different-looking helicopters flying all over the sky, thousands of them going everywhere, stopping and taking off again. I think they took the place of cars and trucks and I saw no trains or boats anywhere, but I did see a lot of people. Millions of them all still were wearing the same silver kind of suits moving around through the haze on some kind of sleds or scooters, one or two on each one. Some were standing and some were sitting on small seats behind the one in front. Everywhere I saw was green, every square inch of the ground was green, and it looked like no one was walking on the grass. The top of every building was green and the scooters or sleds traveled on narrow paths that were four wide, with two going each way. I think they were magnetic.

Then as I sat and looked at my windshield, a sort of revue passed in front of me showing the slow change to the human body as it grew smaller and the heads grew larger. But not really larger, they stayed the same size but the bodies were so much smaller it seemed as though the heads were larger and their eyes grew larger from straining to look through the pollution and humidity and their arms and legs seemed to shrink because they never did work anymore. The hair disappeared from their heads and it was almost impossible to tell the men from the women. Their mouths had changed to a much smaller mouth because they no longer ate solid food and it looked to me as though their teeth had slowly gone away from not being used because they had no need to chew anything. Their voices had all became a sort of high pitched soft sound that hurt my ears when they called to me through the projection. Then the projection stopped and the lights came on in the--- - - whatever it was. Now I know it was some sort of time machine and all those flying UFOs were just the people from the future coming back to see what it was like when humans were still humans, maybe trying to figure a way to stop it from becoming what it will become.

Also, I now know the wreck in Roswell, New Mexico, in 1949 was a time machine that made a wrong adjustment trying to keep in one position as the earth rotated. It was too low and when it blinked out to come back on track, the earth had moved and the elevation had changed, causing it to hit the ground at exactly one thousand miles an hour, the speed of the earth's rotation. It was shown in the projection but until only a few months ago I didn't know what it was showing or how the time machines worked.

It took me a while to figure out what they were all saying to me. They were putting their hands on the windows and calling to me through the glass.

I got out of my truck and stood looking at what had become of the human race and almost cried as I figured out they were saying, "Please help us!! Please help us. We don't like being like this. Tell them, don't destroy the planet ..."

Uncle Richard's Funeral

I had only seen him once when he came to stay with us for a few days. I think he had just gotten out of jail or out of the service when I was very young, maybe six or seven, maybe eight, but I still remember him standing in the front yard holding his clothes in a green bag with my Dad yelling at him to get off his yard, he called him a bum and said, "Don't ever come back here trying to bum money."

Now I don't know if he was bumming money or just visiting, I don't really know, but I remember watching him walking down the driveway and out of the barnyard then down the road, He had his bag on his shoulder and he was whistling "Jimmy crack corn and I don't care," then he stopped and waved back to me and I didn't see him again for several years.

My mom was crying about it and telling my dad he didn't have to tell him to leave. Then, a few days later we had to move from the farm ourselves because the man my dad worked for refused to pay him or something. Anyway there was another big argument and we ended up loading all of our stuff into a truck and moving to a housing project. I think the houses were old Army bunk houses made into apartments after the war was over in '46. There were ten buildings and twenty apartments. There was a lot of talk about how much the man owed my dad and they were suing him, then my mom went to work at a hospital for kids and my dad went to work doing some kind of construction work, I think he was building service stations of which there are no more of.

It wasn't too bad there in the project, it was a little project. I remember almost all of our relatives lived there, or they just came there all the time, but Aunt Ruth and her two kids lived

237

there, we threw a mouse into the bathroom when she was taking a bath and she ran out into the front yard naked. That was sort of fun until we got our butts whacked for doing it. She was real skinny. If I remember, my mom's sister and two of my dad's brothers and all their kids lived there, for a while. I kinda liked it because there were no chores to do and no cows to milk or pigs to feed at four-thirty in the morning.

We just went to school and hung out with the other kids for a couple years.

Now I'm not saying I was a perfect kid or a perfectly rotten kid, I was kinda both at different times. I think I was ten and my brother, nine, then. I hung out with the older crowd and he was still a kid. A kid who loved to tell on me for everything I did (like smoking). So I loved to punch him in the belly every time he told on me and he finally quit snitching. Then one day my dad got all dressed up in his one blue suit he wore when they went dancing and put on a tie with a horse's head painted on it and he and my mother went off to court. When they came back, they were all happy because they had won a lawsuit for several thousand dollars from the man my dad used to work for. Then the next day, they had a lot of money and bought some new clothes and a pretty new truck (I think it was a '48 Dodge). Us kids never got anything if I remember right, but my dad got drunk! I remember that, he drove his truck up on the sidewalk and it fell through the boards and got stuck in the mud, they had to jack it up and put boards under the wheels to get it off the sidewalk and my dad had to pay to have the sidewalk fixed. I remember him cussing the guy who was in charge of the houses because he wouldn't let my dad and his brothers fix the sidewalk and he had to pay the guy to do it. I think it cost about fifty dollars which is equal to about six hundred today.

But anyway, a few days later, we moved again. My dad had bought a piece of land across from a huge field he rented to farm and he and his brothers started building a house on the half acre. It was kind of fun, we all lived in a little trailer house with no bedrooms or anything, I think it was about fifteen feet long but we (my older brother, older sister, me, younger brother and one younger sister, maybe two younger sisters, I remember them fighting over something). Anyway we all slept outside in a tent. It was a huge big tent from the Army or somewhere, it was huge and we had it for a long time, people who came to pick beans in the fields used to live in it. The man was a really good guitar player, his mule was Eddy and his daughter's name was Jill, I think she had a crush on me because she used to follow me around all the time and she always asked me if I wanted to go out in the woods and do something. I never did know what she was talking about so I told her no. Anyway, it took until the springtime to get the walls up and the roof on the house and the beans, and corn planted in the field but we all did it and had a pretty good first year in the house that had no inside walls, I remember it was so funny, we had blankets hanging on the studs, no sheetrock, just blankets but the doors were all installed, so if you walked through the blanket instead of going through the door you got in trouble. Now that I think of it, it was pretty funny living in that house.

But I had something going for me for about a couple years. Down the road was a family named Wilson and the Wilsons had four daughters, two of them older than me and two of them younger than me, and I was maybe 11, and, the only guy around who smoked Lucky Strike cigarettes, and I did it under the bridge down the road about a half mile. I learned a lot about the anatomy of a female that year and a few other things too. And I learned to regret telling I felt like a doctor. See an operation, do an operation, teach an operation. Those girls were all good teachers and good students right up until Mary Wilson, the second from the oldest, was teaching me something and my dumb brother came and caught us. Mary pulled her skirt down and I pulled my pants up and we both got into big trouble. I remember my dad whipping me with a belt and he had a big grin on his face while he was doing it. Then the Wilson girls were not allowed to walk down the road where our house was, they had to go to the other road and go to school that way. But Doris, who was three years older than I was, still snuck over to see me and have a smoke under the bridge once in a while. So then I had no girls to smoke with and no chores to do, so I went to town and stole two candy bars from Payless Drug Store, a Three Musketeers and a Snickers bar, and got caught, then got beat for that too. Then I had to get a job to pay for the candy bars. I got a job sweeping out the shop room at a piano store for 50 cents a hour because I had to pay the store five dollars each for the 5-cent candy bars that I never got to eat. I worked two hours a night and eight hours on Saturday polishing and cleaning the dust out of pianos, and I learned how to fix pianos but I never used what I learned. I earned about eighteen dollars every two weeks at that job which was a lot of money in that year of 1953 and my dad charged me five dollars a week to live in his house. That went on until after Uncle Richard came back home.

I think I was fourteen when I stopped working there. That was a day to remember. I had sat and figured out if he had used the five dollars I paid him every week he could have had the house all dry walled but he spent the money on horses and beer and when I showed him the paper I had made up, well you can guess what happened. !@#%%$#@#@! Thank you very much!!

We were all outside the day he came back and I think it was Saturday, no; it was a Sunday because I didn't go to work that day. My dad had just got a new horse and everyone was looking at it, a big painted black and white gelding named Tarzan. So anyway, we were all outside looking at the horse and this huge brand new black Lincoln drives up into the yard and stops, then Uncle Richard got out and walked around the back of the car with everyone staring at him.

He looked like a movie star standing there.

Everyone just looked at him and finally my dad said, "Who are you? What do you want?"

"I'm your brother-in-law Richard," he said, smiling.

Then my mother ran over to him and hugged him and started crying and everyone else went over to him and shook hands and hugged him. Uncle Dick tried to steal the diamond stick pin he had in his tie and he got caught. Uncle Richard yelled at him and called him a god damn moron and told him if he ever tried to steal anything else he would shoot him and he showed everyone the gun he had in a shoulder holster under his coat. Uncle Dick left and never came back for a long time and when he did he stayed a few feet away from his younger brother.

Mom asked him if he was a gangster and he just laughed. He looked so good I just stood there staring at him. He had a real nice suit with a while shirt and silk sort of real light pink tie with that big diamond stick pin in it and his shoes were real shiny and his pants had a crease so sharp you could have cut paper with it and he had the neatest hat, one like all the PIs (like Boston Blacky) wear in the movies and he had four rings and one big earring in his right ear with a huge chunk of gold hanging from it. He looked like he had just walked off of a movie screen. I decided then and there, that's what I wanted to look like when I grew up. Compared to the rest of them, he looked like a picture window and they looked like they all fell out of a second-hand store. But he had some beer with him and a couple bottles of

Four Roses Whiskey and that broke the tension. Pretty soon everyone was talking and telling jokes and asking him where he had been and how he got there and how much the car cost and all kinds of other things but no one told him to get off the yard this time. He drove my mom to the store and they bought a huge sack of big steaks and some different things and we all had a huge dinner out in the yard and everyone got a little bit drunk except for me and I snuck off to smoke a couple Lucky Strikes with Mary Wilson who I saw walking through the back of the barnyard. She asked who he was and then took off back home and I went back to see what was going on.

It was quite a homecoming. The funny part of it was everyone invited him to come and stay with them when before they all told him to get out. I guess the money made a difference, huh? Anyway, I was so impressed at him and the way he looked, plus each time he reached into his pocket and took out that huge roll of fifties I go more impressed. I had managed to save almost twenty dollars in a year and a half. If this is how a rich man dressed and acted, then I wanted to learn all I could while I had the chance. I finally got to talk to him and I ask him how he got so rich.

"I ain't rich kid, I'm just on a hunk of good luck, I got lucky selling some land and now I got to get smart before I end up like the rest of these people here."

"How are they?" I asked.

"Oh, they're all right, but none of them have any real chance to do anything, you want to go to college?" he asked me.

"I don't know, I never thought about it."

Then he told me, "Go ask your dad, if you go to college, will he pay for it?"

"I already knew the answer to that. He don't have any money," I answered.

242

"So there you are. Get my drift?"

Then he said, "If you want to go to college, you ask me, and if I got the money, I'll send you to college, and I might send you even if I ain't got the money."

"How you going to do that?"

"I'm on a hunk a hunk kid," he smiled and told me, "Go get me another beer." Then he asked, "Hey, you know how to play pool?"

I answered "no" and went and brought him back a beer but he was talking to one of my aunts so I went off and sat in a corner, then went outside and looked at his car. I got into it and sat on the big leather seat and felt the comfort of it. It was a wonderful car and it smelled like new leather, the inside was so big you could have put one of my dad's cars inside it. I sat there for a few minutes and Doris Wilson, the oldest of the girls, came and looked in at me.

"Whose car is this?" she asked.

"My Uncle Richard's," I answered.

"Is he really rich?" she asked.

"He says no, but he sure has a lot of money in his pocket."

Then she asked if I had any cigarettes under the bridge and I told her yes, so we went down to the bridge and smoked a couple Lucky Strike cigarettes and talked about that suit he was wearing and that big diamond in his tie, the car he was driving and that big handful of fifty-dollar bills in his pocket and that was it for the night. Doris made it a point to let me know she was wanting to do something with a boy like kissing and feeling and then she told me if I wanted to I could tell my uncle she lived up the road and walked by here all the time. Then she put my hand on her boob (she liked me to squeeze them when we smoked cigarettes) and then ran off. Doris took off and went back home about nine, worried her dad would find out she was smoking again, and I sat there for a while and smoked a couple more Lucky Strikes and then went back. Uncle Richard had left and everyone was still talking about him and drinking the rest of the beer he had bought.

Then when I asked about him the next morning no one wanted to talk about him. It was like he was a stranger who had just stopped by and was never coming back again. Then I asked, "So why didn't he just stay here last night?"

And my dad said in a really sour voice, "He has to take a shower every night and we don't have a shower or towels dried in a dryer."

"What?" was all I could think of to say.

"He's too good for us now," Mom said, then turned her back and walked away. That was it; I couldn't believe what I was hearing. They were jealous of him.

It was about a week later when he came back and everyone treated him like he was some kind of bad guy, they talked about him saying he was a know-it-all and a show-off and things like that but I thought he was a swell guy, he always talked to me and the other kids like we meant something and we knew things, he asked our opinions and bought us all things, nothing big, but a few things. Then one day when I was walking home from working at the piano store, he came by and gave me a ride and my dad got mad at him. But I thought he was a swell guy. Now I know he was waiting for me so he could ask me about Doris Wilson.

I told him she had big teats and when she walked they bounced and when she ran they really bounced so she ran with her arms folded across her chest.

Then, a few days later he asked me if I wanted to go play pool and we went to the pool hall downtown. He was a really good pool player; he called his pocket money 'chump change'.

244

He could make all the balls without missing almost every time. No one in the pool hall wanted to play with him and he told me he made a lot of money playing pool while he had been gone, but when I asked him how he got so rich he told me he had been really broke and camped out in a field a mile or so from a railroad and found an artesian spring on the property, then he found out the property was for sale real cheap because there was no water on it. and he bought it for a hundred dollars down and then dug up the well. I asked him how he got the hundred dollars and he told me he cleaned out chicken houses for five weeks and didn't eat anything every other day and saved three hundred dollars, then bought the land for ten thousand dollars. He said he worked for almost a year and a half cleaning out the chicken houses, eating peanut butter and grape jelly sandwiches and worked on the well every night. Then when he got the land so it could be irrigated, he sold it, and made $88,000. He bought the car and some new clothes and came back. He was pretty disappointed in the family from the way he talked about them. He said they were all mad because he didn't want to loan them any money. "People have only as much money as they can take care of," he said, "and those guys got none. If I loan them money they'll never be able to pay me back. That don't make them bad, it just means they don't do well with money. They all got too many kids. I got to find something to invest in or I'll just go broke."

"So why didn't you eat some chickens?" I asked.

"See, that's what I'm talking about, when someone is talking about money, you talk about money, nothing else, got it?" he said.

"Yeah I got it, but why didn't you eat a few chickens?"

I thought about that for a long time but I never said anything about it.

Anyway, we got along good but our friendship was sort of on the QT, and Doris Wilson kept asking about him and then one day when he was leaving our house, she was walking down the road and I saw him stop and pick her up. Then after that they were together a lot. I think she was seventeen then, I'm not sure, but she had big boobs. I remember those, they bounced when she walked and really bounced when she ran. She ran with her arms folded across her chest. It was funny.

Then about a month later or so I was talking to the man who owned the piano store and I told him about Uncle Richard and wanting to invest in something. So he told me to tell him to come and talk to him. I thought he was looking for someone to put some money in his store but he told Uncle Richard about a hotel down close to the river that was for sale and Uncle Richard went and bought it. It was an old run-down place with the wallpaper coming off of the walls and the paint was all chipped and the roof leaked and all sorts of things were wrong with it but he bought it anyway, he said he paid $41,000 cash for it. I said "It sure needs a lot of work."

"So what," he answered, "Everything needs a lot of work, even things that are really nice need a lot of work to keep them looking nice."

He asked my parents and the rest of the family to come and help him fix it up but no one ever came to help him, in fact, I was the only one who even went to help or visit him. This was in 1953 and he paid me $4 an hour for painting. My dad only made $2.25 an hour for building gas stations. I kept the money hidden there in the hotel in his office.

Then Doris Wilson graduated and got a job at the J.C. Penney store and moved out of her folks' house and into the hotel. Boy did everyone talk about that! Every time I went there, she was always in his apartment but she had a room of her own.

He worked on the hotel for a couple years and had it all fixed up really good. I thought it was a swell place with nice carpets in the hallway and all the walls were nice with new wallpaper and the doors were all varnished and shiny. He put big brass numbers on the doors and brass mailboxes beside them with the people's names on them. What I liked was the front room where you walked in, when you opened the door, a chime would ring. He fixed the front desk, it looked really nice, all shiny and in back of it he had all the keys hanging on little wooden pegs. He rented one room next to the office to a guy named Joe O'Malley who was a barber, so there was a barber shop right there next to the office. I liked that hotel a lot and I intended on going to work there when I got out of school.

I think I was thirteen when had his grand opening and invited a lot of people, including all of our relatives. My Aunt Ruth and Aunt Alice were the only two who came. I think my Mom wanted to go but Dad said no. Uncle Richard was really sad about that, he had a big table full of food and lots of bottles of different kinds of booze. There were about fifty people there and my boss from the piano company came and I came. I had to leave early because I wasn't old enough to stay, but Doris Wilson was there without her parents.

I spent a lot of time in that hotel for about three years until I was maybe sixteen and I got to be a really good pool player. Then on a Monday night I remember as well as if it was yesterday, he was standing behind the front desk and when I came in he asked me, "Do you want this hotel?"

"What do you mean?" I answered.

Then he told me he had some kind of cancer and he was going to die in a few months and he was going to give the hotel to me. "Why me?" I asked.

"Because you're the only one who has any interest in it," he told me.

I told my Mom and she told my Dad and he told the rest of the relatives and they all started going to see Uncle Richard and offering to help him do this and do that but he just told them no. They even started treating Doris Wilson like she was a nice girl again, talking to her and not calling her a shack-up, and things like that.

So a week after I turned sixteen, on the 20th day of June 1958, Uncle Richard died and we had a funeral on Monday. The following Thursday, an attorney named Bibs called everyone and said he was reading Uncle Richard's will in the hotel lobby at four in the afternoon the next Monday and everyone needed to be there. Everyone, all the men and women and kids, all thirty-three of us.

It was the most awful day of my life as I sat there in the lobby. Me and Mr. O'Malley had gotten some chairs and sat them in a few rows so everyone could sit down and the attorney opened a paper folder and took out a bunch of envelopes. He called each of the kid's names first and gave them an envelope. Some had a hundred dollars in it and some had two or three hundred dollars in them depending on how old they were. He never called my name and everyone kept looking at me funny. I didn't care, I had almost eight hundred dollars in the box in the office and I didn't expect him to give me anything. He gave my mom five hundred dollars and my dad a hundred. All of his sisters got five hundred and all the men got a hundred and a card that said "Go have a few drinks on me." Then it was down to me and Doris. Everyone was looking at me like I was some kind of a thing from outer space.

Then the attorney handed an envelope to Doris Wilson and he gave her the hotel but he gave me five thousand, three hundred and fifty dollars. All in cash, all the money he had left, and the car.

Then I sat here really proud and really sad and really numb all at the same time for about three hours, because my dad took the money and the title to the car. Everyone else just got up and walked out, but what really made me mad and made me not ever want to see any of them again in my life was everyone of them except my cousin Cathy just dropped their envelopes on the floor, or left them on the chair, and left.

My dad drove away in the car, leaving me there in the hotel with Mr. O'Malley, Mr. Biggs, and Doris. We all just sat there for a while and Mr. Biggs said, "That was quite an experience, wasn't it?" and he left.

Mr. O'Malley asked me if I thought I'd ever get the car or the money and I said "no".

Doris asked us if we wanted a drink and we both said "yes". I got really drunk drinking rum and 7-Up and I got sick and threw up.

I got up the next morning, and took my money from the office, and came to Seattle and went to work washing dishes in a hotel downtown, then joined the Navy. When I went home four years later, everyone was just like they were when I left. No one had any money and the car was long ago sold but still today I can see all of those envelopes scattered all over the floor of the hotel lobby. Doris still owns the hotel or she did the last time I was there about fifteen years ago.

The Ghost of Mary Freeman

It was in 1980, February, when I came back to Seattle completely broke with exactly $6.17 in my pocket at three in the morning in the middle of a snow storm. I had been in New Mexico and my car had gotten stolen along with everything I owned in it except the eighty-four dollars I had in my front pocket. I had no choice but to return to Seattle where at least I knew some people and I had hope one of them might let me stay with them for a while until I returned back to Alaska to work in April. I had no luck that night. I walked the streets and headed for the Fisherman's Terminal where I thought maybe I might get some work on a boat that would normally include a warm bed out of the weather. I spent two days walking around the boats asking for work but found none and was now completely out of money with no food. I did find a stairwell under the back of a old hotel out of the rain and wind where I slept for several nights.

The fourth day, I walked about two miles to a day labor place and they put me to work cleaning out a building a contractor was building and I slept in the building for a week and saved enough to rent a motel room and take a shower. Then I got something to eat at a Denny's Restaurant and they had a sign "Dish washer wanted." I took that job also, and then I had enough money to stay out of the rain and I got a meal at work, so I thought I could survive until April.

I purchased a nice warm sleeping bag and stuffed it under the stairwell and I slept there three nights and rented a motel room one night. I worked at day labor during the day until four and then washed dishes until midnight for two weeks and was doing pretty good. I had over a hundred dollars in my pocket and had just settled in to go to sleep when this man who later became a wonderful friend to me shined a flashlight in my face and asked what I was doing there.

"Trying to sleep," I answered.

Then he said, "Don't I know you?"

"Maybe," I answered, "I been around here for a few years."

"You're from Alaska, aren't you? he said then asked, "What the hell you doing sleeping here?"

I explained to him what had happened and he opened the back door to the old hotel and brought me inside.

Now, let me stop and describe the hotel to you so you'll kind of understand how it all happened. During the early years when Seattle was a boom town and there was a great fishing fleet there, a lot of small hotels were built and most of them had a business on the lower floor and rooms on the second floor> This old place had in years gone by a bar on the street lever and a house of ill repute on the second floor. In its day, it was a very lavish place with twelve rooms on the second floor and a waiting room in the center just at the head of the stairs. The leather couches were still there, worn but still useable, and there was a row of small lights on the table in the center that a person could turn on and a corresponding light would also come on in a room. I hadn't seen the second floor but now on the street-level floor was a storage room filled with mattresses and fixtures from other stores and a lot of what 1 would call junk. The man who happened to own this place was also the man who befriended me and allowed me to stay there in the street-level room.

The conversation went kind of like this, and bear in mind, he was then eighty-two years old and completely a junk-collecting miser millionaire whose only thought in life was to make more money and never spend a dollar. We entered the room filled with junk and he said, "Here, you can stay here."

"How much do you want to rent it?"

251

"You got any money?"

"I got about sixty dollars."

"Then I want fifty-five. When you going to have more?"

"I'm working two jobs. I think I could pay you about three hundred a month."

"Then I want three hundred a month, and whatever you sell out of here, I want the money, and don't steal anything, OK?"

"I'm not a thief," I answered.

"Alright then. Sleep on those mattresses or make yourself a bed. There's a shower in the back."

So there I was, I had two jobs and a place to live in less than two weeks. I had made the right decision to come back to Seattle.

The man whose name I cannot mention came back the next day after I was gone to work and moved some things out of the room and when I got back from working, there it was, a red brick wall along one side of the fifty-foot deep room. I decided then and there I wanted to stay here and make a studio out of it. Then about three or four days later, I got another lucky break and the day labor place I was working for told me they had a good paying job for me if I wanted it, a regular job in a drywall plant that played nearly as much as I made working in Alaska. I was pretty happy for two reasons, one was the place I liked so much, second was the job, and third, I could walk out the door and get on a bus and it went right to the front gate of where I was working. The ride took fifteen minutes.

So during the next month, I helped my friend clean out the remaining things he thought were so valuable and then I had an empty room to start on. Nineteen feet wide and fifty feet deep, a very large place for what I was paying, $350 a month.

I bought some furniture from him for nearly nothing and started making my studio. I made myself an easel and got some paints and began painting and writing on a old typewriter that was left in the room. It was fun to try and write, that is where I first started writing and painting.

I hung a swing from the old water pipes that ran along the ceiling and bought a few throw rugs he had gotten from who knows where, but knowing him as I do now, they came out of a dumpster. I cleaned the brick wall and the windows and put up a divider to separate the back twenty feet of the room and made myself a small bedroom there. I didn't have to cook because right across the street was a wonderful restaurant and a very good cook who liked me and gave me nice big meals for not too much money and I bought my lunches there also. So it went very well during the first seven months and all through the summer. I was having a wonderful time, working and writing and painting and fixing things. The wall was almost full of pictures and people were stopping by just to stop in and sit for a while or sit in the swing and look at the pictures. I had money and had even bought a car, a rickety old Oldsmobile convertible '56, and I loved it!

Then one day, my friend who owned the place, came by as he did almost every day and told me the wall looked real nice and he had some pictures upstairs he wanted to hang on the wall and sell, I was more than happy to do that. So we went upstairs and got about twenty pictures all of them were old and in fancy frames that needed a little repair work and I was more than happy to do it.

But, among the pictures, which consisted of several partly-dressed girls from the house upstairs was one of a young auburn haired girl dressed in what looked like a light blue velvet dress sitting on the couch that was in the entryway upstairs, a real piece of history, I thought. She looked to me like she was maybe nineteen or twenty years old but it was hard to tell. The picture was hand painted by some unknown artist but it was a good job and he had done a almost perfect job on her eyes, they looked so sad to me like she hadn't wanted to be painted or didn't want to be where she was in life.

Most of the others that had the frames all in one piece I hung on the wall and put a price tag on them.

My friend wanted to make the prices a lot higher but I sort of talked him out of it. It didn't matter because none of them were ever sold; he ended up taking them all out.

During the months I was in the studio, there was a man, kind of a homeless man named Billy, who rode around on a bicycle with a little trailer on the back of it. He was a fat guy about twenty something, from Georgia, and I later found out he was wanted by the law down there and he went back in handcuffs, but before he was arrested, he went around and took things out of trash bins and some of the things were pretty good, lamps and stuff people had thrown away. And he would come and sell them to me for a couple dollars or whatever. I learned later he had at one time been climbing up the outside stairs and in through a window and sleeping in one of the rooms on the second floor. So then a few days after we had brought the pictures down, he came in with a few things he wanted ten dollars for, I think there was a radio and a couple little pictures and some pots and dishes, did I tell you I also had a little second-hand store going there? Well, I did, that was why I bought the things from him, but when he saw the picture of the girl on the table where I was fixing the frame, he stopped dead in his tracks and turned gray in the face.

Then he said, "That's a picture of Mary Freeman, ain't it?"

I don't know," I told him then ask, "Do you know her?"

I seen her upstairs, she's a ghost," he said and stepped back a few feet. "What the hell are you talking about?" I asked.

"She's a ghost, I saw her walking around upstairs. This picture is about fifty years old," I told him.

He answered by saying, "I don't care how old it is, I seen her walking around upstairs, she's a ghost."

And he left and never came back into the studio again. He would come and stand on the sidewalk outside and I had to go out there to see what he had collected. And the price I paid went down, then he got arrested and gave me everything he had stored away in a vacant lot a couple blocks away. I left most of it there but I got a few good things.

A few days after Billy told me about the picture, the neighborhood police officer came by and asked about if I had seen Billy and I told him he wouldn't come back into the studio because he saw the girl in the picture walking around upstairs and thought she was a ghost, and the police officer simply smiled at me and said, "She is. Her name is Mary Freeman, some guy killed her upstairs in 1939."

"And she's really a ghost?" I asked. "Yes, she is," he answered.

"Have you seen her?"

"Not walking around, but I saw her looking out of the window upstairs a couple times," but he was smiling and I thought he was just putting me on.

"You saw her? You really saw her?" I asked.

He just smiled and said, "If you're here long enough, she'll come around," then he said, "If you see Billy, you tell me I got a warrant for him."

"If I tell him that he'll take off," I answered.

"Yeah I know, that's what he said," and walked out. I really liked him after that, but Billy got caught anyway and they took him back to Georgia for whatever he did.

Then I was really curious about the picture and half afraid to have it around. Then I dreamed I saw her walking around the studio, but I woke up and I was dreaming. Then I really saw her a few nights later looking out of the window right above the door to the studio. I swear I saw her plain as day. I saw her and I told the man who owned the building and he laughed and said he had seen her lots of times, then his son, who I did not know very well but did not like, told me he had lived upstairs for about two weeks and she would come into his bedroom at night and just stand there by his bed and he moved out after he saw her three times in one week.

So I believed she was a ghost, but I still wanted to fix the picture frame and I worked on it for about a month and finally finished it, then hung it on the wall. With all the stories about her, I thought I could get a lot of money for it, so I put a little price card on it of $5000. But every time I put the card on the picture, it would be on the floor the next morning and after about ten times of putting it on, I stopped.

For about two weeks, a lot of people came to look at it, and then one morning, it was turned facing the wall and every morning when I got up, the picture would be turned with the picture facing the wall. I guess she didn't like people looking at her, so I left it facing the wall for a long time and when people wanted to look at it I just let them turn it around and look.

Then I saw her myself. I was in the shower and she was standing right in front of me watching me take a shower. She wasn't in the shower with me but outside the door and I could see her over the top of the door, she was just standing there by my bed looking at me. She looked real, not like a ghost but like a real person standing there. It scared the holy beejeeberies out of me, but she just stood there looking at me and sort of smiling like she liked me or something. She just stood there as I started to dry myself then thought better of it and put on my pants with no shorts and no socks and no undershirt. I got dressed and got out of there. When I was outside the door, I looked back and she was gone. It took me a few hours before I had enough nerve to go back in. The picture was turned face out and I swear, she was smiling at me. Before she wasn't smiling, just looking sad, but now her eyes were turned straight ahead and she was smiling.

I stood in front of the picture looking at it and said, "At least you still have a sense of humor." And I swear as sure as I'm writing this, someone kissed me on the face, right below my right eye.

Then I was not so scared but really curious. I stood there for a long time until a friend came in and asked me what was going on. "I'm talking to Mary," I said.

"Then ask her who killed her. If she tells, then we'll know it's a real ghost."

"It's a real ghost," I answered.

We just sat around and drank a couple beers and a couple more people came in and the night passed and the next few nights without me seeing her, but then on Tuesday night a week later, I was getting ready for bed and she was standing right there in front of me, not five feet from me, smiling.

I looked at her and said, "Hello, Mary." She didn't move, just smiled at me. Then I got real brave and told her "I wish you weren't a ghost. You're really good looking." Her face changed and she looked like she was sad again and she went away. I laid in bed that night and didn't sleep well. I was trying to decide if I should move out of there but by morning I had forgotten about moving and was thinking more about how to really talk to her like she was a real person. I went and had some breakfast and when I came back she was standing right in the center of the studio at the big table I had there and she was writing on a drawing pad. I walked over and watched as she drew out the words:

It's like wanting a cigarette really bad and no one will give you one. Then she went away.

I showed the letters to a lot of people but no one believed me. I really didn't care if they did or not, I knew what I saw. I took the sheet of drawing paper and put it in a frame, then hung it on the wall next to the picture of Mary. The next morning under the words she had already written was:

You're nice and I wrote under that:

Thank you, Mary, you're nice too.

I went to work the next morning and when I came home both her picture and the frame with the words in it was gone from the wall. No one ever admitted to taking it but I know it was the guy who owned the building, thinking he might make some money from them some day. But he got a big surprise because the building where he kept his things stored caught on fire the very next day and burned to the ground while I was at work. I came home and everyone was standing around looking at a big pile of ashes.

I never saw Mary Freeman again. I moved out of the building about a month later.

Him

He came from upper New York State in 1768 at the age of three and with three other families settled in a part of Mexico now called southwest Texas. It was a hard winter the second year and eight of the thirteen people starved to death while three of the others froze, leaving Him, one woman, and a small girl. They tried to walk across the vast prairie in the blowing snow but the woman died of starvation and one week later the girl finally died also.

He was alone in the great flat land of Texas and just almost six years old when he was found by a small band of roaming people who kept goats and he lived with them for three years until he was seven and then Indians killed the family while he was out gathering firewood.

He returned to find them all dead...

He walked off into the open countryside with only the ill-fitting clothes he wore and survived by throwing rocks at birds and rabbits. He became so good at throwing rocks he missed only once in maybe fifty throws. Not only was he extremely accurate, but he also could throw a fist-size rock nearly one hundred yards with deadly accuracy. By finding abandoned campsites of Indians, he discovered things they had left behind, remains of plants and different objects, and this was how he learned to survive so well by himself.

He was about nine or ten when he became a sort of spirit person, a super warrior, a wild man/boy, one to be feared and left alone. This lesson was sorrowfully learned by the Indians when they tried to capture him after seeing him near a small water hole on the prairie. He of course ran and they followed him into a hill of rocks where he quickly and very accurately threw rocks and bounced them off the heads of the fourteen Indians at great distances. Then, he gathered up their bows, arrows and other things, and then their horses and sat on the top of a huge rock with his arms folded and his legs crossed, watching them as they one by one regained consciousness and sat up feeling the large bump on their heads, and seeing the blood from the wound caused by the rock.

One by one they saw the small boy sitting up on the rock, smiling down at them and as they gathered into one group, he began to laugh at them and show them he had taken all their things including their horses. They of course tried to go after him but turned back after four of them were again hit with a huge rock. At first bewildered, then hesitant, then outright frightened by this small boy who looked like a wild animal sitting on the rock laughing and sounding more like a coyote than a human boy. They ran off back to the water hole carrying the three who had again had the misfortune to raise his head up and look at the boy, and tried to decide what to do. To go back to the village without horses or weapons would be so shameful they would be laughed out of the tribe. To go back and try to take back their things might be a worse thing but they had no choice. So after much deliberation one was chosen to go and try to catch the boy. He was almost instantly knocked on the back of his head with a rock and fell halfway back down the hill. The second and third and fourth suffered the same lump on the head experience and again all of them gathered back at the waterhole and tried to decide what they should do, flee or stay and try to fight.

Morning came and they found their horses and weapons had been placed a short distance away from them and no sign of the boy was to be found. But the legend had began about this, whatever it was, the Indians called 'Him' -- who was it? It was Him!!

So naturally, when the young braves returned to the camp, it was soon found out that they all had large lumps on their heads, the story of the boy turned into the story of this great huge man who had came charging down from the hills throwing huge amounts of huge rocks as he ran down the hill, tearing out trees and brush and crushing boulders with his hands and throwing them down at the brave warriors who tried to fight but was no match for the huge thing who had (as the story was told and re-told) become as tall as a small tree and stronger than ten horses with long black hair, huge black eyes and arms as big as the back leg of a horse. They had no way to escape whatsoever. Only by sneaking back in the dark of night did they manage to steal their horses back and escape with their lives.

After this, the boy was seen here and there and the stories grew and grew. He was also very good at hiding himself and doing things to the Indians like stealing their food and horses and even a couple of young women, it was told. Every time something turned up missing, or a young girl began to show a enlarged belly, the blame went out, and the cry was "It was Him!!"

Well, as the west grew and cowboys began to drive cows north to market he was seen here and there and as he grew older, the spotting became more and more widespread. He was spotted almost every day in some part of the great western states. Sometimes just sitting on a rock laughing like a coyote, sometimes running across the open range as they called it, creating such a huge swirling windstorms behind him they named dust devils that were blamed for cattle and horses being sucked up into the sky and lost forever. If a town caught on fire and burned down, it was him!!

Someone had seen him. If some chickens were gone and the farmer would stand out and listen he might hear him out there laughing like a coyote.

He was a problem all right, and he caused a lot of problems in the western states. From about 1850 until around 1900 from Texas, to Arizona, New Mexico, Oklahoma, Nevada and in California too, and sometimes in all of them on the same day or in the same week. It was said he was the one that ended the Civil War by telling a certain General where to take his men and make his stand because when Sherman surrendered and was asked who was to blame he simply said, "Well it sure as hell wasn't me, it was him." And he looked away at the hills.

Santa Anna said the same thing when he returned to Mexico City in his underwear after losing Texas. And on and on it goes. He was blamed for everything.

Then one day this tall, long-legged cowboy named Ukulele Bill saw him asleep on a rock and he snuck up and tied him up with his rope and then sat there and waited until he woke up. Well, when the kid, who was now a teenager, woke up, he was really mad at first but then after a while he figured out the guy wasn't going to skin him or scalp him so he took up with him, learned to wear clothes and boots with spurs on them and they went around the western states for a few years punching cows and punching cowboys and poking cow girls and getting into all kinds of trouble.

Then as luck would have it, this bunch of bad guys was robbing a bank in south Texas and it was not a really big bank. It only had about fifty dollars in it but the building was really big with big windows and two big doors and one big fat teller of big fat lies, and two clerks, who took in money but didn't like to give any out. So when this gang of robbers came in to rob the bank, both clerks started arguing with them and told them there was no

262

money in the safe but the robbers won the argument when they shot at one and hit the other one on the head with a chair. They took the fifty dollars and mounted their horses and started riding off into the sunrise (it was nine in the morning). So this guy who they called Him and old Ukulele Bill were walking out of a house where there were these nice-girl entertainers and just as they got out the door and down the stairs someone yelled, "They robbed the bank!!" in a big loud deep voice and of course everyone heard her.

Then old Ukulele Bill whipped out his six-shooter and was going to dismount the robbers but He picked up a few good-sized rocks and bounced them off the heads of the robbers and knocked them all as silly as the US government has became in the last couple decades.

Well let me tell you, He was a hero. He saved the last fifty dollars left in South Texas and it was all there was between all those cowboys having a good-time drink and not having one.

So men started talking about it and some fool wrote about it in a book and the word spread around. Then a paperback ten-cent book came out about it, telling how he had thrown the rocks and the distance got further and further and the number of men got bigger and bigger and he became more and more famous. So then someone came and invited him to go back east and tell his story and they would pay him for doing it.

So he went back to New York and began throwing rocks, first at targets, then someone tried to hit one of the rocks he had thrown with a stick, and then it became a paid game. Each man was given three chances to hit one of the rocks with a stick for a dime. So after that, men made their own sticks and because really good round rocks were hard to find, someone took some leather and sewed it into a round ball and he began to throw it as men tried to hit it with the stick they had made. You take it from there.

Slo Joe's Golf Game

So how many men have you ever known named Slo Joe? I knew one. A big guy over six feet eight inches tall and as slow as any person I ever met, and about as funny and as aggravating as any man I ever knew, but still as funny as any of the old-time comics. He had timing. And he sang that song all the time, "Timing, a' tick a' tick a tick a' tick a' timing."

He talked in commercials. You had to be real careful when you talked to him because if you mentioned any product sold on the open market he would quote the commercial related to it, the guy drove me almost crazy every time he pointed his finger at me, got this stupid looking smile on his face, and then repeated a commercial related to whatever product happened to have been mentioned. And most of the time he sang it in this high voice that sounded like he had been inhaling helium gas.

This isn't a short story of any kind, it's just one of those things that happen to a person and sooner or later, you got to get it out of your head. I have dreams about him singing and I wake up in a full sweat, shaking. It's terrible!

We went to play golf once a few years ago and he just happened to be there when I was invited. "Can I go with you? Please? I always wanted to play golf," he begged.

"You got any clubs, Joe?"

"Well, no ... but I guess I could get some somewhere," he answered.

"Where?"

"The second-hand store?" he asked.

I didn't say anything, hoping he would just forget it, but not Slo Jo. He spent the day going around and came back with about forty golf clubs and not one of them matched, but he had a whole set, one through nine and three or four sand wedges and four or five drivers and two or three woods and all of them were in a Ping golf bag along with six putters of every name you can think of, all with different colored grips. Some of them even had head covers on them, but the best part was the shoes, those brown and white golf shoes and the checkered shorts and tall socks. It was an emotional sight to see, but we tried not to laugh at him. He was as serious as a heart attack and he had come to play golf.

"Just how much did you pay for all that stuff, Joe?" my friend asked him.

"About a hundred," he answered proudly, then went into a commercial about something, I don't remember what it was, but I almost fell over laughing.

Then my friend told him flat out, "Joe, no commercials on the golf course, it's illegal. You can't say them," he thought for a second then added, "Or sing them".

So, very hesitantly we left to play golf with six foot eight inch Slo Joe in the back seat of Al's car. We got to the course and the first thing that went wrong was they told us it cost $65.00 to play and Jo had fourteen dollars, so we chipped in and paid for his round. Then he had to have his own cart because he was too big to fit in one with the two of us. Then the next thing that happened was we stopped at the putting green to practice and Joe kept hitting the balls clear off of the green and out onto the walkway and into the parking lot and in every direction, I don't think he hit one putt less than fifty feet and he never hit one into a hole.

So then we went to tee off. Now you have to use your imagination, a guy six for eight inches tall wearing a pair of plaid shorts, knee high socks, a pair of saddle shoes like golf shoes that didn't fit, and he had to bend over halfway just so the club would reach the ball, but he hit it the first swing and it went

266

about three hundred yards, straight as any golf shot I have ever seen and it ended up about seven feet from the hole, on the fourth green.

"Hit another ball," Al told him, and he did after swinging at it about ten times, he hit it about fifty feet and was starting to get frustrated and mad.

"Joe," I said, "don't try to hit it so hard, just hit it easy but use a bigger club."

He had three or four 1-woods in the bag and he took out the one with the biggest head on it. Swinging kind of easy, he hit the ball and it took off straight down the fairway about two hundred fifty yards. It was a good golf shot for anyone, but the next shot was about a hundred yards from the green and he bent four club shafts trying to hit it. He kept hitting about a foot before the head got to the ball and he was swinging so hard every club just bent right above the head. We left the first green with four bent clubs laying there.

The second hole went a little better, it only took him about twenty swings to finally get the ball in the hole and he was happy. I was trying as hard as I could to keep a straight face for fear he might just twist my head off if I laughed at him. Al kept laughing and telling him he was pathetic, hopeless, and too oversized to play golf. During the first nine holes, Joe bent about eleven of the clubs, lost eight or nine balls, threw three clubs into the lake, and walked off twice, only to come back and try again.

He said several times. "I don't care if you laugh at me. I'm having fun even if I ain't no good at it".

"You got the last part right, Joe," Al laughed and I thought Joe was going to hit him with a club, but he didn't, he just teed up another ball and hit it, two feet from the hole two hundred seventy-five yards away, then he went and put it in for an Eagle four.

"I did good on that one, huh?" he smiled.

I was laughing at Al because he was half mad and so surprised he couldn't talk, he just kept saying, "What is this, a F!@##$$% joke?"

Slo Joe played out all eighteen holes and made three birdies and two Eagles, more then I or Al have ever made in all out years of playing golf. I've never made a Eagle on any hole and if Al told the truth, I don't think he has either.

What's the point. I don't know, it's just something I think about and laugh at once in a while.

Slo Joe is a stunt man in Hollywood now.. He jumps off buildings and gets paid about ten thousand dollars each time he does it.

My Opinions

Sometimes I set and look at a blank screen trying to think of something to write about and a million thoughts pass through my mind. I'm not going to write them all down but here's a few.

The situation this country is in. Silliness has taken over common sense.

Too many boys are being raised by their mothers without a man and they grow up thinking like women.

It's all about me. And the lack of the moral character in this country.

Why is it? Money!! Too many taxes spent on silly things.

Credit cards. Everyone is so far in debt they have no time to think about others or being honest.

Welfare, just get drunk and arrested three times. Go to 20 days of treatment three times and you're on the payroll for life. $640.00 every month, plus food stamps.

It's the public's job to take care of the people who work for the government. Not the government's job to take care of the people. Huh??

What's to gain about wanting to control everything? When we all, sooner or later, end up in the same place? I've yet to see anyone lying in a coffin with both hands full of money.

There is such an insecurity complex among the people in this country; everyone is afraid to step out and let others see them for fear of being shamed or ridiculed.

The fact that 7.5% of all the people in the US are without a home... that's craziness!! The fact that 67% of all the people in this county work for the government... that too is crazy. What happened to the employment offices? Now if you don't have a computer and can get on the Internet, you have a hell of a time getting a $5.50 an hour job.

I don't think Ken Lay is dead, I think it's a fix. His death was just too convenient.

People are drinking too much coffee and paying too much for it. Too many people say what they have been conditioned to say or what they have heard others say and not enough of them think about what to answer before they speak.

Dancing has turned from an art form to gyrations. Singing has gone from finding a person with a nice-sounding voice who can deliver a message with feeling, to a lot of sound-alike obnoxious noise.

Walt Disney made women and children think animals were human, now it's completely gone overboard.

This country is becoming a country of talkers and non-doers. No public official should ever be re-elected after one term in office. No one over fifty should ever hold an elected office.

60% of the fish in the sea, rivers, and lakes are gone. There is maverick kelp taking over the entire coastal areas of the eastern oceans and now it has moved to the coast of California and soon (by 2012) it will have killed 75% of all the fish in the oceans.

Cell phone towers are causing all the bees to become lost and unable to find their way back to their hives and that could in ten years deplete the amount of food on this planet to only fifteen percent of what it is now.

People don't seem to realize that everything has equilibrium. Soon there will be no humans and the earth will be a lot better off because of it. What took a thousand years to build will be gone in only ninety, after the human race is gone. Cities and town and roads and bridges will all be overgrown and decayed away. Too bad!!

Shouldn't the leaders of the country try to teach and set a good example for the people? So why do they all try to show how powerful they are by destroying others?

I think every president just has to kill at least a couple people, just because he can get away with doing it. The ultimate crime of power.

I wish a space ship would land on this planet and then everyone would join together and try to kill the aliens instead of each other.

Abomination; Something made up of parts that don't fit together and has no natural function or purpose in the world. Look up the word in the Bible.

Child molesters; Kill every one of them after the first offense! Abominations!! I think people's heads should get as fat as their bodies are, proportionately.

Every person in prison should have to go to school every other day and work every other day sorting and recycling garbage. One day of school, two days off their sentence, if they keep their grades above 3.5.

No shot should ever be fired by an American soldier in any other country.

The quickest way to ruination is to spend more time minding other people's business then you do your own.

I like thin line things.

There is a thin line between a human animal and a human being. Unfortunately, the former outnumbers the latter by a hundred thousand to one.

There is a thin line between loyalty and stupidity.

There is a thin line between being firm and being overbearing.

There is a thin line between being loyal and being stupid.

TV teaches kids how to talk and make excuses but not how to think or do things. But it does teach them a lot of good excuses.

Here's something to think about. All those courtroom shows are teaching people what they can get away with and how to cheat and not get caught.

They have taken all the honesty out of the younger generation, teaching them that anything they do is alright if they don't get caught, and who watches them? Fat lazy people on welfare who have three or more kids all by different men who don't support them. No instead they go to jail and get supported themselves... by us...

Anyone who is thinking about buying any exercise equipment should take two hours and think about how it will look at their garage sale before they buy it.

Example: someone sells someone something that is no good. Do they have to tell the person buying it, it is no good? No. It's all up to the buyer to check it out before buying it .. Is that right? I don't think so.

Someone steals from you but you don't see them do it, but you tell the cops and the person says, "I didn't do it," even though it's sitting right in their front room. But the cops can't come into their house to retrieve it.

What if the President of the United States took forty-five minutes and went on the TV every week, maybe on Saturday morning, and talked to the children and told them to do the right thing??

Doctors who do eye surgery are more important the heart doctors.

George Bush could have converted every licensed car in the United States to natural gas for less money than he spent in Iraq.

I don't play the lottery. If you don't play, you can't lose.

Shoes you buy at the Goodwill last as long or longer than new ones and they only cost four dollars.

"Every man is entitled to write one good book, have one good woman, and one good dog." I'm overdue.

The smartest people on earth are only one tenth as smart as they think they are and the others are below them.

Religion is the worst thing ever thought of by man or woman or whoever thought of it.

Why is it all the animals on this planet can understand what people say and we can't understand any of them?

It used to be if a family or the head of a family had a problem, he went off by himself and thought until he came up with a way to fix the problem. Now everything is so.... what's the word I'm looking for? Choreographed? There's a book that tells us all how to live, eat, think, even wash our bodies. They tell us in which direction to rub the washcloth, and where to begin and where to end, what to do and what not to do, how hot to turn the water and how long stay under it, what to say and what not to say. Then when you do say something, you have to be very careful not to offend someone who is so insecure that anything you say can make them jealous and they'll condemn you for saying it or turn it into a negative.

I call that silly.

No one looks for something extra to do, they look for a way to do less and get more. That's not just silly, that's wrong in every sense of the word. But I wonder what's the point of trying to ruin everything everyone else has??

I listen to all the news all the time and that is one of the worst things a person can do today, nothing good ever comes from the news on TV. They have to make it sound as interesting as they can, even if they have to stretch, twist, and turn the facts around in their favor so people will stay tuned in and listen to the advertisements.

Most of the good parts of my life took place after I was twenty-one and before I was thirty-one, so the good parts were short and sweet. The rest has been a sort of wondering and searching experience. What I have been looking for? I still don't know. A perfect love? Maybe a magnificent thing to do? A super challenge? Who knows? But I feel lucky. I'm still here after 68 years and I can still run and jump and laugh, but I think most things I see and hear now are pretty silly. This country has gone from an energetic, constructive country to a country made up of greed, low morals, and laziness. The people are getting fatter and dumber every day. It's horrid! I hate to see it, but then, as they say, "You get what you deserve," so I would guess the next few generations are in for a hell of a hard time.

My Friend, D. B. C.

We promised we would never tell until one of us was dead... Well, my friend died on December 18th, so I'm going to tell you. There were four of us and I'm the last one, and the only one of us that smoked, but I was a singer and I used my lungs a lot so I think that might have helped me. I'm 68, almost 69. We all have talked about this a thousand times during the last thirty-five years and if they find out who I am I might even have to go to jail after all this time, but it was just a joke. No one got hurt. And no one suffered except the egos of a few cops around Seattle. And life is a joke. So what the hell?? At my age, if they lock me up, how long can I be there? Two or three years and I'll be dead too. So let them do what they want. I don't believe they could ever prove I was a part of it anyway. It ain't like I was making a written confession to the cops, I'm just telling a story. But I got the proof stashed away if I ever need it and if I can remember where I put it. Then again, if someone gave me a million dollars to prove I was there when it happened... But I doubt that is ever going to happen.

We were both driving race cars at that time of our lives. I was from Oregon but had just moved to Seattle and he was from Vancouver, BC. The other two were from Seattle. Not only was he a good stock car driver but my friend was one of the very first ever skydivers. I used to go and watch him on the weekends. He was amazing; he could land in the back of a pick-up truck going fifty miles a hour down a dirt road.

He used to use two or three parachutes and as he fell, he would cut one loose, then cut another one loose and fall almost to the ground before he pulled the third one. He was one of the first to jump off buildings too.

Believe it or not, but it started out he wanted to steal a race car. He wanted to go to Indianapolis and steal an Indy car and the truck it came in, then a fighter plane from the US Navy. Before that he stole my coat.

That's really how we met, kinda, and got to be friends. I liked him because he was so weird. He was also the vice president of a huge insurance company.

I had bought this coat, an elk skin coat made by an Indian on the coast of Alaska. It had beaded designs on it and it cost $750 in 1968 so it wasn't just a coat to me and when it was stolen from the truck at a race track in Vancouver, BC, in June of 1969, I was pretty mad. I called the police and everyone in the pits was searching for it, but no one found it and I went back to Seattle pretty disappointed about the whole thing. I called it my "girl pick up coat" and it worked very well. Seven or eight months later, maybe March of 1970, when my friend and co-driver was down in Seattle, we went out in the evening and had a few beers and hung around in this bar on the waterfront where a band was playing. When we were ready to leave, he stopped me and said, "Wait a minute, I want to steal a coat."

"What!" I didn't believe what he had said.

"I got this thing in me. I like to steal coats."

"Not when you're with me, in my car, you're not," I told him.

"Ok," he said, but it seemed like I had hurt his feelings pretty bad.

Then, after we had gotten nearly back to the shop where my race car was parked it sort of came to me and I asked him, "Are you the guy that stole my elk skin coat last year?"

"Yeah I did!" he sort of laughed then said, "I was going to give it back to you for Christmas."

You can use your imagination to hear the words I called him, but he came back down the following weekend and brought back my coat. It was in a plastic bag and as good as new. He said he had never worn it and was keeping it for me. I still wanted to knock a couple of his teeth out.

So then all was more or less forgiven, but he still stole coats every time I didn't get a chance to stop him. He would leave earlier or later than me, or us, if there were several of us in wherever we were. We all tried to break him of it but he just liked to steal coats and other things also, we all found out later.

We were in a motel in Eugene, Oregon, when he told me was he was going to stowaway on a airliner in the wheel well and then jump out over Hercules, the nuclear power plant located just north of the Columbia River. But he needed someone to pick him up in a boat and take him back to BC. He had it all planned out. He was going to have a strobe light and whoever picked him up was going to guide him in with four strobe lights on four floats in the center of the water. He did it perfectly... right in between all four floats and ten feet from the boat.

The man known as D. B. Cooper is now dead, but he gave us thirty-six years of fun knowing we had gotten away with the first and only skyjack in this country.

What happened to the money? He dumped it all in the river except six twenties, one for each of us to keep as proof we did it. He didn't want the money; he just wanted to get away with dong it.

Here's how it happened... I'm not going to name the three others who helped us do it, they're all gone now. One was killed in a car wreck outside of Tacoma, Washington, killed by a drunk driver, one died of cancer, and the third one died racing Sprint cars in North Carolina. But for me, I'm just including this in a book of short stories to get it off my mind and after all this time I just want to tell what really happened that afternoon in Seattle, in 1971. It really started in the shop, located in an area of Seattle known as Fremont, on the street named Leary Way, just around the corner from the main town center. We had started an auto repair business and also built our race cars there. My wife at the time hated it and everyone I had anything to do with, especially the guy this story is about, I think because he just didn't like her and he told her he didn't like her every chance he got. He used to call her mouthy, but we liked him and so she didn't like us and finally got a divorce from me after I had left her about three or four times. Every time I would go off to drive race cars, she would throw all my things out of the house and leave, so when I came back, I would have to find out where she was. Finally I just quit looking for her and looked for a different woman.

We were sitting in the shop drinking beer and supposedly working on the cars when it came up. Someone asked him, "What's with you anyway, stealing coats?"

"I don't just steal coats. I steal a lot of things," he sort of laughed.

"Like what?" It was me that asked him that question.

"Canoes," he laughed, "boats, stuff that I can steal and have no need for... I don't steal money."

"How the hell do you steal a canoe?" Not me, but another of us, asked him.

"Put a sales slip in your teeth. Put the canoe on your head and have one of the salesmen open the door for you. I've done it eleven times," he laughed.

"Then what do you do with them?"

"Stick them in the back of a pick-up truck," he laughed again. "So someone comes out and finds a canoe in their truck." He thought it was really a good thing to do.

I just sat there and looked at him and remembered my coat. "You're a sick man," I said.

"Some of us have to have fun even if the rest of you don't know how," he answered and then he said, "You know what I really want to do? Jack an airplane."

"What??" all four of as asked at the same time.

"Yeah I do. I want to jack an airplane and then jump out of it."

"What kind of an airplane," someone, not me, asked.

"An airliner. Like a 727. I got it all figured out. I know exactly where and when to jump and they'll never catch us."

All four of us said, "US? What do you mean US?" at the same time.

"Oh, I'm just thinking," he laughed.

Then one of the guys who was the main mechanic on the car told him, "I might be in on it. You'll probably get killed, so I want to be there and see it," and then he said, "Can I have your car?" He had a 63 Jag XKE and it was in perfect shape.

He sort of laughed then got up and left.

We were going down to look at a modified offset roadster car in Salem, Oregon, with the intentions of maybe converting it into a Sprint car to run on asphalt tracks in California that weekend and he said just before he left, "I'll show you where I'm going to jump." Then he said, "Piece of cake! Evil ain't the only one!"

We left Saturday morning and it was raining like hell but when we got to Kalama we stopped and had coffee and some ham and eggs, then we went on and when we got to where the power plant was, he pointed to a huge log raft and said, "Right there! I'm going to land right in the center of the river right there. I just need someone to be there and pick me up." Then he said, "We'll be back in Seattle drinking beer by the time the plane lands in Reno."

"You're really serious?" I asked.

"50/50," he sort of laughed and said, "I got to jump first and see if I can make it. I don't want to land in a tree."

"And how are you going to accomplish that?" I asked.

"I got a friend in the Air Force who's going to let me jump out of a transport. I just need you to come and pick me up."

"Yeah right! Hell, you are nuts," I answered and from then on for the rest of the weekend, I was pretty leery about his sanity. But he bought the car and we brought it back to the shop and started working on it. It was a very well-built car and I liked it and couldn't wait to get it on a track. Unfortunately, that never happened, because a few weeks later in August, he came to the shop and was carrying a canvas handbag. He put it in the office and sort of slid it out of sight.

"What's in the bag?" I asked him.

"A jump suit."

"Jump suit?"

He smiled and answered, "Yeah, what are you doing tonight?"

"I don't know, what are you doing?"

"I'm jumping out of an airplane. You want to come and bring me back?"

"From where?"

He smiled and said, "I got to show you this. I made it. It's a glide suit."

I followed him into the office and he took the suit out of the bag and laid it out on the floor. It was a pair of canvas coveralls, but in between the arms and legs he had sewn what looked to me like leather wings. It had thin round plastic poles running through the outside edges of them, and even between the legs, there was leather sewn in to make the whole thing a sort of kite, I guess is the best way to describe it. Then on the back was a parachute in a bag.

"You are crazy!" I said.

"Maybe, but this is going to be a lot of fun. I figure I can glide about three and half miles if I jump from 10,000 feet and still be high enough for the chute to open."

"And if you ain't?"

"Then you can have my car, and I put a check made out to you for all the money I have in the bank in case I get killed." He handed me an envelope.

"You go jump, I'll just go cash this check," I answered.

"The check stays here. If I don't come back, it's yours. If I do, then we'll know I can do it and maybe..."

Then he stopped and asked me, "You in or out?"

"I got to talk it over with the others," I answered.

"We don't need the whole world knowing about this or it won't work," he said.

"Well, I'm not going to go by myself," I answered and he sort of walked out. I guess he went to eat or something. When he came back, I had asked the others if they wanted to go and watch him get killed and they all said yes.

When he came back, he was not very happy that I had told the others, but then when they said they all were going to meet him and watch him get killed, he was happy again and he showed them all the suit he had made. One of the guys called it the 'Rocky Bullwinkle suit'. And that's what it looked like; a flying squirrel suit with a large pack on the back of it.

He left and told us to be out on the water at 10:30 Sunday night and have the lights set about a hundred feet apart but not to turn them on until 10:20. He figured it would take him eight minutes to fly from the plane to the river and land. We figured we would never see him again and I was going to make sure I cashed the check the next day if he never showed up. I figured he was going to chicken out and just stay on the plane and then

281

come back later. Too bad! I was already going to have the money however much it was.

To this day I don't know if there was one dollar or fifty thousand on the check.

We left Seattle at eight in the evening August 19th and was on the log jam at 9:45. We used a small boat that was tied up there, whose it was we don't know, to set out the four small rubber floats he had tied together in a bag. We turned on the lights at 10:20 and waited.

At 10:28, he came splashing down right in the center of the four lights and then nearly drowned because of the suit. As soon as he hit the water, it got wet and began to sink. We got to him in the last second; his head was already under the water and we just managed to grab him and pull him out and into the boat. The current had gotten a hold of the parachute and was taking him downstream as we tried to row to him. Then he got tangled in the rope he had the lights tied together with. We had to cut the lines on the parachute to free him and none of us had a pocket knife so we had to just hold him up while one of us swam about fifty feet back to the log raft, then climbed up on it, ran across about a hundred moving logs, then up the bank and about another fifty yards back to the truck, got a knife from the toolbox and then ran back and across the log jam and threw the knife out to us in the boat. It was pretty scary for about fifteen minutes. The guy who was rowing the boat to keep us from going down the river was getting tired and he kept saying, "I'm going to kick the shit out of you when we get you back to the shop."

He never admitted it, but I think he was pretty scared he was going to die right then. When we finally got him into the boat all he said was, "Piece of cake!!" but he was freezing his butt off all the way back to Seattle.

I still don't know who the boat belonged to but I've always wondered what would have happened if the boat hadn't been there? Or what if we hadn't had the knife in the truck? Or what if when he threw it to us, it had missed the boat? and he drowned. How would we have ever explained it?

If the boat hadn't been there he would have just landed in the water and drowned. I kind of think he had put the boat there sometime before or had someone else do it because it was pretty convenient and he was a scammer.

So after about an hour, he had gotten warm again, and he was laughing and trying to tell us how it had felt to just sort of glide across the sky in that suit.

"I could have made it another four or five miles," he said, "it was just like floating on air. I could see the lights as plain as hell and I just floated right to them and when I was over you guys, I pulled the cord and came down. Piece of cake!!"

So we stopped and had a couple beers at Kalama and then on the way back to Seattle the wind caught the parachute that we had just stuffed into the back of the truck and pulled it up and out of the truck and out onto the freeway. We had to stop and run back and get it, with a Highway State Patrol man sitting across the freeway watching us. We got it stuffed back into the truck and laid a tire on it.

He repacked it in the shop a few days later after it had dried out. So that was about it for the first part. Had we known what he was really going to do, we would never have gone along with it, but we didn't know so we did, and on that afternoon in December, 1971, all four of us left in two trucks heading for the log jams at Longview, Washington, across from the power plant. He was going to stowaway on a flight going to Reno, so he said, but as it turned out he told the plane to go to Reno and fly at 10,000 feet and he even told them what time to leave because he

283

had to meet us when he said he was going to meet us, why no one figured something out about that, I have never figured out myself. They said there were two Air Force jets following the plane and they never saw him leave it but...?? So anyway, I don't know about that part. All I know is what we did. We all knew a couple guys in Longview who built racing boats, so we wanted to go see them. We stopped in Centralia and had lunch which consisted of a few beers and a hamburger then we went on to Longview and by the time we got there it was all over the news about some guy trying to hijack a plane at Seattle Airport. The first words said, and not by me, were, "It can't be? Can it?"

And I answered a big fat "No!" then "God! I hope it ain't".

And someone else said, "I bet it's him. Shall we stick around here or go home?"

Two said 'stay.' two said 'go home,' and I was a 'go home'. So we flipped coins. Odd man out and I lost, so we stayed and drank beer and listened to the radio and then went to a tavern and watched TV but nothing was on it about the plane so we went back and waited. He was supposed to meet us at 9:45pm and to tell you the truth, I don't remember what time it was because I got pretty drunk and I was cold as all hell from the snow and half asleep on the log jam when he came down. He woke me up screaming at the top of his voice as he came down right in front of me, nearly hitting the log jam. The chute hooked on a post used to tie up the logs and he just pulled himself up onto the logs and climbed out of the jump suit. Then he stood there laughing and doing a sort of dance.

"I told you I could do it!" he laughed, "A piece of cake if I ever had one".

"You're F$#@#$ing crazy!"

"I dumped the other chutes out and let the wind blow them a few miles east. They'll think I jumped and got killed." he laughed.

"You're nuts!!"

I think all of us said it at least five times while he was taking all the money out of the pockets in the jump suit and throwing it into the water.

"How much you got there?" one of the other guys asked.

"I don't know," he laughed. "A couple hundred thousand. What difference does it make anyway?" He was tossing bundles as far out into the water as he could throw them.

"Some of them are going to turn up somewhere downstream," someone said.

"Yeah, and some of them will turn up over there in the mountains where I tossed them. When they find it in about ten years, they'll think I'm dead. We can't spend it. They know all the numbers," then he handed each of us one twenty and said, "A souvenir! One for each of us and don't ever spend it! If we never spend them, they'll never know who did it! This is a day to remember, guys!" he laughed and danced a few more seconds and then one of the guys said, "Yeah, well, good!! Let's get the hell out of here and get rid of that suit somewhere."

"Hell, no! I'm keeping it!" he said, "I'm going to hang it right in my closet and keep it until I die."

If he did or if he didn't, I don't know; I wasn't there when he died, but knowing him as I did he was probably buried in it.